Remnant

Roland Allnach

ALL THINGS THAT MATTER PRESS

Remnant

ISBN 13: 9780984629701

Library of Congress Control Number: 2010915754

Cover Photo: NASA

Cover design by All Things That Matter Press
Published in 2010 by All Things That Matter Press

To my family and friends,
for their patience and support

All the Fallen Angels

I

...there she stands, among the whispers of ruin, caught between so much anger and hurt and betrayal. So dark, that night: the whisper of the wind, the patter of the rain, the steam of humid air; it had the feel of dissolution, of tears and loss and futility. And there she stands among it all, among the whispers, dehumanized, for what is her life—any life—but the lost murmur of whispers in the dark?

She was only nine. I shot her anyway.

The nightmare snapped away as it always did, stunning the mind of the man that had been held in its sway. He rose up in bed—not bolting, but more a slow, steady bend at the waist to sit upright, like some undead creature of old. The comparison, he thought distantly, was not all that off the mark.

He turned in the darkness to let his feet slide out from under the sheets of his bed. There was no curious glance over his shoulder to look upon his wife; he knew by now that she was a heavy enough sleeper, and that she had grown accustomed to his often troubled sleep. Yet it bothered him nonetheless, waking a petty notion in the lonely recesses of his heart, a petty notion of jealousy to sleep in apparent peace.

With a sigh, he departed the bed and staggered with the stiffness of his bad leg towards the little kitchen of their captain's cabin. He moved with familiarity, not turning on any lights, yet still able to silently gather his customary mug and the hot water to make his tea. Then he settled himself at the small table beside the portal of their cabin, one hand on his mug, the other on his com. He looked out to the cold points of starlight in the black void. He blinked. The sound of water, the soft tinkle of running water, came to him. He looked to the sink, but he had turned off the faucet.

He closed his eyes.

The com vibrated under his hand, startling him. His arm folded like an old mechanism to bring the little black communicator to his ear. He could hear the breathing on the other end of the call. He knew who it was, but not how she knew to call, and she always knew; she always called when he woke, but she never spoke. Too many bad things dwelled between them, he knew. *Where does one start? When all that's left is broken, which piece do you pick up first, and more important, why that particular piece?*

But then something changed: she spoke his name, her voice a thin rasp in his ear.

"Stohko?"

He blinked. His lips parted. He put the com down and keyed it off, but stared at it for several seconds, his face settling to stone. His eyelids slid shut, and when he opened them, he was looking to his side to see his wife standing by the teapot, arms crossed on her chest, her long blue nightshirt hanging to her knees. "Nightmare?" she said through a long yawn.

He stared at her.

She rubbed her face before walking around the table to hug him from behind, her arms wrapping around his shoulders. Her dark hair slid forward to brush against his cheek. He barely breathed. His eyes had not moved, holding where he had seen her, as if she still stood there.

He laid his hand over the com.

"Stohko—"

"It's my burden, Pallia, not yours."

"But it's here, with both of us." She let her breath go. "You took your pill?"

He shifted in his seat, uncomfortable at once, but nevertheless confessed to her. "Last two days. Something's changed. I don't know. I've been sleeping well for the last few weeks. No headaches, no nightmares, no calls—"

She straightened, her dark hair trailing across his neck as she receded from him, but her hands remained on his shoulders. "Those pills are old, you know. Expired, I would think. Maybe you should see Piccolo tomorrow. At least you could sleep then."

He frowned.

She said nothing. After several moments she went back to bed, the only remaining imprint of her presence the sudden chill of his skin where she had touched him. He crossed his arms over his chest to lay his fingers on his shoulders, sensing the dissipating warmth of her hands. He looked over his shoulder, but as he expected, she was gone. With a frown, he let

2

his hands slide down to lay on his thighs as he looked back to the mug of tea.

He sat for some time, alone, in the dark, his eyes burning. He pushed the com away, his arm holding a moment before he settled his hand in his lap. He rested back in his chair, gazed out the portal to the emptiness of space, and took a sip of tea.

A shrug, slight and almost involuntary, pulled at his shoulders.

***

He blinked, coming to his senses at the sound of snapping fingers. His eyes darted about to place him in his usual pub within the engineering section of the inter-system shipping nexus where his freighter was docked. He looked across the regular customers until his eyes fell on the man sitting across from him.

"Hey, Jansing, you still with me?"

Stohko looked at the man for a moment. He glanced down at the beer mug he realized he held in his hand. He looked back at the man across from him. "My credit's good, Piccolo."

Piccolo rubbed his beard, a grin seizing him as he lounged back in his seat. He was a dock foreman, but he was also a marketeer, and despite Stohko's reliance on him, Stohko held no illusion about Piccolo's nature. "You know, I like you Stohko," Piccolo said, but sighed as he opened his hands on the table. "It's just this stuff you need, you know, it's not in my regular catalog of goods. That means I have to have it brought in special, and special considerations, well, that means special costs. If it wasn't some exotic designer thing, it would be different, but being that I have to have it made, well, you understand. There's only so much consideration I can give a former Navy man."

Stohko stared at him. "My credit is good," he said again.

Piccolo's grin faded to a crooked frown. "Is it? I hear your business is real soft lately."

Stohko's eyes narrowed on Piccolo. "I know you have the pills."

Piccolo's face settled. "I like you." His eyes wandered over the black ceiling before settling back on Stohko. "Tell you what: I have a little job for you—do it, and I'll extend your credit."

Stohko sat. He didn't blink, he didn't flinch; in fact, he felt nothing, nothing but the heavy weight of *inevitability* pressing down on his shoulders. He sipped his beer. "What?"

Piccolo grinned. "Simple. Just another walk around."

"Just another walk around," Stohko echoed.

Piccolo opened his hands. "See? No problem. Meet me back here tonight, late. Until then, fare thee well, Captain Jansing," Piccolo said with disarming whimsy as he raised his mug. He emptied his beer and stood, laying his hand on the table before withdrawing it to his pocket.

Stohko stared at the plastic bottle Piccolo had left on the table. After several moments his hand settled on the bottle and drew it into the depths of his long black coat.

"That's a good boy," Piccolo said and patted him on the shoulder before leaving.

Stohko stared into his mug. He pulled the bill of his black cap low over his gaze.

***

He emerged to his senses standing beside the dock link to his freighter, the armored transport *Solitude.* Pallia stood several steps off to his side with their executive officer from the *Solitude*, a man Pallia had often relied on during Stohko's time in the Navy. His name was Lucas Owen, and he and Pallia shared a comfortable demeanor that made Stohko's heart jealous in its muted recesses, despite the hidden hypocrisy of the emotion. Nevertheless, his eyes narrowed on Owen's fit, officious frame as Owen stood by Pallia—too close, perhaps?— haggling with a dock engineer about repairs to one of the *Solitude*'s thruster assemblies. Stohko looked away to return his gaze to the similarly officious, slender man before him, who wore an impeccable Internal Security uniform. It was deep blue, with red piping about the collar. If there was one thing Stohko missed about the Navy, it was the feel of a crisp uniform, the sense of *meaning*, of purpose, that it conveyed.

The IS officer was talking, he realized. He looked down to find a file folder in his hand.

"Well?" the officer said, prompting him.

Pallia turned.

Stohko cleared his throat and blinked before his eyes settled on the folder. "I don't think so," he heard himself say. Pallia's lips parted, but he shook his head, and at the will of his subconscious memory of what the IS man had been saying, he grew certain of it, sending Pallia back to her negotiation. He looked up to the annoyed officer. "Colonel Osler, I don't do military subcontracting."

The IS man tipped his head, perplexed. "Your business is collapsing, or need I remind you that your wife's familial endeavor has had its reputation ruined by her unfortunate decision to remain with you?"

Stohko stared at the man. He knew it was true.

The lack of his response only seemed to fuel Osler's ire. "I could have all your shipping licenses revoked," he said, waving a finger to accentuate the threat. "You're free on probation only under the auspices of IS and my conduct reports. I know you have associations with a certain Jason Piccolo. That alone is enough to revoke your release papers."

Stohko studied Osler, a slow dissection from his gaze that unnerved the IS man. "Tell me, Colonel, of all the firms here, why is it so important that I take this contract?"

"You do claim to specialize in high risk transport, do you not?"

Stohko tipped back his cap and rubbed his forehead. "There's high risk, and then there's military high risk."

Osler glanced at Pallia, Owen, and the engineer before grabbing Stohko's arm and leading him out of hearing range. Stohko followed, but his glare at Osler's hand made the IS man recoil as if stung. "Orders have been filed," Osler said, keeping his voice to a hiss. "This job is to be done—handled—and little note made of it. The scripted fee should offer you enough evidence of that. It is only out of respect—no, pity—for your wife that I'm even offering it to you as a paid shipment. My initial inclination was to simply order you to do it or send you back into custody, so that you could rot out the rest of your despicable life in prison. Do you understand me?"

Stohko pursed his lips. That sense of weight on his shoulders returned, amplified as Pallia came up beside him. Owen trailed two steps behind her. "Is there a problem here?" she said.

Osler smiled on her. "Not a problem, but an offer. Paid, priority. You would leave as soon as possible."

Owen shook his head. "We're in no shape to go anywhere."

Pallia frowned. "Owen's right. We're not space-worthy without that thrust assembly in working order."

Osler tipped his head. "I'll see to it."

"We'll need fuel," Pallia said, taking her clipboard from under her arm. "Provisions—"

Osler waved a hand. "Done, done, whatever it is, done."

Stohko shook his head and handed the file folder back to Osler. "You're too eager." He looked to Pallia. "We'll find another job." He turned back to Osler. "You can go away, IS man."

Pallia's mouth opened, but it was Osler who spoke first. "I'm not going—"

Stohko turned a threatening glare on Osler. The man fled at once.

The surprise, though, was still clear on Pallia's face. "What are you doing?" she asked, her eyes wide. "What the hell are you doing?"

Owen opened his hands. "We need the job, Captain." He hooked a thumb towards the *Solitude*. "Most of the crew is running out on their contracts—"

Pallia glanced over her shoulder to silence Owen before looking back to Stohko.

"You have to trust me on this," Stohko replied.

She shifted on her feet, laying a hand on her forehead as she looked back to the waiting engineer before leveling her gaze on Stohko. "We can't go on like this," she said, voicing her frustration. "We'll lose everything—what little we have left—we'll lose it all. You can't do this to me," she added, her voice trembling. "Stohko, I've been loyal, I've been patient, I *stayed*. After all that, you can't do this to me."

He closed his eyes. He remembered his meet with Piccolo. "I have to go."

She gasped. "Stohko? Please!" she said, grabbing his hand.

He shook her off with a grunt before realizing what he was doing. He turned back to her, the hurt plain in her eyes. For some reason, some cruel twisted reason, it gave him a remote satisfaction as Owen registered in his sight, standing behind her. Shame usurped him at once.

Remnant

His throat locked. What was there to say? How could he explain anything to her, if he couldn't remember it, explain it, to himself?

He lowered his head and walked away.

***

His feet carried him about the dock nexus as he navigated the many decks and interconnected tubes. He left the dock links and entered the Concourse, a comparatively spacious, bustling row of shops that, with its midst lined by a string of small trees, almost made one forget that the nexus was an entirely artificial structure, a massive station orbiting a sea-green gas giant in the barren depth of space. Like railroad towns of ancient Earth, the nexus existed only for the circumstance of intersecting shipping lanes; existed because it was a messy convenience to transfer goods, existed in the commercial lawlessness that was reality off the solid surface of a planet, far out on the very limits of humanity's reach into space. The irony, Stohko knew, was that it was up to men like Osler to maintain a basic order, to hold back the complete subversion of order by perverse elements embodied in people like Piccolo. Even so, Stohko sympathized with Osler. He had held a similar duty in the Navy; likewise, it was that previous life, or his attempt to make order where order had failed, that had pushed him under the thumbs of people like Osler and Piccolo.

It was not that he held any particular grudge against Osler—even if the IS man would periodically threaten him—but more that he knew the reality of men like Osler: as with Stohko, he was in business with Piccolo. In was unavoidable. A man like Osler, he had to make a choice, a dreadful choice, to either dance with the demon to keep it in check, or blind the sensitivities of morality and justify a brutal cleaning by keeping the end in sight. The latter had been Stohko's choice when he had been forced to make the decision, and the results had been disastrous.

You can't fight the tide, someone once told him, the voice whispering through his mind with bitter sentiment as he entered his preferred eatery. Like all stores on the Concourse it was cramped, but the owner, a man under Stohko's former Navy command, kept a table for him. It was not a pleasant place, the unsettling question of cleanliness concealed beneath the dim lighting and the dark resin tables and chairs. None of it bothered Stohko, but then, little bothered him anymore. It was not his choice; it was what he had been made.

He sat in his chair with a frown as that thought drifted through his head. It was why he went there—when he would go there—to sit in the shadows and lose himself in the blurry traces of old memories and thoughts. He hardly noticed when the bowl of seasoned rice noodles and the large cup of tea were set before him, as his eyes were fixed out the portal beside him on the little pinpoints of distant stars. When he looked down at the bowl and tea he contemplated the reality that this was yet another bill he couldn't afford to pay. His life, the new life he had tried to create in pathetic imitation of his old life, was collapsing, sinking in the mire of his past crimes.

You can't fight the tide.

He leaned an elbow on the table and twirled his fork in the noodles before stuffing them in his mouth. Then he sat back and chewed, letting them sit on his tongue before swallowing them. A sip of tea washed them down.

You can't fight the tide.

He thought of the job Osler had offered him. If it had been anything else, he would have snapped it up without a second thought. But the job Osler had, it would throw his old life and the mockery that was his new life into each other's face, and in the process, tear open every wound in his mind that had been sewn shut after his war-crimes trial. It was a deal he had made, handing himself over to Military Research as a test subject so that his physical life would be spared. Then again, he considered with another mouthful of noodles, perhaps all this was, in some greater sense, the punishment, the fulfillment, of the things he had done, that these last few years had only forestalled.

He sipped his tea. He stared at the stars. He thought of the pills in his pocket, of how he had been told if he did not take them, his mind would deteriorate, an unfortunate side effect of the tests he had endured. He thought of the pills, and how they made him an apathetic zombie, so repugnant even Pallia found it difficult to deal with him. He thought of the pills, and he remembered the voice on his com that would find him in his sleepless nights, and the nine year old girl he had shot dead, and the disgusting smile on Piccolo's face.

He sipped his tea. He looked up at the vandalized poster framed on the bulkhead across from him. It was an old travel poster for Hermium, the planet where he had been stationed. A lush planet of pristine white sand shores and crystalline blue oceans, it had been settled as a resort world, the most remote human settlement in space. Within a decade of its establishment a labor revolt erupted against the local Navy stations that managed the planet, festering until it was deemed an outright war, with his crimes serving as the grisly climax. In the end, the bureaucrats back on Earth had ordered a forced evacuation, resettling all Hermium's residents across space and listing the planet and its system's access as forbidden. It seemed a bit much to him at the time, but then he had come to understand after his trial that with the public disclosure of what he and his men had done, nobody was interested in vacationing among the echoes of those sins.

He licked his lips. Now that he thought about it, he never knew where he had been imprisoned after his trial. Had Osler given something away? Did it make a difference?

He stared at the stars. He thought he heard something, something very remote, a thing that was *in* him. He closed his eyes, his jaw clenching as he fought to focus on the trick he decided his ears were playing. *What is that? I know that sound, heard it in my head last night, like tinkling, like air bubbling in water...*

There was no sense to it, he decided. His eyes opened to the portal.

He took his pill, and forgot why he even cared about the whispering dream of reality in his head.

***

The blink of his eyes served to return him to his senses.

Startled, his gaze darted about as he realized he sat on a bench. It was one of a short row, perched atop a low veranda at the edge of the common square on one of the civic decks. His gaze lowered to take in the sight. A large set of stenciled blue letters on the bulkhead across from him spelled out their collective home: NEXUS 9. It seemed an odd, obtrusive reminder of where he was in space. And then the letters were lost, obscured in the passing crowds of the late day rush as people returned from the various duty decks to their cramped little residences. Across from him, a battery of lights blinked above a set of doors that hissed aside on their hydraulic pistons. Several IS personnel stepped out, clearing an area of the crowd before the sound of children rose up: school was out for the day.

He clenched his teeth and swallowed. Perhaps no one had seen him—

"Colonel," a voice said in greeting.

He blinked and dared to look to his side as an IS man sat beside him. He didn't recognize the man, but no one greeted him by his old Navy rank, except some of the scattered remnants of his former counter-insurgency command. His head sank. "I'm sorry," he said, fighting to find his voice, "but I don't remember you."

The IS man lounged back on the bench and nodded as his eyes surveyed the crowd below, watching parents as they gathered to retrieve their children. "That's okay, Colonel. I heard the rumors, that they did things to you after the trial. I always thought you got a raw deal, to tell you the truth, Sir."

"I'm not your CO anymore," Stohko reminded him.

The IS man nodded again. "I know. I just wanted to say that, so you wouldn't misunderstand me."

Stohko closed his eyes.

"You know it's a violation of your release to be around the school," the IS man said.

Stohko opened his mouth, but then closed it, yet in his next breath he heard his voice, and he could not be sure if it came from his throat or not. "This wretched pile of metal is no place for children to grow. They should know fresh air and the open sky."

The IS man sighed. "Shouldn't we all."

Stohko trembled. He hated himself for having wandered to the school, but he refused to hold his silence, and his voice came in a hiss. "She was like a daughter to me," he said, his hands closing to fists, "and *still* I shot her. If only I could take that back."

"But you can't," the IS man said with a tip of his head. "And since you were convicted of murdering that child, the Navy Judiciary ruled you a threat to all children."

Stohko frowned and closed his eyes.

The IS man turned to him. "Look, Colonel, you have to go, understand?"

Stohko looked to the children. They were kept in rows, filing into a merge to slip away one at a time through the IS men to their parents. His face fell, his curiosity nagging him, for the sight seemed somehow familiar, but in the end his attention was drawn to their complexion.

They were deathly pale, for they had never felt the warmth of a sun. He pulled the bill of his cap down and walked away.

***

"So there's nothing else?" he asked again.

Choykin, the beefy Transit Officer of Nexus 9, looked to him over the glasses that sat low on his great bulbous nose. "I told you three times already, there's nothing here for you. They hear the name Stohko Jansing and they book with anybody else. You're a goddamn pariah, you know that? And by the way, when do you plan on paying your link rental? You think I'll let that decaying tub of junk of yours sit on one of my links until you get something?"

Stohko scratched his forehead as he stared across Choykin's large, cluttered desk to the TO's nose. "What about waste hauling?"

Choykin laughed. "Oh, now you must be desperate," he said with a shake of his head, then cursed under his breath. He pointed to the window of his office, which looked down into the refuse processing pod of the nexus. "You know we replaced waste hauling with canister dumping into the giant's atmosphere back when we got the refuse pod added to our structure. Ruined my view." Choykin's chair creaked under his weight as he settled back and tossed the heavy outbound roster's clipboard onto his desk. "Look, Osler's job is all there is for you, so either suck it up and take it, or I have no choice but to appeal to him as the chief IS officer to revoke your link reservation. Tell you the truth, at least then I'll have some business running off your link instead of the nothing you got going on." He fell silent, looking over the cramped confines of his office before settling back on Stohko. "Ah Christ, you are one sorry son-of-a-bitch, you know that? Listen, because I think you should have got a reward for kicking ass on Hermium, I'll give you a little break."

Stohko closed his eyes.

"This military transport that Osler wants you to tow out, the *Chrysopoeia*, I think there's some kind of toxic shit or something on there and Osler's covering it up. You know these dock link rats we got up here, those big hairy gray bastards, they're the toughest things in space, and on this ship's link, all the rats, they're turning up dead in the three days since that damn transport showed up. One of Piccolo's boys put himself out an airlock a few hours ago. No explanation. Just as well—another one of Piccolo's grunts, but now I've got a mountain of paperwork to fill out. Take Osler's job," he ordered, "take that thing off my nexus, and I'll give you an extension on your back fees for your link reservation. Otherwise, I'll have *you* towed out."

Stohko leaned forward in his seat.

Choykin opened his hands. "Well?"

Stohko stood and stepped to Choykin's window. He looked down into the garbage pod at the large mechanized operation. Recyclables were sorted out for further processing, but the rest of the waste was pounded together and then smashed into gray canisters. They passed along in rows by their processor receptacles to merge by the airlock control before being blown out toward the gas giant beneath them. He remembered the school, and with disgust understood where that strange sense of familiarity had come. He lowered his head and turned.

Choykin waited, drumming his fingers on his belly. "So?"

"I have a meeting to go to," Stohko said and walked off.

Choykin slapped his hands on his desk before pulling his bulk from his chair. "Hey! Jansing! Next time send your wife! I'd rather deal with her pretty face!"

***

Stohko made his way back to the dock links, but didn't return to the *Solitude*. Instead, he worked his way from link to link until he found the object of his curiosity, the little military transport *Chrysopoeia,* alone on the terminal end of a vacant four-link dock extension. The lights had been powered down due to the lack of traffic—and, no doubt, for Choykin's annoyance at the troublesome transport's presence—so that he found himself a solitary shadow standing at the head of the ribbed rampway leading into the extension. At the far end, through the viewing portals, he could make out the dark outline of the transport.

His heart began to pound.

His eyes narrowed as he laid his hand on his chest, curious over the riot of anxiety that mounted within his body, for it was something he had not felt in a very long time. At first he questioned the pill, wondering if between Osler and Choykin and Piccolo and Owen it had been decided to do away with him. Perhaps Pallia had been part of that decision. She had, after all, urged him to see Piccolo—

No. She would never do that. How could I even suspect her?

His mouth went dry. The old paranoia stirred within him like some waking monster.

His chest began to tighten as he stared at the transport's outline. He knew the class of ship; it was a local hauler, underpowered for deep space routes. Two man crew. *Two man crew.* His eyes darted about. And in a moment, what he believed was his worst fear manifested from paranoia to apprehension to clear certainty to form a single unnerving thought within his head.

Siona… You're here, not just a voice on my com now…

There was something else with the thought, something that nagged him, burning at the base of his skull and knotting his stomach. He thought of what Choykin had said about the dead rats and one of Piccolo's men going out an airlock, and it only served to crystallize a new suspicion within the muddy memories of his post-trial torture in the military's research labs.

Siona, you're not alone…

He gasped and forced himself away. If he thought he could confront himself, force himself to accept Osler's contract as the only way out of so many binds, he had fooled himself. He broke into a cold sweat as he backed away, anxious to put the extension far behind.

***

He sat at a table towards the back of his pub, waiting on Piccolo behind the vapors of a teapot. The walk down to the pub had been uneventful, but he was aware of it, which was something of note for him. It was not the pill, he decided. Something else was happening, something *within* him, and he was entirely aware of its coincidence within the maturing web of circumstances enmeshing him. It was the weight of Inevitability he felt on his shoulders, and even though it grew, it was transforming over the course of this rather strange day, transforming him, as if waking him to something that had long slept within him, so long he had forgotten its existence, so that it was a thing strange and unknown to him, and unpredictable as to where it might lead him.

He closed his eyes and breathed in the vapors of his tea. It had been a long time since his mind had worked with any kind of energy, the thought evident for the very nature of its consideration: his mind and *its* thoughts, as if he were some dissociated witness to himself. But he knew that sense, remembered that sense all too well, for it was central to his nightmare, and enveloped him whenever his memories tortured him with the sight of that young girl beneath the flash of the gun in his hand.

"Jansing."

Stohko opened his eyes to see two men settling in chairs to either side of him. They were two of Piccolo's enforcers, dockhands he knew only as Lugnut and Spanner. It was typical of Piccolo, which was to say it was typical of personnel on a shipping nexus. The claustrophobic confines of the nexus, the striking and stark delineation of the massive hull's remote inner space against the harsh expanse of vacuum, the inescapable surroundings of machines and equipment, the ever present hissing of hydraulic systems and the subtle moan of air circulators all served to reduce people to labels from random objects.

You can't fight the tide.

Stohko tipped his head.

"Piccolo's on his way," Spanner said.

Stohko nodded. *I hate this place.* The simplicity of the thought stunned him, but at the same time stirred his suspicions. "Piccolo said it was just a walk."

Lugnut laughed. "Hey, it thinks."

Spanner grinned. "A walk? Yeah, well, things changed, Piccolo said." He grabbed the teapot and sniffed the vapors before shoving it across the table towards Stohko. "Looking scary isn't enough this go around. Time to *be* scary."

Piccolo emerged from behind some men standing by the bar to pace toward their table. He looked them over. "Let's go," he said, tension plain on his face.

They walked the corridors of the nexus and took a serpentine path to make their way into the less traveled service corridors, empty now in the late hour of the artificial day imposed within the nexus. Nobody spoke, the only interaction between them when Piccolo came to a halt before a residential deck's lock to hand out black hoods. Stohko stood there with the hood in his hand, his heart sinking as he began to realize that indeed this would not be a simple walk around, that his menacing presence alone would not suffice to get Piccolo results. No, if the presence of Lugnut and Spanner was not enough to rouse his suspicion, then the hoods finished the work.

He looked to Piccolo. "Where are we going?"

Piccolo glared at him. "Move," he said with impatience.

They emerged from the lock and followed Piccolo down several corridors. If their previous path had been twisted, this one was as direct as possible and in short time they stood before a residence's security door. Piccolo went to work on the door's card reader, bypassing the door's security to push it open.

Stohko paced down the short, narrow entry of a typical residence. Like most rooms on the nexus, it was cramped, but efficient in its use of space, so that the constant rubbing of elbows did not instill too great a sense of claustrophobia. Despite that, it was not comfortable for four men and furniture, as they had little space to move. Piccolo shifted about with his anxiety, checking the kitchen and bedrooms while Spanner and Lugnut pulled on their hoods. Stohko gazed over the domesticity of the little residence and was reminded of the school and its crowd of children. It drove his memories back before his trial to his time in the Navy and his duties, of open air on a planet, of a warm sun and the innocent laughter of a little girl—

His eyes widened, the sight they beheld intersecting his reverie with a numbing collision. Before him on the wall, on a little oak mantle, sat a set of framed pictures. Although the presence of any wood was a sign of luxury on the nexus, that detail was forgotten as his eyes focused on the pictures themselves. They were of Osler, not as the annoying officer that Stohko knew, but as a family man, pictured with his wife and son. And as much as those pictures unsettled Stohko as he realized in which residence he stood, it was the last picture that seemed to vaporize his innards and leave him a gutted zombie of fractured memories.

It was a picture of Osler and his wife, their son a mere infant, dating the picture. And huddled with them, in that clumsy smiling way of familial portraits, was a young woman with her daughter.

He turned a caustic eye on Piccolo.

Piccolo stepped from the kitchen and caught Stohko's gaze, but when he saw the pictures behind Stohko he shrugged. "What?" he said before blowing out a breath. "You can't tell me you didn't know. Are you that spaced out?"

Stohko pursed his lips.

Piccolo stepped before him and snapped his fingers in Stohko's face. "That's right, Osler's half sister was Ellen Fortas. Remember? Her daughter's name was Elena, the same ones you took up with during your time on Hermium."

Ellen—

Stohko's memory flashed. "I never betrayed my wife," he said between clenched teeth.

Piccolo stared at him for a moment. "So you do remember," Piccolo said under his breath. "Well, do you remember the rest of Hermium? Did you forget it was the uprising, and Melogo Isla, your supposed negotiating partner and friend, that were responsible for blowing up Ellen and Elena and nearly killing you? It's what set you loose, the reprisal campaign of Stohko Jansing, founder of the Fallen Angels death squads. Did you think we all just went away?"

Stohko blinked. "You, all of you, you were all there?"

"Goddamn right," Lugnut said from beneath his hood.

Stohko shook his head. "No, no... That's behind me, that's all gone now."

Piccolo blew out a breath and slapped the back of his hand against Stohko's chest. "We're all over the place on this nexus! Why do you think you get so many breaks? If you were anybody else I would've had you out an airlock a long time ago—but that's *exactly* why we're here right now, Jansing."

Stohko ground his teeth.

Piccolo shoved him against the wall. "Listen! Osler had something brought here on that goddamn transport, something that shouldn't be here, and I don't want it here. So for that he has to pay and you have to get it out of here to get that fat bastard Choykin off my back." He paused, but when he saw the look in Stohko's eyes, he frowned. "That's right, Osler's kid, too. We're cleaning house. If you won't kill the boy I'll take him and sell him off. There's a market for that, don't forget."

Stohko's lips parted as his eyes came to rest on the picture of Ellen and Elena. He thought of the transport. He thought of Pallia. He thought of Siona, and then he thought of Siona on the transport, and how Ellen and Elena had died... And then he remembered how he had exacted his terrible revenge on his good friend Melogo Isla by murdering his daughter in front of him. His head tipped back. Things connected in his head at the will of his paranoia: the coincidence of the transport, of sensing Siona, of his memories sparking to life within him. The odd sensation of waking from some long stupor came to him once more, and with it came an even greater sense of Inevitability's weight upon his shoulders. He shrugged.

As confusing as it was, it all made a certain sense to him.

Piccolo stared at him. "You're good?"

Stohko turned to him. "I'm good."

Piccolo nodded. Stohko pulled on his hood.

They did not have to wait long. There was the sound of voices outside the door before the lock released. Light from the corridor revealed three shadows, stretching in from the doorway between Lugnut and Spanner.

"Can I stay up?" came the boy's voice, but Osler's wife piped up at once. "It's very late," she said with a maternal tone. "Now quick, get ready for bed."

The family emerged from the walkway into the sanctity of their home.

They never knew what hit them.

Lugnut moved first, crumpling Osler with a vicious punch to the gut that lifted him off his feet and doubled him over. Stohko seized the boy and yanked him aside as Spanner slapped his large hand over the woman's face and whipped her around to slam her head into the wall. The boy yelped, but his cry was muffled by Stohko's hand while Stohko's other hand covered the boy's panic stricken eyes. His mother flopped to the floor as Spanner let go of her, Spanner's big hands seizing Osler by the collar so Lugnut could drive another crippling punch into Osler's stomach. Vomit erupted from the man's mouth.

Stohko turned, spinning the boy away from the scene before pressing the boy's face against his side. He looked back over his shoulder to see Lugnut and Spanner throw Osler against the wall. Spanner pulled Osler's handgun free, only for Stohko to snatch the gun from Spanner's hand. The man gave him a murderous glare but Piccolo stilled him with a smack on his shoulder.

"We're against the outer hull of the nexus," Stohko hissed. "You could vent us into space!"

Piccolo looked to him. "What are you waiting for? Take care of that!" he said, waving a hand at Osler's son.

Stohko shoved the boy toward a bedroom and closed the door behind them. The boy staggered back, trembling, tears running from his eyes. Stohko dropped the gun into a pocket of his long coat and crouched before the boy. He took off his hood and looked the boy in the eyes. He put a finger to his lips before speaking in a whisper. "I'm not going to hurt you," he said, opening his hands. Then he reached out, slow and gentle, to lay his hands on the boy's shoulders. He pulled him close so that he could whisper in his ear. The boy nodded, and, still trembling, hid in his closet.

There was a knock on the door.

Stohko stood, took out the gun, pressed it to the boy's pillow on his bed, and pulled the trigger.

A few heartbeats after the muffled pop of the gun there was another knock.

He opened the door, but stood in the doorway to stare eye to eye with Piccolo.

"Your hood," Piccolo said.

Stohko shrugged. "No witness."

"What about the outer hull?"

Stohko stepped past Piccolo and closed the door. "I wanted the gun."

Piccolo chuckled and walked over to Osler as Lugnut held him against the wall. Piccolo punched Osler in the side, causing Osler's body to warp and a groan to slip from his lips. Spanner had rolled Osler's wife over and was fumbling with the suspenders of his utility suit as she lay on the floor, clinging to consciousness. "You can have a turn when we're done," Spanner said to him, then looked to Lugnut and laughed.

Stohko turned to Piccolo. "Old habits don't change, do they?"

Piccolo punched Osler again. "The Fallen Angels ride!" he said with pride. "Just like old times!"

"Just like old times," Stohko echoed.

He frowned.

He shot Spanner in the temple, swung his arm, and shot Lugnut between the eyes. The two of them were dead before they hit the floor. The small caliber of Osler's service gun left little red marks where the bullets smashed through their skulls, the rounds lacking enough power to blast out the opposite sides of their heads. Piccolo blinked at the sudden eruption of the gun, the two pops so close together he failed to discern them until his eyelids rose to the blinding white flash of the barrel's snout. Blood ran from the hole in the middle of his forehead, down his nose, to drip on his shoes. His knees buckled and dumped him to the floor.

Stohko lowered the gun.

He listened to Osler as the man fought to breathe.

He looked down at the gun in his hand. He looked at the three men he had just killed. His face was blank.

Osler's wife groaned.

Stohko wiped the grip of the gun on his shirt before kneeling and pressing the weapon into Osler's shaking hand. The IS man's eyes bored into Stohko, but Stohko ignored him. Instead, he slipped off his coat, draped it over Osler's wife, and helped her to her feet before whispering for her to see her son. She dropped his coat and fled the room. Osler struggled to his feet, sucking in shallow breaths to come to a hunched stance against the wall. Stohko looked back to him. "You saved your family," he said to Osler. "You're a hero. I had nothing to do with it. I'm not here."

The gun fell from Osler's hand.

Stohko picked up his jacket and slipped it on. Osler's wife emerged in the doorway of their son's bedroom, holding the boy close at her side, his face turned into her as he clung to her. She stared at Stohko for several moments before she found her voice. "Thank you, Mister —"

"You have to go," Osler interrupted. "Now. My men will be here —"

"Nobody heard a thing, not through these bulkheads," Stohko said with clear confidence. He looked to Osler's wife. "Close the door. I need a moment of your husband's time."

She glared at Osler, but he waved her away.

Stohko waited for the door to close. He looked to Osler. "Tell me about this transport."

Osler bowed his head, his eyes darting about the residence.

"Tell me about the transport and I'll take it away," Stohko added. When Osler hesitated, Stohko tipped his chin to the floor. "They were here because of that transport."

Osler stared at the three bodies sprawled about Stohko. "If you did this you have to know," Osler said, his voice tight. He looked at Stohko. "The order came from up above: get rid of the transport. You know who's on board that thing — Siona Hutchins and Jason Bhandhakar — they have their orders, too." He pushed himself off the wall and pulled out his com.

"Nothing more?"

Osler looked at Stohko as he keyed in a call code. "I can never repay you for what you did here tonight, but that doesn't translate beyond us. Look, this transport didn't just show up here, it was *sent* here specifically for you to take it in tow along the rest of its route. The Navy, they're settling all accounts." He glanced at his com. "I'm calling Choykin. We're going to clean up this mess so that nobody knows what happened to Piccolo. It's in our best interests. But after that, you have to go."

Stohko nodded. He looked back to the pictures on the mantle.

Osler's eyes narrowed when he discerned the focus of Stohko's gaze. "Ellen Fortas was my half-sister," Osler explained. "That was my niece that died next to you. I guess you could say I have an agenda to meet as well. But that doesn't make what you did right." He paused, letting out a sigh. "We have to talk, Stohko. All this, all these things, they have to end."

***

After Osler called Choykin, Choykin came with his secretary and several men.

Osler sent off his wife and son with the secretary. The boy looked at Stohko as his mother led him away, the wide-eyed look of a child who just learned that reality is a vast ugly mess, that innocence is a lofty, angelic dream.

Choykin's men swept over the residence, but it was Choykin, Stohko and Osler who loaded the bodies into a janitor dolly Choykin's men had brought with them. Choykin led them down to his office, then beyond to the refuse pod. And once there, Choykin and Stohko donned heavy rubber aprons and attempted to stuff the bodies into the little gray waste canisters. When they refused to fit, Choykin hefted a heavy mallet used to seal the occasional canisters kicked off the automated line and smashed the hips of each body. Osler had grabbed an apron, but at the dull crunching of the mallet at work the IS man lost his nerve and faded into the shadows. Choykin prodded Stohko with an elbow and joked about it, saying that he knew where the son got his wide-eyed look.

When it was done Stohko took the mallet from Choykin. Choykin and Osler watched as the canisters floated away, sinking to the crushing, senile depths of the green gas giant beneath them. Osler turned to Stohko, and without a word, handed him the shipping terms for the *Chrysopoeia*.

Choykin laughed. "Deal's a deal," he said as Stohko left.

***

Stohko found himself sitting at the little table in his cabin. His com was on the table beside his cup of tea. It was late. He was exhausted, but sleep would not come, denied by the muddied wash of memories welling up in his mind.

At some point Pallia shuffled from their bed, rubbing her eyes with the sleeve of her long blue nightshirt as she leaned on the bulkhead framing the kitchen's entrance. He looked at her, waiting for her to say something.

She sat down across from him and took a sip of his tea. "Can't sleep?"

He pulled out the *Chrysopoeia*'s terms and slid them before her.

She blinked several times as her sleepy mind fought to make sense of the papers. When she did, her eyes grew wide before rising to meet his gaze. Her lips pulled to a small smile. She pushed herself up, kissed him on the forehead, and whispered in his ear. "Come to bed. You'll need your sleep."

He grabbed her hand. "Pallia?"

She tipped her head at the sudden urgency of his tone, but when he failed to speak she laid a hand on his cheek. "You did the right thing," she said and went back to bed.

He looked at the terms. He thought of Osler's son, of the look in his eyes. Then he thought of Osler, and the things Osler had told him.

He frowned and looked out the portal.

His com vibrated. Without looking he turned it off and sipped his tea.

II

He woke in the still quiet of his cabin. The patter of soft rain from his old nightmare echoed in his ears until he shook his head to clear his senses. He glanced over his shoulder to make sure Pallia still slept, then slipped from their bed. He pulled on his bodysuit, taking care to slowly close the zipper as not to wake her. That done, he made his tea, took his com, and left the cabin.

For some time he walked about the ship, deceiving himself with the idea that he was doing a little inspection, as was a captain's wont, even on third watch, when all but a few second tier personnel on the bridge were fast asleep. Satisfied that he had not succeeded in fooling himself, he stood before the lock he thought he would have avoided, but accepting the futility of that, he keyed the lock release and stepped through.

The link bubble was a small protrusion from the ship's hull, a little hemisphere of heavy ribs and plexi panes that allowed for direct viewing of the *Solitude*'s burden, coupled in hard-lock beneath the hollow curve of the ship's belly. Beneath him, clutched to the hull in the transport's massive actuated coupler arms, was the little burden of their trip, the *Chrysopoeia*. With a frown, he settled into the bubble's chair and pushed aside the terminal console's arm to get a clearer view. For behind the *Chrysopoeia*, and filling the empty void of space beneath them lay their destination: the planet Hermium, its oceans a glittering blue expanse under the light of a pale yellow sun.

They had settled into orbit two hours before third watch, initiating an exhaustive set of navigational chores. At Owen's urging and Pallia's agreement, he consented to let the ship pass into the sleep period of third watch. Starting first watch would come the long task of atmospheric entry preparation, consuming most of the next watch as the crew did a full inspection of both ships before penetrating the atmosphere and settling on Hermium's abandoned surface. It made his skin crawl at the very notion of returning, but it was the letter of the orders Osler had given to Stohko. Worse, he would have to insist on boarding the *Chrysopoeia*, something he had avoided during their trip, and something for which he had serious misgivings—the disruptions the little ship's presence had caused back on Nexus 9 had seemed to dog them on their way to Hermium. As the watches passed he witnessed a pattern that was disturbingly similar to things he remembered from his time on Hermium: petty fights had erupted among the crew, while other men who were normally focused and capable, had grown distracted and lax in their duties. It reminded him of something, something that woke like a screaming child from his memories to stir him from this latest of uneasy sleep periods: *Hermium euphoria.*

He sipped his tea. In a moment of clarity, he debated jettisoning the little ship, and letting Hermium claim it, but circumstances would not be so convenient. He could only release the coupler arms from the bridge, and Osler had made a point of informing the *Solitude*'s junior officers that the *Chrysopoeia* be left on Hermium intact. As to what the ship contained, it bothered Stohko, for like Siona, it seemed like a remnant of his torture come back to haunt him. Then again, he figured it must haunt the Navy as well; the confidential shipping terms Osler had furnished him held special clearance codes to bypass the armed drones at the edge of Hermium's system. They were the Navy's solution to secure the planetary blockade after the forced removal of the resident population.

He clenched his fists. For all the vastness of space, he felt the claustrophobic confines of his narrow little life, trapped between Choykin and Osler and his own past, his disastrous past on this place that now hung beneath him.

I shouldn't be here, but Osler was right. It has to end.

His com vibrated, startling him.

He pulled it from his pocket, but with an unsettling feeling his gaze was drawn back out the plexi, down beneath him to the bridge panes of the *Chrysopoeia*. They had lit, and standing there, to his discomfort, he recognized Siona.

He narrowed his eyes to see her put a com to her ear. Despite his reluctance, he followed suit. "Hello Stohko," she said, her voice calm.

He forced himself to swallow.

"It's good to see you," she continued. "It's been too long."

His skin began to tingle. He laid a hand over his face as he leaned forward to rest his elbows on his knees, his eyes locked on her.

She splayed a hand on the bridge pane before her, a tinge of sadness on her face. "You never called."

"There's nothing to say," he replied, the rasp of his voice surprising him.

She dropped her hand. "I led you back to her."

He squeezed his eyes shut.

"Have you forgotten that as well?"

His eyes popped open as he jabbed a finger at her. "You led me back to nothing! It was all a trick!" He sucked in a breath, his heart pounding. "The things you did to me—you used her as the carrot for the mule, and I never understood until too late!"

She frowned. "I'm sorry you feel that way."

He shifted nervously in the chair, but found himself riveted before her. In that moment he hated her, hated her because of what he had done on the nexus, hated her for the pills in his pocket and their incessant whisper, hated her for keeping him alive during his torture, dangling from the memory of Pallia without ever telling him he would be hopelessly isolated from her. All for some precious research, which had obviously failed, given that he was assigned the task of dumping it on a forgotten, forbidden world.

He stood and smacked his fist on the plexi. Even with the vacuum between them, it made her step back, her eyes blinking and widening in surprise. "You should have let me die!" he said, his voice laden with guilt and shame.

She came back to the pane, and her voice returned with its deceptive calm. "Do you believe that? That's not what Pallia said."

His breath locked in his throat.

"She came aboard, once, after we left the nexus. And do you know what she did, Stohko Jansing? She thanked me. It was remarkable. How soothing it must be, how soothing it could be, more than any pill I could give you, to be loved like that," she added, her voice almost inaudible over the com. "If only I could be, if someone..."

He slumped in the chair. He dropped the com in his lap.

She stared at him. The bridge lights went out, and she was gone.

He lingered in the bubble, locked in the paralysis of his own thoughts. He pushed off his cap, his eyes squeezing shut as his hands clamped over his head and clawed at his scalp. Visions began to spark within him, dreams of realities that had come and gone, that had been ripped from him during his torture to leave only wounds, like photo-negative bas-reliefs that spawned color and filled, not with the puss of shame and guilt and resentment, but with the blood of life, the confused life he had lived from the first moment he heard the name Hermium and the planet set its odd spell about him.

He sank into his seat, and he felt himself falling, falling through a wave of pain into a mindless stupor to confirm what he had feared all along, that seeing Siona would be the trigger, the trigger that would let his memories wake within him, a chaotic eruption of jumbled moments in time...

***

"Please state your name for the record."

Stohko looked down from the ceiling panels above him to regard the Navy barrister sitting across the table from him. The barrister was an angular, proper little man, another of those bureaucratic types Stohko had come to hate. He could not help but let out a short, singular laugh at the idiocy of the man's question.

"Please state your name for the record," the man repeated, his eyes fixed on the papers before him.

Stohko frowned. He stared at the barrister's expressionless face, annoyed by the man's mechanistic repetition of the question. Stohko's temper, long left unrestrained by his reckless flippancy, vented once again. The formalities were a torture—he knew what was coming, that he had traded a death sentence by handing himself over to the military for their research. He would have his life, but he would be their test rat first. It made a mockery of bureaucratic formalities such as the barrister's pointless question. He slammed his palms on the table, startling the barrister, and stood from his seat.

The door to the little interrogation room opened to reveal a slender woman in a dark Navy uniform that bore no rank or insignia of any kind. He studied her for a moment, his eyes narrowed with violent rage, as he contemplated how quickly he could make it out the open door. The clumsy barrister gathered his papers and stood back from the table, disarmed by both his fear and the woman's apparent ease. The man opened his mouth, but she raised a finger to him and smiled, then stepped aside and motioned for him to leave. "If you would," she asked, but her large dark eyes remained on Stohko.

The barrister fled at once.

She closed the door and opened a hand to Stohko's chair. "Please, sit. Your leg, does it still hurt? It was a grievous incident, from what I hear."

He clenched his teeth, but stilled himself, knowing the obvious futility of his prior urge to attempt an escape. It was a clever maneuver on her part, he decided, reminding him that he would not get far with his leg as it was: the limitation of his body was a more immediate thing than the abstract thought of guards and security locks. And it told him something else: she was thinking of more than the crimes he had committed. *Grievous incident*—she was looking at the whole situation; she was speaking of Ellen and Elena.

He tipped his head, not sure what to say, but he studied her nevertheless, scrutinizing her with the same dissecting stare that had withered others in his final terrible days in the Navy. This woman, though, did not flinch, instead meeting his gaze and holding the ease of her smile. She had a pleasant face, framed by long dark hair that fell past her shoulders. From a distance, she could remind him—

He forced himself to swallow.

"Why don't we start from the beginning, shall we?" she said, her voice snapping him from his thoughts. Her congenial tone sounded more as if they had gathered to reminisce over a quiet afternoon tea. She offered her hand in greeting. "Stohko Jansing, my name is Siona Hutchins."

***

Stohko paced with rapid, excited steps about his captain's cabin, waving his hand to the portal and the distant stars as he spoke. "This is a real opportunity, Pallia. You have to believe me. I know it'll be time away, and you'll have to manage things, but Owen, he'll be a great help. This could open so much for us."

Pallia sat at their little table, her hands resting on either side of their logistics reports, a pencil bobbing between her fingers. "It's the military," she said as her only explanation. "We're doing fine. Business is up. At this pace, we can even consider another ship in a year or two."

"Or three or four," he replied. He put the open recall letter he held in his hand on the table before her. "Read it, please," he said after calming himself. "It's not a draft. The Navy wants to recall some officers; they went to their reserve pool, and my name came up. They're not looking at mandatory service. I decide if I go, and I decide how long I stay, in three month terms."

She glanced at the paper and pushed it away. "That's now. How do you know how this Hermium mess is going to pan out? Yes, it could be a little six-month show of force to quiet the locals, or it could become another one of those full-blown labor insurrections. What do you think they're going to do then with all their volunteer officers? You'll be hooked in and that will be that."

He shook his head. "It's a resort world. Some waiters and cooks are unhappy, so what? It's barely a hundred thousand people living on that planet. They have no industry, and they're isolated way out on the very edge of human space. What kind of fight can they mount?"

She shook her head. "Goliath," she said, glancing to one side before glancing to the other, "meet David. Oops, that wasn't supposed to happen," she added with sarcastic whimsy and looked back to him.

He frowned and sat across from her. "A few months, that's it." He leaned toward her and took her hands. "Business out here, on this nexus, it's all about who you know. Aidan Keane, of Keane Supply—he's General Keane, now—they made him senior commander of the whole operation! If I can make a few contacts during my service, make myself known to him as part of the solution instead of part of the problem, think beyond adding a ship, think of having other people run the ships for us. We could *live* on Hermium. It's beautiful," he said as she rolled her eyes. "Tropical heat, yes, but a genuine white-sand-beach paradise, bright and warm."

She stared at him.

"We agreed this nexus is no place for a child, all cold and metallic and confined as it is," he said under his breath. "I hate being here. I hate that *you* have to be here—"

"We *both* decided it was best for the business," she said, her stubbornness flashing in her eyes.

They looked at each other. The moments passed.

In the end she relented, and despite her reluctance, nodded. "For us, then," she said with a sigh. She clutched his hand. "Get our piece of heaven so we can make some little angels," she whispered beneath her widening gaze.

***

Melogo Isla was a lean man of average height, his welcoming smile almost hiding the guile in his large, dark eyes. Nevertheless, he was the president of the Hermium Laborers Coalition, even if the office translated to only a passing authority on the chaotic group. He sat in Stohko's office, watching him rummage about to straighten the mess of records his predecessor had left behind. "Forgive me," Stohko said with some embarrassment, having hoped to impress Isla with some of the prestige invested in Stohko's recent promotion, "but I have only just arrived, and not all is how I would have it."

Melogo gave that disarming smile of his and opened his hands. "I could furnish you with office staff, if you would welcome it."

Stohko glanced over his shoulder to Melogo. "Thank you, but that won't be necessary. I contacted the Navy logistics pool and some help is to be billeted for these offices."

Melogo chuckled. "And do you think all your Navy comrades are as ambitious or efficient as you seem to be, Colonel Jansing?"

Stohko looked back to the file draw he was fingering through. "As a matter of fact I already have some help here; they arrived this afternoon."

"Do you mean Miss Ellen Fortas and her assistants?" Melogo chuckled again. "Those are my people. I sent them over, as a courtesy."

Stohko looked back to him. "I was not aware—"

Melogo waved him off. "No bother. Such is life on Hermium. I came here twenty years ago on a work contract as a janitor, and still I remain. You will find this world has a way with people, a way to make all things that seem straight and linear to become tangled and convoluted. It is such confusion that people refer to as the 'Hermium euphoria', that delirious sense of disembodied content so many travelers have felt here. But they are only visiting, and we live here, so the befuddlement is not all as it should be. Even the simplest little things become impossibly complicated here. That is why your predecessor let my staff run these offices for him. You will find Ellen is more than capable as an office manager."

Stohko blinked. "The HLC staffed the offices of the Navy peacekeepers sent to stabilize the insurgency of radical HLC factions," he thought aloud. "Now that's interesting."

Melogo shrugged and looked out the windows to the evening rain. "We are a world of laborers far from any labor source. It's only natural that the Navy subcontract work to local sources." He bobbed his head to either side, seeming to debate some matter with himself before letting out a low sigh. "It's a shame he won't see Hermium in bloom." He glanced at Stohko. "You're predecessor, that is."

Stohko shook his head. "He was an officer in good standing. He had a tenure that started several years before the insurrection. He was a valuable resource. His suicide was tragic."

Melogo opened his hands and smiled.

"Does that humor you?"

Melogo's smile vanished as he turned a very serious eye to Stohko. "No, not in the least. But you didn't know him as I did. He held no value or interest in family. Family is very important on our world, as there are so few of us. He was not a family man, as I am. Are you a family man?"

Stohko was caught unaware by the direct nature of Melogo's question. He turned once more to face this man he was finding fascinating in an odd, disarming way—the way of Hermium, he decided. "No, not yet," he said slowly. "But maybe one day."

"Wonderful!" Melogo exclaimed and clapped his hands together. "Then my daughter and I must have you as our guest. Ellen and her daughter will join us as well. We'll go fishing."

Stohko shook his head. "You're the president of the HLC—"

"Fancy that," Melogo interrupted.

"I'm the Navy representative on this world," Stohko continued.

"If you say so."

Stohko was perplexed that Melogo failed to understand the obvious conflict of interest such a gathering could embody. "I thank you, but I cannot accept the invitation."

Melogo frowned. "But this is how we do things here, we do them informally, with merriment, over fresh cut fish filets, with iced drinks of our local herbs. This is a resort world, and it is our way to convene as if we are all family—it is our tradition."

"Hermium has existed as a settlement for barely three decades," Stohko said. "You people haven't been here long enough to have tradition."

Melogo sighed. "Ah, now that's what your predecessor would have said."

Stohko looked to him.

"He rejected our Lady Hermium," Melogo said with lament. "Such a shame. In the end, he became such a *lonely* man."

***

Stohko sat on the edge of his bunk in his little white cell, his eyes hovering over the sensory cap he held in his hands. "So all I have to do is wear this while I sleep?"

Siona nodded. She was sitting on a stool across from him, her legs crossed to the side, her hands crossed in her lap. The cap was reflected on the lenses of her rectangular glasses. "You won't feel a thing," she said with a small, assuring smile.

He frowned.

She took a breath. "And I thought we had established some trust," she said, mock hurt in her voice. "I don't want you to feel quite so alone here; this is not adversarial, so we may have some trust."

"There's trust and then there's trust," he said, still studying the cap.

She stared at him in thought before replying. "Yet, you volunteered for this research."

"I volunteered not to die. So all I do is put this on?"

"And sleep," she added. "Dream, if you like. We would prefer you dream."

"So you can read my mind?"

She smiled. "Now why would we want to do that?" she asked, but then held up a hand to allay his suspicions. "Dreaming amplifies certain brain activity while you sleep, which makes our research somewhat easier to accomplish; but no, we are not reading your mind."

He looked up to her. "You know I don't sleep much anymore."

She tipped her head to his pillow. "Those pills will help."

"And this won't hurt?"

She did not blink. "You shouldn't feel a thing when it's done."

And with that, he put the cap on.

"No other questions?" she asked, perplexed by his sudden and unexpected acquiescence. "If you like, I could get Doctor Bhandhakar—"

He shrugged and held up a hand to dismiss her concern. "I agreed to this. It's this or I never see my wife again."

"You must have very strong feelings for her," she said, her voice low.

Moments passed. He stared at her, dwelling on the vague wording she had chosen for her question. She specified feelings, but had not specified *what* feelings. It only took a heartbeat for him to decide he

31

would keep the truth to himself; it was the only thing he could claim for himself after the things he had done. "Well," he began with a thoughtful tone, deciding to play his own game, "maybe I love her, and I'm making this sacrifice, taking this risk, to get back to her. Or, maybe I despise her as some people think I despise the rest of existence, and by doing this to spare my life I'm thinking only of a way to hurt her by surviving, to spite her by my own wretched existence."

A troubled look crept across her face. "So little thought for the love, and so much for the hate." Her concern faded away to a grin. "See, you can share things with me," she said, using that low, private voice that so often followed her pleasant expressions. "I've enjoyed our little talks so far, and I think you have as well, yes?"

He looked to her, his eyes narrowing. "I'm not sure how to answer that, because no matter what I say, you'll read something into it, won't you?"

She tipped her head back, studying him. After several moments, her knowing little grin returned. She blinked and took a breath. "Now, as I said, you have strong feelings for your wife. Perhaps one day you will tell me which?"

"If you tell me where I'm being held."

She leaned forward in her chair. "So many times you ask this. Why such concern?"

He shrugged. "Space is a big place. Captain's instinct; I like to know where I am."

She pursed her lips, but shook her head. "I'm sorry, but that's confidential."

He opened his hands. "Then so are my feelings."

She laughed; it was a welcome sound. "Well then, we shall leave it at 'perhaps one day', some day when we may talk at ease, yes?"

He eased back and put his head on the pillow. "Perhaps one day," he agreed.

"Then it's settled," she said with a small clap of her hands. "We can sit, and have tea, some place warm and sunny. Yes?"

He looked to her.

She grinned once more. "Goodnight, Mister Jansing."

Remnant

***

The sleek hull of a Navy interceptor sat off the link beside Stohko's transport, the military vessel's smooth lines in sharp contrast with the utilitarian, angular outline of the *Solitude*. Stohko turned to Pallia and settled his duffel bag by his feet. "That's my lady for the next three months," he said, rolling his eyes to the interceptor.

Pallia gazed at the interceptor, crossing her arms on her chest as she shifted her weight from one foot to the other. "Stohko—"

He put his hands on her shoulders. "I'll be careful," he said, repeating it yet again. "They're bringing me in as a lieutenant, that's it. Under the new unified service rankings between the Army and Navy, I'd have to be promoted to colonel before they send me planetside to command ground forces."

She poked her finger into his chest. "And we both know how you can be when you get involved in something," she reminded him. She bowed her head, but then looked at him, patting her hands on his chest before smoothing out the shoulders of his uniform. "Just make your business contacts and come home to me in one piece, okay? No crusades, please?"

He shook his head. "Pallia, I'm on patrol to enforce a blockade on a planet with no shipping of its own. We'll be spending time calibrating lock pressures just so we don't go crazy with boredom." He embraced her, gave her a quick kiss, and then bumped her with an elbow as he grinned.

She hesitated for a moment, but then hugged him, holding him close. "Come back to me," she said in his ear before slipping away from him. "Don't leave me marooned here."

He picked up his bag at the sound of the interceptor's boarding klaxon. "Three months," he said as he backed into the link. "So short, it's not even worth saying goodbye, right?"

The lock closed between them. He was alone. He came to a sudden halt, his eyes blank and frozen on the dull metal of the lock. "Pallia," he said, his voice a whisper. "Pallia?" he repeated to the emptiness, but only the lock was before him now.

And then it hit him: she was gone.

***

He sat on a pier looking across one of the many scenic inlets outside the main settlement of Hermium, a picturesque town by the rather unimaginative name of Seaside. What lay before him, though, was a sight to behold. A bay of clear blue water washed over white sand, the depths speckled by exotic rainbow colored fish beneath a blue sky dappled with the rose ringed clouds of early evening. It was warm, but not uncomfortable, as the sea breeze helped break the clutch of the air's humidity. No insects served to annoy him, for they had not yet evolved on Hermium, and the Navy kept a strict policy to maintain the planet's evolutionary primitivism. Regardless, by any measure, it was perfect, and the expansive hotels and resorts built into the terrain to disguise their presence were testament to the expectations held for the planet. That was before the HLC fractured, however, before the insurrection, before things had gone so maddeningly wrong.

But there was fishing, and he had come to enjoy it on that pier in those first moments that Melogo had given him a pole and he had dropped the lure. It was something he remembered from his childhood, seeming so long ago, fractured from Hermium across the gulf of space to old Earth and a Scandinavian dock looking out on the Baltic Sea. And despite himself, as much as he felt meeting Melogo Isla in such an informal manner so soon after arriving planetside was a mistake, he could not help but feel relaxed, disarmed, *welcome*. It was why, he decided, their fishing parties had become something of a routine, and yet, as comfortable as they felt, he always felt beneath his duty the guilt of his time away from Pallia.

As if his unease had summoned her, Ellen came up behind him and put her hands on his shoulders. "Any bites?"

Seated on an overturned bucket, he craned his neck to look back at her. His gaze rose up to her, her light brown hair drifting off her shoulders in the breeze.

She studied him, her growing curiosity unmistakable. "What's bothering you?"

He looked back to the water. "How long have I been here—planetside, I mean?"

She rubbed his shoulders. "I don't know. A year, something like that."

He pursed his lips.

She patted her right hand. "No, it's just over a year. This is Elena's tenth birthday, and I remember Melogo appointing me as your office manager just before her ninth. Yes, that's it. It's so confusing, maintaining the standardized Earth calendar alongside our local calendar. Why do you ask?"

"I—"

Melogo came up beside him and handed him an iced drink, pale green in color. "Any luck?"

"He hasn't caught a thing," Ellen replied.

Melogo held up his hands and let out a yelp. "My good friend Stohko! But you must catch something! How can we have a fish bake without the fish?"

"We have the other ones in the freezer back at the offices," Ellen reminded them.

Melogo waved a hand in dismissal. "I wouldn't want to put our good colonel back out in the cold. *Thermae et vitae!*"

Stohko glanced at him.

"Warmth and life," Melogo said, leaning toward Stohko.

Ellen laughed. "Translated, that is, from Melogo's own personal bastardization of too many languages to name."

Melogo clapped a hand on Stohko's back. "Well, in any event, we need to talk later in your office, my friend. There's some concern among my people about some new dictates from the Navy regarding our supply deliveries."

Stohko looked back to Melogo. "Your 'people' made incendiaries and torched one of my patrols outside of Seaside. We can't have that, and you know it."

Melogo shook his head. "But you cannot in one sweep deny all our agricultural supply to feed ourselves," he said in disbelief. "We must have our supplies."

"Then let my people work with your people to patrol the spaceport better."

"Then our own HLC security people will be seen as collaborators," Melogo said with a sigh. "This will inflame the attacks."

Stohko let his head hang. "Why can't it ever be easy?" He glanced at the water. "You'd think with all this beauty around here, people would just calm down. We've managed it, why can't the rest?"

"The Lady is their world," Melogo said with a shrug. "It is not yours to understand."

Stohko shook his head. "You people talk of this place like it has a soul of its own," he said under his breath. "It's getting on my nerves."

"If you don't learn to know her as we do, then you'll never know us," Melogo continued, trying to explain himself. He sipped his drink and patted Stohko's shoulder again. "We have solved more problems in the last six months than at any other time during this difficult situation. You have been a blessing to our world, Colonel Jansing. I know this, because Hermium herself whispers it to me in her breeze. We will solve this crisis as well, so we will talk later. But now, fish!" he added with a laugh and walked off.

Stohko waited until Melogo was out of hearing range before turning to Ellen. "How long have I been here?" he asked again.

She crouched down beside him, putting her arm around the small of his back. "It'll be okay. You and Melogo have always found a way to work things out."

"I've been here too long," he said quietly, her words not registering. She looked to him.

He gazed across the water. "I think I've lost my way."

"But you're so much a part of this place now," she said, dismissing his concern. "You've accomplished so much. Elena's father was here for so long, and he turned his back on her, on me, on his duties with the Navy, and killed himself. But now you're here, you replaced him in so many ways, and you're more than any of us could have hoped for."

He shook his head. "I made a promise, and I forgot that promise, and for some reason, I'm just remembering it now."

She laid a hand on his cheek to turn his face to her. "Stohko," she said, her voice low.

"Ellen, I've told you, I can't…"

Her eyes held on him, piercing him with their gaze. "You're like a father to Elena. I want you to stay. Stay here; you could stay with me, Stohko, *live* with me, here—"

He looked at her in horror. *Pallia*— "I'm married."

Ellen's face fell.

"I promised her—"

"*What?*" She recoiled from him, clamping her hands over her mouth. "All this time?"

He stood. "Ellen, please, I told you—as a sister, as my closest friend, as the person I trust most here, but that it could never be more than that—"

She stared at him, her eyes going wide and wet. She lashed out, but stopped her slap the moment before she would have hit him, causing him to blink in expectation. But when he opened his eyes she rested her hand on his cheek, the warmth of her skin against his own, and when she spoke, her voice came in a whisper. "I don't believe you. I *won't* believe you," she said. She clenched her teeth, but then she eased, and withdrew her hand. "No one, no one could claim to love another and never mention their name for so long, unless the love was wrong or you were exceptionally cruel and cold. I know you love Elena, I can see it in your eyes, and I know you too well now for you to hide coldness or cruelty from me. So *you* decide Stohko, you decide just who it is you've betrayed all this time, because you've betrayed someone, and you're only fooling yourself until you figure that out."

He looked away in shame.

"I'll leave you now," she said, her voice tight. "Elena's going to want you there for her cake." She fell back a step, but then came back to him, seizing his hand and squeezing it to draw his gaze to her. She opened her mouth, but said nothing, instead turning and leaving him.

He looked back to the water. With a curse he kicked the bucket off the pier.

***

He woke in agony, his hands trembling as they clutched the sensory cap and tore it from his head. He rolled over, drawing himself on his knees before pounding his head against his pillow at the blinding pain in his mind.

The door to his cell opened. He heard footsteps, not the light clack of Siona's shoes, but the heavy thuds of guards who set their hands on him. He groaned and tried to fight them off, but contorted instead. Suffering the sensory dismemberment that came with waking, his efforts were useless. They pulled him from his bunk, struggling with him until they managed to plant him against the wall. By that point he could hear Siona yelling at the guards and arguing with another person, a voice he had heard several times now after waking; a measured, nasal little voice that responded to the address of Doctor Bhandhakar.

It was impossible for him to tell how long the struggle lasted; sometimes it seemed to last for hours. This time, though, they threw him on his bunk after what seemed little time, yet the argument between Siona and Bhandhakar raged on in the background for several minutes until the doctor silenced her with a vicious scream and slammed the door to the cell.

Stohko cared little for the exchange, too busy trying to calm himself from the pain in his head.

Siona hissed his name.

He whipped around like a caged animal, seizing her shoulders and throwing her against the wall. He pinned her there, pounding his forehead against her shoulder to subdue the pain so that he could focus some kind of thought. "What are you people doing to me?" he said through clenched teeth. "My head—what are you doing to my head?"

He heard her voice, but could make no sense of her words.

He banged his head into her shoulder again. *"You lied to me!"*

"I know it hurts!" Siona cried.

He slammed her against the wall in rage. "Forget the pain! You bastards! You stole them away from me! They're all gone now! You took—ah!" He clutched his temples as a bolt of pain erupted in his head. He staggered back from her before falling to the floor in a ball. Siona slipped down next to him, clutching her arm. "Stohko?"

Curled up on the floor, he shook with spasms, clutching his head in his hands, his fingernails pressing into his scalp until he started to bleed.

And then it relented, the agony fading to leave him limp and lame in his own urine.

The door to his cell opened, but Siona turned at once on the guard. "Out!"

The cell slammed shut.

They were alone for some time as they both caught their breaths. Stohko tried to move, but there was nothing left in him to serve as strength, so he flopped on his back. "Why?" he said, struggling to summon his voice. "Why did you take them? Why did you take my memories? Why am I here? Let me die!"

Siona looked down at him, grimacing at the pain in her shoulder. "You can't die."

He began to weep.

"There is a purpose," she said.

He shook his head.

"To get back to her, remember?" she continued. "You have to endure to get back to her." She rested her head against the wall. "Guard!"

Pallia?

"Do you remember me?"

"Pallia?" he said, his eyes sliding shut. "I'll come back..."

The cell door opened. Several guards entered. They hoisted Stohko off the floor and dumped him on his bunk as another guard helped Siona to her feet.

"Give him the shot and put the cap back on," a nasal voice said with perfect calm.

Stohko heard himself whimper.

"Jason!" Siona's voice implored. "You're going to kill him!"

Doctor Bhandhakar didn't hesitate. "We're almost done with him, Siona. Only a few more sessions, and then—only then—you can do your job and put what's left of him back together."

***

He was in his office, alone, late, when Ellen found him typing his resignation by the soft light of his terminal's screen. She sat across from him, her back stiff, her eyes filled with unfathomable hurt. He didn't know what to say; he thought she had turned in for the night, but then he thought of the vicious argument he had instigated with Melogo, and in a heartbeat he understood the source of his hostility and intolerance. Ellen was right, and she had awakened a sense of shame in him so deep that he found it difficult to be in her presence. Her company served as a bitter reminder that he had been absent from Pallia for so long, so unforgivably long. He had buried that betrayal by never mentioning her to anyone on Hermium, all but denying her existence within his own dislocated emotional reality so that he could follow the obsession he had fostered for controlling Hermium. It was a consuming obsession, a blind obsession—as all pure obsessions ought to be—that had afflicted him with insidious perfection before he had even set foot on the planet. There was no discernable reason for it, no logic to it, nothing to it at all but shame and regret and *hostility* for the people of this place—his Lady Hermium—that had come to fill his life.

He was not sure how long they sat in the office that night, sometimes staring at each other, sometimes staring at the floor, but neither he nor Ellen found a word worth speaking. In the end, she wiped her eyes, shook her head, and left him.

He looked out the windows of his office to the luxuriant green growth surrounding the mansion. According to Melogo, if Stohko's resignation posted quickly he would be off Hermium before the planet went in bloom.

***

"This is a huge opportunity," General Keane said with his usual confidence, visiting the bridge of Stohko's interceptor eight months into Stohko's Navy term. "Breaking up that smuggling ring in our supply corps gained a lot of notice, Lieutenant. That kind of dedication, that kind of initiative, we're not getting much of it out here. We need men like you, Jansing."

Stohko blinked, staring in disbelief at the papers Keane had handed him. "General, I'm honored, but such a promotion, skipping rank up to colonel—"

"A sign of the confidence we hold in you Jansing," Keane interrupted, dismissing Stohko's concern. "Your answer?"

Stohko looked up at the orbital display of Hermium, and beneath it, the real time satellite feed of the planet, monitored from low orbit.

"Jansing?"

Stohko rubbed his chin. "Why do my surface scans fail every time we look away from Seaside?"

"Magnetic anomaly," Keane said with a wave of his hand. "Everybody's got the same problem. Navy Intelligence has a team working on that."

Stohko looked to Keane. "I'd be planetside?"

Keane nodded. "Full-time. Is that a problem?"

"No, Sir, no problem," Stohko said, his eyes drifting back to the satellite feed. "General, look at it—sometimes, on third watch, when the ship is quiet—I sit here, in the dark, and just watch it, just watch the beauty of it. It could be like heaven, it should be like heaven. If I could just get my hands on it, just hold onto it..."

He cleared his throat and turned to Keane. "When do I begin?"

***

He was sitting at his desk, the warm sun of Hermium on his back, two months into his post planetside, when he realized it for the first time. As luck would have it, it was the same moment Ellen happened to walk into his office with a stack of folders to file. The look of consternation on his face must have been obvious, for she stopped in her tracks by the file cabinets and addressed him.

Startled, he looked up at her, but then shook his head. "I was reviewing monthly magisterial logs for Seaside, when I noticed that in the two months I'm here there's been—well, at least what I would consider—an alarming number of reports concerning child disappearances. Why isn't this a bigger issue?"

Ellen shrugged, the typical Hermium answer for all things inscrutable.

He opened his hands. "The HLC goes off the wall for something as silly as parking tickets in the visitors' loop at the spaceport, but this goes without a peep?"

Ellen turned to the file cabinet. "She's a mysterious one, our Lady Hermium," she said with a sigh. "We've settled just one little speck of it. Most of it isn't even properly charted. The jungles, the trees, they're deep and dark. Children who wander off, well, you just never know."

"That's it?" He shook his head. "This is insane. These are *children*. Nobody looks for them?"

She gazed back at him and leaned on the file cabinet, their mutual demeanor already having grown quite casual. "We don't have a lot of resources here, Stohko. We keep the visitors happy on their vacations, and keep the rest under the lid, except for the HLC and their gripes. But the rest is ours to worry about, something between us and our Lady Hermium."

Unsatisfied, he frowned and looked over his shoulder, out the window to see Elena playing catch with Melogo's daughter. The Navy offices, in an understated building that looked more like a large mansion, were on the outskirt of Seaside, and beyond the wide lawn surrounding the building, there was only the endless expanse of Hermium's impenetrable flora. He shifted in his seat and looked back to his desk, but could not help glancing over his shoulder once more.

Ellen tipped her head when she discerned his gaze. "Stohko?"

He looked to her. "I don't like them playing so close to the trees."

Ellen waited, her eyes locked with his. She blinked as her lips rose in a smile. "I'll tell them of the Colonel's concern."

She reached out to squeeze his hand, and left the office to get back to her work.

***

A white piece of paper stared at him from his lap. It was his third day on Hermium. He sighed and looked out the window of his bedroom to the rising sun.

Dear Pallia?

No. To my wife? No. To my Pallia?

He put the paper aside and drew his knees up to his chest as he sat in his bed. Why was it so hard to write her? It seemed a simple question, but he felt incapable of acknowledging the answers. He had never told her he was going planetside, had never told her about the promotion. In fact, he knew he had not written her for at least six months. The last time they had spoke, eight months into his duty aboard the interceptor, they had exchanged few words. It was a frigid conversation, not a screaming match. The long, horrible periods of silence said far more than the terse words they spoke, spoken like words scripted for them just so that they would not stare mute at each other through a monitor. They had told each other the same thing: *you don't understand.* And as much as he knew he was right, he knew she was right as well, but not in the way she thought.

What is it about this place?

He had sat in on his first interrogation of an HLC insurgent the day before. The man had detonated an improvised bomb in one of Seaside's sewage plants. Two workers were injured. Yet the man Stohko saw was not some bitter, hard-nosed anarchist, but someone who seemed at ease, who seemed, for all intensive purposes, *happy.* Perhaps equally discomforting and disorienting to Stohko was the demeanor of his own men who were charged with interrogating the insurgent. As Stohko sat and listened, it sounded more like a casual afternoon tea than a serious criminal investigation.

It was a stark education in the ways of Hermium, and he could not help but think of some of the things Melogo had said to him in their first meeting. This suspect, this terrorist, seemed to embody all the incongruence that was Hermium.

When asked about the bombing, the man held up his hands and shrugged. "I hate shit," was his only stated motive. "Listen to the Lady's trees, they'll whisper the same thing."

***

"This is a serious problem, Melogo."

Melogo crossed his arms on his chest as he studied Stohko. They were seated in two comfortable chairs at the end of the long pier reaching into

Seaside's bay, the Navy offices behind them. "Such things as this, they do occur, despite the Hermium euphoria. I know; it is not good for our business."

Stohko looked at him in disbelief. "An under-age prostitute killed a man while his wife was passed out drunk on the floor of their baby's bedroom!" he said, failing to contain his anger. "I don't want to hear this 'Hermium euphoria' crap! Outright prostitution isn't even legal here, and now I have a murder that the magistrates have to prosecute, not to mention the fact that the Youth Protection Ministry is sending an inspector out here. You have to tell your people to straighten out their act or I'm going to have to do it the hard way."

Melogo bobbed his head to either side as he considered his options. "I will make this disgusting matter right, I promise you," he said, reaffirming his intention with a slight bow. "But do not concern yourself with YPM inspectors. They have been here before; they use problems here as an excuse for a vacation on the Ministry's expense. As with many things, this is the way it is. You cannot fight the tide, my friend."

Stohko shook his head. "This girl has to be turned over to the authorities. Let that be known to whoever is sheltering her."

Melogo pursed his lips. "Her parents, they will not be happy."

Stohko put his hands on his face. "Good God, what have you people done to this place?"

"Yes, I know, this is a terrible thing." Melogo frowned. "She is only thirteen, the poor girl."

***

Stohko snapped to consciousness in the middle of a convulsion, guards piled on top of him to restrain him to his bunk. Through the mess of limbs and grunts he perceived the outline of a slender hand, the fingers long and delicate, framed against the one light glowing over him. It was Siona, he knew, come to take him away, to stop the torture, even if she would reinstate it later.

"Enough!" she called out, the guards parting at her order. He felt himself calm at once. When she emerged to sit on the edge of his bunk he fumbled to grab her hands, an incoherent mumble seeping from him as he tried to speak. "Easy," she said, trying to sooth him, but he could make out the tears in her eyes. "You only have to endure tonight, and then you're done."

His heart began to pound.

She took his face in her hands, but the guilt was plain in her eyes. "Listen, listen! If you don't go back, we can't help them."

He blinked. "Them?"

She shook her head. "I'm here with you. But you have to go back now—"

His eyes bulged.

He screamed.

He sat up in his bed. Recognition was instantaneous: another time, another place. The rains of Hermium pelted his windows. The planet would be in bloom in several weeks, Melogo promised. No matter. He would be gone by then.

He spent his morning packing his spare uniforms. There were several pictures on the wall by his bed, little encapsulated moments he valued. In the middle, Elena blowing out her birthday candles. On either side, portraits of Ellen and Melogo standing with their respective daughters. There were scenes from several fish bakes. And last, a picture Elena had taken of him, framed against the setting sun, fishing as he sat at the end of the pier with Ellen beside him.

He felt nauseous.

He left the pictures on the wall but folded his discharge approval and put it in his pocket. He didn't know how to tell Pallia he was at last returning; rather than another awkward exchange he figured it better on all counts—and easier—to just appear before her, and deal with rebuilding their marriage from there. Taking the pictures, he knew, was not a possibility; he had let himself drift into another life, a counterfeit life, and it was time to dispel its existence. So he turned, turned away, and went downstairs to his office to spend the next several hours clearing his papers and finalizing his reports.

Ellen came in once to put away some folders. She said nothing. He understood.

After eating his dinner alone, his car came to take him to the spaceport. He went back to his office to look out the window one last

45

time. A soft evening rain fell from featureless gray clouds. Ellen was still in the outer office. He offered her a goodbye. Unable to maintain her anger, her hurt welled up in its true form, and she wept. Disgusted with himself, and feeling in that moment very tired, and very oppressed, as if some great weight burdened his shoulders, he put his bag down and held her. It reminded him how he had, in fact, never said goodbye to Pallia.

He separated from her. "I have to go."

She grabbed his hand. "We'll go with you," she blurted. "Elena's already in the car. Don't tell Melogo; he insisted this morning that I stay here with Elena until everything was cleaned up, you know, get the place ready for you—I mean, your replacement. I'll finish after you go."

Despite himself, he smiled. "Elena's in the car?"

She nodded.

"You'll be in the car," he thought aloud. He bowed his head, but then looked back to her. "Yes, yes, I would like that very much."

Rain pattered on the windows. And then, with equal ease as the windshield wipers washing away the rain, so, too, the tension in the car washed away, and for a few minutes, at least, things were as they had been. Yet it only reminded him, in those easy minutes of their happiness, that such as it was, it should never have been; that it should have been with different players in the roles, and all of it recreated under the wishes of his old self to what he had originally desired: he and Pallia, and a child of their own. Sitting in the company of Ellen and Elena, considering everything in the midst of his own twisted Hermium euphoria, the more it played through his subconscious, the more the glare of his conscience beat upon him like the eyes of a wrathful god.

But this was a good time, he decided at last.

I did not pursue it; some things just happen. I was caught up.

You can't fight the tide.

He gazed out the window. They were surrounded by trees, a section of road called an 'embrace', common on roads of any length on Hermium, where long stretches left the planet's massive trees to grow around the road to give travelers the sense of being absorbed straight into the heart of their Lady. Such a thing it was that he pondered, the idle reverie of a man lost in his thoughts.

And then the world flashed white, a great greedy glutton that erupted against the side of the car. That was the last he saw of them, Ellen and Elena. They were gone.

He woke up in the wreckage, his leg mangled and burned, the rain pelting his face. His men had filled the area, encircling the remains of the car.

He regained consciousness in his bed. Night had returned. He took the cane that had been left next to his bed and staggered from his room to find Navy personnel swarming about the offices. He was told to rest. He was told to go to bed. Instead he staggered to his office, shouted a dismissal to the man at *his* desk, and resumed control. He opened files he had once felt were best left closed, and produced lists of names—both HLC and Navy personnel. The Navy personnel he had summoned to him, and to them dispensed the HLC lists. They stared in disbelief at his simple orders, but when he barked at them, they moved with sudden vigor and enthusiasm, as if they, too, had been stirred from some fanciful, but corrupted, dream, and embraced their soon to be infamous moniker.

He went to bed. He let the Fallen Angels initiate their kill sweeps while he slept, but he didn't dream, and he felt no rest when an aid came and woke him. He was exhausted, tired beyond any measure he had known or had even thought possible, tired to the point of feeling disembodied, broken and senseless. The aid whispered in his ear, but he shook his head in anger and turned to her. "Bring them!"

The aid returned in short order with several guards, and between them, Melogo Isla and his daughter. Melogo's daughter stared mute at Stohko as he forced himself up in bed and swung out his good leg. He sat there, the scrapes on his arms and face clear to the eye, the white undershirt he wore stained in several places from dressings that couldn't be seen. Melogo began a vehement protest, demanding to know what was happening to the other HLC members that were being rounded up from the city. "Besides," he said to Stohko, "you resigned; you no longer have an official capacity here!"

Stohko's eyelids drooped. He reached under his pillow to slide out his handgun and rest it in his lap, still in his hand. Melogo paused at the sight of the gun, but what caught him more was the emptiness in Stohko's eyes when Stohko looked to him. "You told Ellen not to ride with me," Stohko said. He had to force the words out, his throat was so dry.

Melogo fell silent, his jaw hanging.

Stohko stared at him.

Melogo sank to his knees and began to plead. "My friend, please…"

Stohko closed his eyes.

Melogo's daughter began to cry.

Stohko was very tired. Yet in some odd way, he felt the wearisome weight upon his shoulders shift, alleviated from what he had known but returning as something new. In his state, he cared not for the next, but welcomed only that things were appearing much simpler to him now. Ellen and Elena were gone. He had torn up his discharge papers. The planet's visitors were being collected and deported. He had created, authorized, and unleashed the Fallen Angel death squads, a last resort plan that had long eaten away at him. And with all this in process, there was no way he could leave, precluding the undesirable, yet desperately craved, reality of having to face Pallia.

All was not as he wanted it to be, but it was what he received, and he felt a strange euphoria of a different kind, the strangling freedom of waking to the antithesis of life as he imagined it would be, and as such, felt no bound, no restraint, no judgment to still his impulses.

But Elena, she was gone, and Ellen too, lost no matter what, and it was the barrier of Elena's little body that allowed him to survive even as the bomb tore her apart.

He was not aware of what had happened until he heard the blast of his gun and felt his wrist relax to let his hand droop in his lap. His eyes focused to see Melogo kneeling in the frozen, silenced shock of the room, but where Melogo's daughter had stood there was emptiness, and beyond a red splatter on the wall, covering Stohko's pictures. He blinked to realize she was flat on her back on the floor, looked down to realize he had just shot her in the head.

Melogo wheezed. The Navy personnel in the room shifted about, uncertain what to do.

Melogo opened his hands. "My child! How could you, she was innocent—"

Stohko's glazed eyes bored into Melogo. "*You,*" he began, but then fell silent, reconsidering. He took a breath. "I hate shit," he said, announcing each word with force. "Listen to the Lady's trees, they'll whisper the same." And then he shot Melogo in the head. He looked over the stunned Navy personnel and put the gun on his nightstand. "Clean the pictures and hang them in my office. Let them be a reminder," he added through a haggard scowl. Then he rolled over and went back to sleep.

In the two weeks that followed there was no record of how many were tortured and killed, but he knew one thing, and it was the feeling that he had unleashed something, tapped into something bestial and depraved, a warping of the Hermium euphoria that was allowing his personnel to wake from their listless nature and commit every form of violation he could conceive. Over those days he was both impressed and distressed with himself, for he knew not from where his madness came, and cared even less to understand it or its compulsion. But as he would limp about the mansion on his cane, draped in a long black rain slicker with his old captain's hat on his head, he only felt satisfied with one thing, that soon Hermium would be quiet. The HLC would be exterminated, and that would be that.

General Keane came planetside two months into the massacre, satisfied with the reports that HLC activity had dropped to zero since Stohko had been attacked, but compelled by the increasing number of rumors that the situation had violated all bounds of morality. When he demanded answers from Stohko, Stohko had him arrested. When the entire fleet turned on the planet, Stohko gave them a Hermium shrug and surrendered.

When an irate General Keane had him in a holding cell on Keane's flagship, the interrogation went nowhere. Stohko ignored any questions, gobbling up the last of his stimulants and painkillers to fight the agony of his leg. When asked why he surrendered himself with such ease after having the audacity to arrest Keane, he gave them another shrug.

"What about it?" he said with little care. "You can't fight the tide. Now if you don't mind, I'd like to get back to my work. I'm a very busy man."

The trial became a mess in the months that followed. His merciless detachment on Hermium had transformed to reckless flippancy, to self-destructive disregard, over his own defense. It did not help matters, at one point instigating a brawl in the courtroom that shattered the mending bone in his wounded leg. In private, his frustrated barrister asked him several times if he wanted to die, to which he shrugged, and said that he was complacent with what Fate had in store for him. When it was his turn to testify, it became a spectacle. "Yes, I did all these horrible things, allowed all these horrible things to happen," he admitted, to the great displeasure of his barrister, "but no one cared what I was doing. None of these things were hidden; no effort was made to hide them. Yet I was told I was doing a fine job by my superiors because after instituting my measures, there were no more disturbances on Hermium, and that's what they wanted, that's what the *trees* wanted. And if the end is any justification or vindication to my means, then certainly I'm vindicated: I was well on course with my goal of depopulating the planet to bring peace to Hermium. No more dead children, no more missing children, no more prostituted children. But since I didn't get to finish my job, now the military is conducting a forced resettlement of the entire remaining population. So there will be peace on my Lady Hermium after all, won't there?

"Do I deserve the death penalty?" he asked the stunned prosecutor, who only opened his hands to let Stohko speak. Stohko rested a hand on his chest. "This person before you is not the man who joined the Navy voluntarily to better his business interest in the hope of having a family with his wife. I don't know where that man is anymore, or what happened to him, but I know he would not approve of the man sitting before you now. So I will not object to the panel's decision, and I will not fight it. I would only say goodbye to my wife, because I never did before, and I regret hurting and embarrassing her, and these two things, I think, are among the worst of my sins."

He was sent to a cell. He sat and ate, certain they would execute him at any moment, but instead his barrister came to the cell and opened his terminal. "I don't know why I'm doing this," the barrister said with frustration, "because as far as I'm concerned, they should fry your mass-murdering ass right now. But as your representative, I thought you should see this, in case you want to modify your stance. One of my assistants pulled it up a few days ago; I just got it now."

He turned the terminal to Stohko. Stohko put his fork down and chewed his seasoned noodles, but froze when he saw an image of Pallia. "Why is she being interrogated?"

"Military prosecution," the barrister explained. "They were building character assessments of you, so they went to everyone they could find."

Stohko swallowed his noodles. The image played. He hated himself, then, for seeing what he had put her through. But then she spoke, and he began to understand, in some strange, distorted way, why he had done what he had done.

"My husband is a good man," Pallia said. She fidgeted, rolling her eyes until she could not hide the fact that she was weeping. "He promised he would come back to me. I don't know anything about these things he's charged with; I don't know how the man I know could have done those things. But I want my husband back," she said, her stubbornness lighting her eyes. "Maybe I'm a fool, maybe I'm a tremendous fool, but I won't be accused of being disloyal. I want him back, wherever he is, back to where he never should have left. That was part of the promise we had."

Stohko sat up straight. His eyes darted about the cell.

"The Research people still have their deal open," the barrister said.

"Done." Stohko looked to the barrister. "Thank you. Now if you could give me some time alone, please."

***

The next time he saw Pallia it was a replay of the same video feed, but rather than his trial holding cell, he was sitting in the stark white cell of the research facility. Siona had shown him the video to remind him why he had suffered through the torture they had inflicted upon him.

"It's nearly over now," she said. "Soon you'll be back with her."

He frowned, his eyes lingering on the terminal. He stared at Pallia's image for some time before he had the courage to ask the question that was haunting him. "That's my wife?"

Siona's eyes widened before she caught herself.

He nodded. "Yes, that's my wife," he said, reinforcing the idea of it in his head. "So I did this, to get back to her."

Siona took off her glasses and rubbed her eyes. She dropped her hand, studied him for a moment, and then put her glasses back on. "Yes, Stohko. That was all you ever said through all of it, that you had to continue, to get back to her."

His head tipped to the side as his eyes returned to her image. "Pallia," he said to himself. "I must have," he began, but stopped as he reconsidered. "She must be special, to me?"

Siona blinked.

He frowned and shook his head. "I don't remember her anymore," he whispered and shrugged. He ran a hand over his head, his fingertips lingering over the scars from the sensory cap. "I don't remember much of anything anymore."

Siona swallowed, and when she gave him a simple apology, she had to fight to keep her voice level.

He looked about the cell, blinking against the glare of the lights. "It's very white and bright in here. That reminds me of something." He closed his eyes, and when he opened them, he was looking to Siona. "Did Doctor Bhandhakar get what he needs?"

She fought to contain herself. "No, not really."

He shrugged it off and looked back to her. "I have to thank you," he said, his voice coarse from so many nights of screaming.

She looked at him in disbelief. "What?"

"I didn't give you what you were looking for, but I think you gave back to me what I've been looking for," he said, tipping his head to the terminal. He opened his hands. "It's just a thought."

She sucked in a breath.

"I don't remember what, but I know I did something terrible," he continued, rubbing his forehead. He lowered his hand to look at her. "Will I ever remember anything, before this?"

She looked down and shook her head. "No, no you shouldn't."

He drummed his fingers on the table. He was silent for several moments, pretending not to notice as she fidgeted and peered over her shoulder to the camera mounted in the corner of the ceiling. He knew she was deceiving him, and that it bothered her to do so, but he was not sure what to make of that, or why the observation registered through the haze of his perceptions. "Are those my pills?" he asked, pointing at the little bottle between them.

She blinked as she regained herself. "What? Oh, yes. When you need more, contact me, and I'll see to it; it's part of your terms with us. The details are in your papers." She leaned forward, waiting to catch his gaze. "Stohko, please, contact me."

He stared at her.

"Stohko?"

"I think I know where I am now," he said. He nodded once and looked away from her. "I'd like to go now. I should be with my wife."

The door to his cell opened. Two guards were there, along with Bhandhakar. The doctor glared at Siona. "That's enough," he said, his words tight and sharp with obvious disapproval. Siona glanced at Stohko before lowering her head and leaving the cell. The doctor, though, had his gaze full on Stohko. "And it's enough for you as well," he added, nodded to the guards, and left.

They drugged him so that they could transport him back to the nexus without his knowing where he had been. Their interceptor docked, they handed him his bag, and sent him on his way. He walked down the dock link and came to a stop at the last lock before entering the nexus.

He waited for the lock to open.

Yet, as he stood there, something came to him, and he tipped his head, unable to remember it clearly, or put any definition to it; it was just another muddy memory in the mess that was left of his mind. But he heard himself say something, and he recognized it with painful clarity, and the sensation of a great weight came to rest on his shoulders.

This new beginning, he realized, had looped back to an ending of old. *Had it all happened?*

He cleared his throat. *Of course it did.*

"Pallia?"

***

Underneath, there lurks one more memory, like the stone cast in a pond, and the ripples it sends forth.

It was night, a night like many others in which he could not sleep for the weight of his thoughts and self-recriminations whispering from his hidden guilt, another steamy Hermium night. He walked from the Navy offices across the wide lawn to the pier that reached out into the bay of Seaside. The lights of the city, powered down to a dull glow for the night, were difficult to discern through the humid haze. He sat on the overturned bucket he kept at the pier's end and let his eyes get lost in the silvery reflection of starlight on the calm water. Hermium's little moon was a sliver in the night sky, its odd violet color almost imperceptible in the night. It was a pity, for the diffuse glow it sent through the night when in full phase was considered one of Hermium's wonders for travelers to behold. With that missing, he frowned, and listened to the rustle of leaves in the gentle breeze.

Sleep crept to him, his eyelids drooping.

The sound of the leaves…

Listen to the trees, and they'll whisper.

His ears rose, and his eyes snapped open.

***

He sucked in a breath.

His gaze darted about to discern his location, and he determined he was sitting in a utility bay at the stern of his ship, nestled between the gravity damper controls that kept them in a stabilized orbit. He rubbed his forehead and looked down to find a small duffel bag between his feet. With a deep breath he zipped it open and stared at what lay inside.

We have to talk, Osler had said. *It has to end.*

Stohko rubbed his face before lacing his hands behind his neck, his eyes locked inside the bag. After several moments he dropped his hands and took a deep breath. "It probably is the only way," he sighed.

He reached in the bag. The timer had already started counting on the small detonator Osler had given him. His lips parted in confusion, but he figured that he had set the timer and then forgot the act. Frowning, he reached into a pocket, took out his little bottle of pills, and swallowed several of them dry.

He walked back through the ship, running his hand along the bulkheads. The corridors were quiet and desolate, the ship on third watch. With the absence of commotion he could hear the background noises of the ship, and with his well-trained ear, he knew all was well.

It was a good ship.

He came back to his captain's cabin. He sat on the edge of the bed and watched Pallia. *Please wake. Time is so short now, and I want to tell you before I forget, before obliteration.*

She rolled over, her eyes wide and dilated in the darkness. "Stohko?"

"You're awake," he said in surprise.

She shrugged. "Couldn't sleep." She blinked and propped herself up on an elbow, her other hand rubbing her eyes. "Is something wrong?" she asked, dropping her hand in her lap.

He took off his cap and laid it beside him before turning to her. He opened his mouth, but found himself speechless. Instead, he took her hand and held it, closing his other hand over hers, the way he used to do, in that other life he had lost. He sucked in a breath, trembling as he fought to speak. Hurry! he thought, his emotions mounting with nervous urgency. He had to tell her, had to tell her before the pills took the moment away; had to tell her before all was lost!

She sat up, laying her hand on the back of his neck as she tried to catch his downcast eyes. "Hey, it's okay, I'm here. What is it?"

He threw his head back to look her in the face. "Pallia, I'm so sorry! I never should have left you—"

III

There was the rustle of leaves, followed by the dull patter of soft rain.

Stohko opened his eyes to find himself sprawled at the far corner of his cabin. With a wheeze, he rose on his hands and knees and glanced across the awkward pitch of the deck to see Pallia curled motionless at the foot of their bed. He coughed as he fought to stand. His leg throbbed. His eyes widened on Pallia until he could see that she was breathing.

The cool pings of raindrops on his head pulled his gaze up to look through the cracked hull above him into the gray evening sky of Hermium. He looked about, found his cap, and settled it on his head.

It was very quiet, almost peaceful.

He made his way up the pitch of the deck to reach their bed, stepping over the scattered mess of their belongings. With great care he rolled Pallia over. She had a welt on her head, but she stirred as he held her, blinking her eyes to focus. She grabbed his shoulder to pull herself up, her other hand pushing her hair back as her eyes widened on the gaping crack of the hull over their heads.

"Can't be," she said, looking about in disbelief. "No, it can't be…"

***

By morning they had assembled what was left of the crew, and to their surprise, most had survived. Many had minor injuries; unfortunately they found several who had made it through the ship's fall only to succumb to their wounds on the surface. As for the *Solitude*, it was a total loss. At dawn, Stohko and Pallia had climbed a nearby hill, denuded by the crash, to survey the site. The *Solitude* had come to rest for the most part on its side, its bow and bridge compacted tangles of wreckage against the mound of earth they had plowed up in bringing the ship to a halt. The hull had twisted, torn, and come apart over the heavy armored mass of the *Chrysopoeia*. The smaller ship had suffered no better a fate, having rolled down a hill from the wreck before breaking apart against a small cliff of naked bedrock, leaving a swath of flattened trees in its wake. The stern of the *Solitude* had separated and followed the *Chrysopoeia,* but had missed the cliff face to be lost in a trail of wreckage in the dense foliage. The only sign of what was once their thruster assemblies, engineering section, and gravity stabilizers was a plume of dark gray smoke rising in the morning sky.

Pallia pointed down to the wreck of the *Chrysopoeia*. "They both survived."

Stohko blinked. He turned on his feet in an attempt to get his bearings before coming back to Pallia, his eyes falling on the wreck of the *Solitude.* "This is unbelievable."

Pallia looked at him.

"We should be dead." He tipped his chin to the bridge. "They managed to get us down here in some sort of state, and they died for it. We should be dead, too."

"Stohko?"

He frowned and sank to his knees. Leaning forward on one hand, he scooped up some dirt and watched as it drained between his fingers. *This is all wrong.*

Owen came into sight from behind the wreck of the *Solitude*. Pallia turned, conscious, it seemed, of his presence, and waved him away. The XO hesitated a moment before lowering his head and leaving them.

Stohko wiped his hands clean, pretending to ignore the little exchange. When he looked up, though, his eyes were on the *Chrysopoeia*.

***

"Our inventory's done," Owen said with surprising energy.

Pallia looked up from her clipboard to the list Owen handed her. He sat beside her on a shattered tree trunk, the two of them turning their gaze from the wreck of the *Solitude* down slope to the wreck of the *Chrysopoeia*. Stohko was approaching with plodding steps; Siona and Bhandhakar followed several paces behind him. "You should take inventory down there," Stohko said to Owen, pointing back to the *Chrysopoeia*. He waited until Owen left to look back to Pallia.

"Are either of you hurt?" Pallia asked.

A look of consternation fell on Bhandhakar's face. "I am a doctor," he replied.

Pallia took it in stride. "That's nice. So are either of you hurt?"

Siona set her glasses up on her nose. "No. Fortunately we were able to strap in before we hit the atmosphere. Bumps and bruises, no more."

Pallia nodded and looked back to her clipboard. "Good. Our XO is surveying your wreck. You know, you two could help, and save some time."

"Save time?" Bhandhakar laughed. "Save time for what?"

"Jason," Siona said under her breath.

"We could be here for a long time," Stohko said with a frown, overruling Siona's rebuke. "The sooner we figure out what we have, and how best to use it, the less of it we waste. Basic rationing, that's all."

Bhandhakar turned away. Siona trailed behind him, glancing at Stohko before leaving.

Pallia waited until they were gone to look up to Stohko. He stood in silence, watching Siona and Bhandhakar walk back to their ship. "There is no help, is there?" she guessed.

Stohko turned back to her. "Nobody knows we're here. The route was classified. The bypass codes we had for the blockade drones were for one use."

Pallia's mouth dropped. "What?"

Stohko shook his head. "I had a suspicion, so I checked. Drones, like the ones around this system, they reset their codes on a timed basis. Our codes, they time out tomorrow night. If we go up after that, they'll blast us out of orbit. Any signal we try to send, they'll jam it."

"What about Osler?"

He rubbed his forehead. "Osler won't say anything."

"But won't the Navy—"

He frowned. "All this, this mess, it's all old Hermium business, just like me," he said, his voice low. "The Navy, the military, Osler, *nobody*, wants any of it anymore. They want it to go away, and what better place to bury the memories than a forbidden planet?"

She reached out and took his hand.

He looked to her. "Don't tell anyone about the codes."

"Does Owen—"

"No," he interrupted, "Owen doesn't know, because he does not need to know. Besides, there's work to be done around here, and I don't want things to fall apart because people think our situation is completely hopeless. They'll find out soon enough if we can't get the *Solitude*'s lifeboat going."

"But that's just it," she said. "That's busy-work, a charade, if we're not *going* anywhere. It's just us, and this place." She nodded once, a slight bob of her head. "If that's the way it's going to be, okay. So be it."

He lowered his head, naked with guilt before her.

She put a hand over her mouth and sat in silence for a moment. Then she dropped her hand and looked up to him. "Stohko," she began, but stopped at once.

He looked to her, but could not read into her gaze. Despite that, it was too much to bear. He narrowed his eyes and walked away, pulling his cap low.

***

Later, he found himself sitting on a moss-laden rock in the shadowed wilds about the crash site. He took off his cap and propped his elbows on his knees, frowning as he considered the situation. The detonator Osler had given him should have ended everything; of that he was certain. Making it down to the surface—the very notion of surviving on Hermium—had been beyond all consideration. Worse, having to figure a way to sustain themselves with Siona and Bhandhakar a constant sore on his mind was a recipe for impending disaster. It had seemed so simple when he had talked to Osler back on the nexus; the IS man had been very persuasive, but then, the truth tends to be persuasive. The detonator would be set, the ship would go down, and all the lingering woes of Hermium would be put to rest. As for himself and Pallia, he would trust to the afterlife to make their amends. As for the crew, in hindsight, he hadn't thought of them.

He cursed under his breath, shaking his head as he thought of those notions. Stranded in the harsh reality of having to survive on an abandoned planet with no significant hope of rescue made all his thoughts shockingly petty, selfish, inconsequential, *stupid*.

What was I thinking?

That's the problem. I wasn't thinking. I was in no condition to think, and Osler took advantage of that. So why did he find the existence of Siona and Bhandhakar so distasteful?

His eyes were drawn to the *Chrysopoeia* as the inevitable question formed in his mind.

What exactly is on that ship?

As if his thoughts had summoned the man, Bhandhakar emerged before him. "Captain Jansing," the wiry doctor said, addressing him with a formal tone, "I think it best we talk."

Stohko put on his cap, conscious of the scars on his scalp. "I'm listening."

Bhandhakar tipped his head back. "We need to understand each other, Captain."

Stohko opened his hands. "What's to understand? It's clear enough. We're screwed."

Bhandhakar cupped his hands behind his back and looked down his nose at Stohko. "The crew, Captain. I was speaking of the crew. They must be kept in their proper place. My wife assures me that we can count on you to keep order. Am I misguided in that assurance?"

My wife? Stohko's eyes rose to meet Bhandhakar's gaze. He said nothing, only for the simple reason that the volume of questions that erupted in his mind clogged his thoughts.

"We must be pragmatic," the doctor continued. "If anyone is going to get off this planet, it will only be a few of us, given our limited means. I expect an officer's privilege, Captain."

"Siona is your wife?"

Bhandhakar stared at Stohko for several moments, a cold but comical look growing on him before he could talk. "Do you mean to tell me you never knew?" He laughed. "Oh, that is perfect, that is just perfect."

Stohko rubbed his forehead. "Actually, it makes sense."

"As it should," the doctor said. He glanced at the crash site before looking back at Stohko. "As I was saying, you must keep your crew in check. A riot, a panic, will do us no good."

Stohko waved off the comment. "There won't be any panic. Hermium won't have it."

Bhandhakar tipped his head. "The Hermium euphoria?" he guessed. Contempt seeped from the smile that grew on his lips. "Is this what you put your trust in?"

"I was here," Stohko said. "Don't forget that. I *know* this place."

"So I gathered when last we met."

Stohko's eyes narrowed.

Bhandhakar opened a hand. "Granted, Captain. Your experiences of this world are more intimate, shall we say, than mine. But I am not ignorant, I should tell you. I've read about the Hermium euphoria, I have studied it rather extensively. In behavioral research, it was a rather 'hot topic', fascinating for its very lack of a definitive cause. Some claim it was the chaotic magnetic fields of this place, the same fields that disrupted orbital scans and maddened the Navy engineers. Some claim it was exposure to the insecticides used on everything and everyone coming to this place to maintain its evolutionary primitivism. And then there are some that claim it was the slightly reduced oxygen content of the atmosphere. Who is to say? Then again, with the planet blockaded, who is there to care? The question is neglected, thrown away. Yet if there is ever an explanation, I can assure you that it will probably be something far removed from anything anyone would have thought." Almost as a post-script to his analysis, he gave Stohko a small, but pointed, shrug. "All that aside, I am well aware your experience here was real enough to you, and that you and I, we share a certain history. I hope that will not be a factor in our situation, Captain."

Stohko stood and pulled the bill of his cap low. "You know, I think you should stay on your little ship, and let Siona represent you."

The doctor grinned. "Do you feel threatened by me?"

"No," Stohko replied, and in a moment of carelessness, pointed a finger at the doctor and finished his thought. "My memory came back."

"Did it?" Bhandhakar tipped his chin up. "Now that, I must confess, I find very, very interesting. So tell me, what is it that you remember?"

"That some things don't change. You're still a bastard," Stohko said and walked away.

***

That night Stohko and Pallia sat before a small fire, sheltered under a twisted scrap of hull plate jutting from the side of their ship. Their eyes hovered over the large map they had managed to salvage from the *Solitude*'s auxiliary navigation computers; the survey was based on the limited scans they had managed to cull before the ship had crashed. As in Stohko's past experience, much of the planet's surface was blank, having denied their orbital sensors. Based on distant mountain peaks off to their right, they had been able to calculate a rough triangulation to approximate their position. From their reckoning they figured they were fifty kilometers or so from the outskirts of Seaside, a stroke of good fortune that had allayed some of the immediate tension of the crew. Even so, Pallia had commented to Stohko on several occasions during the day that the temperament of the crew was quite relaxed, to which Stohko had given little reply, except to look about the surrounding trees and offer her a shrug. "It's a good thing," he said the last time she had asked, "but we just got here. The Lady has her ways," he continued under his breath, but refused to elaborate, his exchange with Bhandhakar still fresh in his mind.

Their survey was broken when Owen sat on a log across the fire from them. He waited until they looked up from the map. "We have about two weeks," he said, his tone stark.

Stohko and Pallia gazed at him, but it was Pallia who spoke first. "We'll have to start foraging. We can supplement the food we have with whatever we find here, anything we find here, and stretch it out as far as possible."

"Evolutionary primitivism," Siona said in warning, emerging from the darkness to surprise them. "There's no game to hunt. No insects either, which is probably for the better." She looked up, the first drops of a passing rain plopping on her glasses. "Do you mind?" she asked, stepping under the hull fragment as she dried her glasses on her sleeve.

Owen opened a hand beside him. "This log's not taken."

Siona nodded and sat next to him, settling her glasses before opening her hands to the fire. "It's getting chilly," she said and wrapped her arms about her chest.

Stohko kept his eyes on the fire. "If food is an issue, we could fish." He wanted to go fishing that moment. Sitting there, pretending that they were having a pleasant talk, sickened him. Whether it was the skin-crawling unease of having Siona and Pallia so close together, in the same place, these two that had figured so much in his life, or the nagging jealousy and distrust he felt for Owen's presence in the same place as Pallia, it didn't matter. The only thing worse he could imagine would be for Ellen and Elena to step out from the whispering darkness of his guilt and sit by the fire.

He took off his cap and rubbed his forehead.

Siona studied him. "As a matter of fact, there is abundant marine life here. When the planet was occupied, the residents of Seaside would frequently catch any number of edible varieties and have bake parties on the shore."

"That sounds nice," Pallia said, her gaze falling back to the map.

Stohko shot a glance at Siona, who gave him a minute shrug.

"You seem to know quite a bit about this place," Owen said, turning to Siona.

"Did you do some research here?" Pallia asked, her eyes still on the map.

Siona tipped her head. "I contributed statistical analysis to a few studies, but nothing direct."

Pallia nodded. "So what about your cargo?"

Siona pursed her lips. "That's Jason's life work, not mine. That's why he's staying by the wreck, making sure the generators on the cargo pod keep running."

Owen's lips parted at Siona's implication. "And if they don't?"

Siona gave Owen a glance. "He'll lose some precious specimens he's extensively prepped for long term storage on this planet. He's worked many years with his material. Everything is contained, though," she said to assure them. "Nobody's at risk."

"You know," Pallia began, looking up from the map, "I have to tell you, I really don't find that too comforting. Besides, we could use the power for something else, or conserve it."

Siona opened her hands. "Jason won't have it."

"Is that so?" Pallia said, her tone combative.

Owen cleared his throat. "I'll get a work detail started on the *Solitude's* lifeboat," he said, trying to defuse the situation. "Its power cells were damaged in the crash, but we might be able to get it up and running with the *Chrysopoeia's* generators. It could be the only way off this place."

"I'm sure the doctor will consent to *that* power diversion," Pallia remarked.

Siona gave her a polite smile. "Yes, I'm sure he would."

Pallia nodded. "That's good. Then we won't have to order him to do it. He doesn't strike me as someone who takes orders well."

Siona laughed. "No, no, that's not Jason. He could be his own research subject," she said, but caught her mistake by pressing her lips in a tight line.

"So what is his research?" Owen asked.

Siona shifted somewhat and took a deep breath. "Behavioral studies." She blinked and turned to Owen, clamping a hand on his thigh. "Oh, I think I know where we could get more supplies!"

Owen glanced down at her hand.

Stohko glared at her again.

"Well?" she said. "Couldn't there be something left in the Navy office building you used to work in?"

Stohko sat in silence, but he felt Pallia and Owen waiting for him to answer. "They would have cleaned it out. We're better off fishing." He stood. "I'm tired. I'm going to sleep," he added and rested a hand on Pallia's shoulder.

Pallia didn't miss the rather blatant cue. "I'll turn in as well, I think. We might have a long day tomorrow."

Siona nodded. "Sleep well," she said with a dreamy tone. She gave Owen a smile before leaving, her fingers trailing off his thigh.

Owen watched her go, craning his neck to keep an eye on her before she was lost to the night. He turned back to Stohko and Pallia with a plaintive look in his eyes. "She seems nice," he said, a nervous edge to his voice.

Pallia grinned as Stohko stepped around her. She tipped her head as Owen stared longingly at the fire. She stood. "Get some sleep, Owen."

Stohko paced back to the crack in the hull that led into their cabin, ignoring the rain that fell on him, but conscious of Pallia following close behind. Once they were inside he failed to hold his tongue a moment longer. "I don't want you to start in with her," he began.

Pallia looked to him in confusion. "What did I say?"

Stohko shook his head. "If it was up to me I'd seal her in the hull of the *Chrysopoeia* with that son-of-a-bitch Bhandhakar and weld the thing shut. You have no idea what those two did to me!"

"I didn't think you were so bitter towards her—"

"They *tortured* me!" he said, looming before Pallia. "I didn't understand what she was doing; she was the only kind hand during the whole thing. But what they did to me, the things they did to me —"

"You shot a child," she said with disarming calm.

Stohko stared at her. His temper dissipated in a heartbeat.

"You know, I never pretended to understand what happened while you were here," she continued, "and I refused to listen to most of the trial. This place did something to you: that's the way I looked at it, that's the only way I could look at it. So even with the things you did here, I wanted you back. Maybe it was selfish, maybe it was unrealistic, but in the end, I got you back—not as I had known you—but I got you back, and in the scope of things, how could I debate the morality of that?"

She kept her eyes on his until he lowered his head and turned away from her, but she stayed on him, determined not to let something that had never vented slip away. "I despise them for what they did to you," she said, drawing his gaze back to her. "But I know one thing, had it *shoved* in my face with all those mysterious late night calls and your refusal to ever really discuss her, that she had played some kind of role in keeping you going. You're a good man, I married a good man, and *that* man must hate himself for the things he did, and hate himself more for being alive after the lives he took. So it only seemed natural to me that you'd hate the hand that saw you through the penalty you paid." She sucked in a breath, bracing her hands on her forehead as she stared at him. "And sometimes I wonder, in all the quiet brooding moods you've had, that maybe, maybe for staying alive to come back to me, that you've come to hate me too."

He gasped as if she had stabbed him, her words unnerving him as they echoed what he had once said in deception to Siona. Yet, he had no idea what to say, if he could have said anything, for the one thing he wanted to say, he felt he had no right to voice or feel. "I could never hate you. Research wasn't my punishment, it was my choice. I chose it to get back to you; I had to get back to you, because I never said goodbye."

She stared at him, her eyes wide.

And then he did something, something that shocked him for its brazen nature in the decrepit trap of moral equivocation into which he had condemned them both: he reached out and put his hand on her cheek before drawing her in and holding her close, the way he used to, the way he had not done since returning. She put her arms around him and turned her face to hide her tears as she thumped her fists on his shoulders.

She struggled to find her voice. "I finally found you," she said at last. "I always thought, always knew, I'd find you here."

***

He woke with a start.

He sat up in bed and put his face in his hands. There was the gentle patter of water dripping through the hull onto the deck. Hermium's little moon, in full face, cast an unearthly glow in the night.

With care he slid from the bed into his boots and made his way through the crack in the hull to stand outside. A lazy breeze stirred the leaves in the upper canopy of the surrounding trees. There was no other sound, for there was nothing else, not a bird to flutter, not an animal to snap a twig, nothing.

And yet—

He squeezed his eyes shut and clapped his hands over his ears.

A hand came to rest on his shoulder.

He gasped and spun around, stunned to see Pallia standing behind him. She seemed not to notice him, her eyes wide and searching the violet depths of the trees' shadows. It was only then that he realized he had not looked back to see if she was sleeping when he had woke.

"Pallia?"

Her eyes still on the trees, she put a finger to her lips to quiet him. After several moments she took his hand and pulled him close, leaning into him to whisper in his ear. "Do you hear it too?"

He recoiled from her.

She blinked, her eyes opening halfway before they settled shut again. "The trees, Stohko, listen to the trees." A smile spread across her lips. "Oh, I know you hear it," she said, turning to him. "It's like the tinkling of bubbles in water, but more gentle."

He pressed his palms over his ears.

She raised her hand. "That's it! Children, like the laughter of little children."

***

He woke with a start, bolting upright and then covering his eyes against the dawn.

"Good morning," Pallia chirped and handed him a cup of tea. "The fire outside burned through the night. The tea, to boil the tea."

He stared at her. His hand rose to take the cup.

She looked at him before tipping her head. "You look tired. How'd you sleep?"

He blinked. Had it been real? "I, I think I was dreaming."

She smiled. "Then I think we had the same dream."

He looked about in confusion before turning back to her. "That doesn't bother you?"

She fell back a step, her eyes closing as her hands opened before her chest. Her nostrils flared as she took a deep breath, her eyes then opening as she let it go. "You know something? I don't think I could explain it if I wanted to, I don't know if I actually care to explain it, because it feels—I feel—well, good." She sat down on the bed next to him, so close their hips touched. "What I heard last night, it reminded me of a conversation we had before you left for this place. Do you remember what I asked you, what you promised?"

He nodded.

"Well, call me crazy if you want," she said, her voice low as she studied him with a sidelong glance, "but I heard *them*."

He forced himself to swallow. He thought of the welt on her head from the crash. It was not that he wanted to be cruel, but she had to understand. "Pallia, what you think you heard—"

She held up a hand. "I know, I know. Did you think I never read about Hermium euphoria while you were on trial? I read everything there was to read on it—most if it's written by Siona and Bhandhakar, did you know that?"

"What?" He closed his eyes and shook his head. "No, I didn't know that."

67

She nodded. "Feeling is believing. And now I believe, and with belief, I think I found a little faith, and with faith, maybe hope?" She shrugged and took his hand.

He eased as he felt the warmth of her skin. He looked to her.

They were startled by a clang on the hull. Owen stepped into view through the crack, sliding a large wrench into his leg pocket. He wiped his face with a rag before stuffing it in another pocket of his bodysuit. His sleeves were rolled up, his hands black with grime. "Good morning," he said with a lazy wave. "I salvaged the uniloader from the wreckage of the cargo bay. I worked on it all night."

Pallia shook her head. "You didn't sleep?"

Owen scratched his chin. He opened his mouth, but then closed it. He looked over his shoulder to the uniloader. He shrugged and shuffled away.

Pallia and Stohko exchanged a glance before making their way out of the hull to follow Owen to the uniloader. It was a burly little truck, compact and high to maneuver between stacked crates, with the driver's cab mounted atop the power plant and wheels. Behind the cab sat a rugged cargo bin and the remnants of a hydraulic loader arm.

Owen turned at their approach, rubbing his forehead before pointing to the arm. "That's a loss. Had to cut it off. It was mangled between two girders. Only way to get the loader out and running again." He patted a hand on the side of the cab. "Cells are in good shape; have a full charge in them. It'll run for days, no problem."

"Good work," Stohko commended. His jaw clenched after the words left his mouth, the old whisper of jealousy coming back to him.

Owen gazed at him before nodding. "Thanks Captain. I'll get going on the lifeboat when the rest of the crew is ready to move."

Stohko looked to his XO, and in that moment, found himself at a complete loss as to how he could foster any jealousy of this man, not for any shortcoming of Owen, but for the simple fact that there was no malice in him, nothing to make him untrustworthy. It was what had prompted Stohko to make Owen XO in the first place. The resentment, the jealousy, and the hypocrisy they dwelled within, withered in the recesses of his heart. An old thought welled up from his memory to echo in his mind.

Some things happen of their own way.

Siona stepped out from behind the uniloader, startling him. "This is great," she said with obvious excitement. "Now we can go scouting for supplies."

Stohko looked to her. "Pallia and I will go. The cab only sits two."

"Oh." Siona pointed to the bin. "I'll ride—what is it?—oh yes, 'shotgun', I'll ride shotgun."

Stohko shook his head, ignoring her as his eyes studied the work Owen did to cut the loader's arm. "No, you can stay here and help Owen. Pallia knows what we need, and I know the layout of Seaside." He leaned on the uniloader's headlight grill. "It's best this way."

Siona looked to him, then glanced at Pallia as she and Owen crouched behind the loader so that Owen could explain some of the repairs he performed on the drive motor. She looked back to Stohko. "I see."

Pallia and Owen emerged from behind the loader, Pallia waving to get Stohko's attention. "Owen wants to show me the skimmer," she said and pointed back to the *Solitude*. "He had a work detail on it. It should be good to go."

Stohko nodded and watched her go with Owen.

"What's the skimmer?" Siona asked.

Stohko turned back to her. "It's a little gravity sled to move the loader when we don't have a good landing flat. We're going to need it to get the loader to the road."

"The highway to Seaside's power plants?"

He looked to his tea. "It's not much of a highway, but it's better than this dense growth."

She nodded and crossed her arms on her chest. She took a step closer to him, drawing his gaze up to her. "Why do you resent me?" she asked with a soft voice.

His eyes narrowed on her.

She did not flinch. "It was a tough experience, for both of us. But it doesn't—"

"It's done with," he interrupted. "It was what it was. We each did what we had to do."

Her lips parted, a stunned look in her eyes. "That's it? After all we went through?"

He shook his head, Pallia's words from the night before burning through his mind. "I don't know what you want me to say. The things I did, all of that, it has to sleep somewhere. I'm with Pallia, my wife. You helped me get back to her, except there wasn't much of me left for her. But that's done now," he added. "Is this what bothers you, seeing me with her? Is that why you keep throwing things at us, to complicate matters?"

She looked about, jarred by his response. "I, I just thought—"

"Thought what?" he pressed, but knew the answer was too discomforting for either of them to voice. "You had to know, *had* to know, that would never happen, not if I had any wits left in my head."

She pursed her lips, her gaze sinking to the ground.

He closed his eyes and took a deep breath, holding it before letting it go. He couldn't help but pity her, and quickly came to peace with that dilemma. Only then did he look at her again. "You never should have stayed with him."

Her eyes snapped up to meet his gaze, boring into him but finding no purchase on his impassive expression. "And what concern of that is yours? You just stated your disclaimer, didn't you?"

He shrugged. "That man—your husband—is evil, and you know it, knew it when you saw what he did to me, knew it the way he treated you. I knew it, even in the state I was in." He glanced over his shoulder to make sure Pallia was still with Owen by the *Solitude*. He looked back to Siona. "The project you two ran on me, it didn't stop with me, did it? I bet you two kept at it, and whatever happened, it got so bad, now not even the military wants anything to do with it, right?"

She took a breath, but said nothing.

"So what is it?" He pointed past her. "That's the secret of the *Chrysopoeia*, isn't it?"

She shook her head. "I can't tell you."

He waved off her claim. "That's crap. Look around; we're not going anywhere. Sooner or later I'll know. So just tell me."

She looked at him. "The name of the ship, 'chrysopoeia', do you know what this term means? I didn't think you would. It's an ancient term from old Earth. It was the name of our project; it translated to the transport, since that's all that remains of the project. 'Chrysopoeia', it was the mythical process of alchemy to transform lesser things into gold."

He frowned. "That was a fool's quest."

She tipped her head. "So it was."

They stared at each other. The moments passed. Pallia came up beside Stohko, looking between him and Siona. "Skimmer's good to go," she said. "We can leave for Seaside once it's rigged to the loader."

Siona gave Pallia a curt smile and opened her hands. "Well then, that's good news. You two can be on your way. Please be careful."

Stohko nodded. "We'll be fine." He looked to Pallia. "We'll have to outline some duty schedules for Owen to follow up while we're gone. For one thing, I would like a party to survey the surrounding area since we couldn't get any results from our orbital scans." He looked back to Siona. "Is the *Chrysopoeia*'s cargo secured?"

She glanced at the ruined transport. "It appears so."

"Good," he said with a nod. "We wouldn't want to upset the doctor, would we?"

She blinked. Then she walked away.

Pallia laid her hand on his back and tipped her chin to Siona's retreating form. "What was that about?"

He sipped his tea. "Nothing," he said after some thought.

***

Late in the morning they sat with the crew for a small break, portioning out some of their ration packs in expectation of finding more in Seaside. Stohko outlined what he expected of the scouting party, but he was caught off guard when several of the crew demanded to open the *Solitude*'s weapon locker to make an armed sortie. Stohko hesitated, but they were in the high risk shipping business, and his men were comfortable carrying weapons. Rather than argue with them that there were no predators or animals of any kind, he only reminded them of this fact and consented to their carrying arms. Bhandhakar, who had joined the break with Siona, voiced his disapproval at once. "They're going to shoot each other," was his simple statement.

"Almost to a man, we're ex-military here," Stohko said, his tone sharp. "They know how to handle their weapons. My crew knows their business."

Bhandhakar looked the crew over before settling on Stohko. "That's what I'm afraid of," he said with resignation. "Very well then. But I should inform you that, as an officer, I, too, will be armed from here forward," he announced and backed away. Siona hesitated, but grew uncomfortable under the inflamed scrutiny of the crew. She retreated as well, following Bhandhakar back to the *Chrysopoeia*.

The *Solitude*'s locker was opened and the repeaters dispensed. Owen stood by Stohko while each man in turn went through a weapon check and took three clips of ammunition. Behind them, half the crew formed up for the sortie before pacing off into the wild green expanse of Hermium. Owen and Stohko watched them go while the rest of the crew set about rigging the skimmer to the uniloader.

Owen rubbed his forehead. "Is this the best idea?"

Stohko glanced back at him. "The weapons or the sortie?"

Owen shrugged. "Chicken and the egg—one leads into the other."

Stohko nodded, his gaze trailing away to the foliage that had absorbed the sortie. "I want to know what's out there. I was never allowed during my time here, and it always bothered me." He looked back to Owen. "If something's been out there all this time, I want to know what it is."

Owen opened his hands. "And then what?"

Stohko looked to him as if the answer was obvious. "It ruined me. Time to return the favor."

***

Clouds gathered in the early afternoon, but with the skimmer ready to go, Stohko and Pallia clambered into the uniloader. Stohko stashed a repeater behind the driver's seat and waved to the pilot of the skimmer. He and Pallia buckled themselves, the cables snapped secure, and then they were up in the air, dangling beneath the skimmer and cruising over the high canopy of the trees. In short time they spotted the highway, overgrown as it was in green Hermium embraces, and were set down. The skimmer departed, off to survey the power plants of Seaside.

Comfortable on the ground, Stohko powered up the uniloader to send them rumbling toward Seaside. A small storm gathered over them, pelted them with a downpour, and then quickly departed. Pallia curled up in her seat and slept in the steady bob of the cab. By evening the clouds broke and the sun emerged once more, low and with a rosy cast on the fringes of the sky. He rolled down his window to get some fresh air. It was humid, but cool after the rains and fragrant with the lush growth around them. It reminded him of something, something from his time planetside: *Hermium in bloom.*

Pallia stirred, rubbing her face before blinking and looking out the windshield. When she saw the clear sky and the bare sun she smiled. She released her seat buckles, threw open the cab's roof panel, and stood through the opening. "What a beautiful evening!" she called down to him.

He nodded and glanced at her. Before he knew what was happening he realized he was smiling, and his intermittent glances at her lingered, until his eyes were on her more than the road ahead. She unzipped her sleeves and detached them from her bodysuit. Turning her face up to the sun, she closed her eyes and stretched her arms, drinking up the long warm light of Hermium's evening. The wind blew, her hair trailing off her shoulders. "Is it like this all the time?"

He blinked. Looking at her, he began to ache, so much so that his voice was lost.

She dropped down into her seat and ran her hands through her hair. She looked happy. He tried but failed to remember the last time he had seen her so in his company.

His heart trembled. He wondered if he was dreaming.

"Are we close?" she asked.

Her voice startled him, but it was the looming reality of her question that served to both still his emotions and disrupt them in a whole new way. He looked out the windshield as they mounted a hill. He extended the pointer finger of the hand he rested atop the wheel.

And then they were there.

He brought the uniloader to a halt as his eyes widened on the drive that led to the old Navy offices, the mansion still visible from the highway. He struggled to swallow, his eyes drawn down the highway to the embrace that lay in the distance, where he had almost died. He closed his eyes, but they sprang open, darting about. Before he put any thought into what he was doing his hands dug out his pills and clutched the little bottle to his chest.

"Stohko?"

He sucked in a breath.

Pallia put a hand on his shoulder. He cringed, recoiling from her until his eyes focused to reveal her over the flashing images of his memories. He blurted her name as he clutched her hand. He looked about before sitting up straight. "I'll be okay." He nodded his head. "It's okay. We'll check the basement stores, do what we have to, and we'll go."

"Do you want me to drive?"

"No." His eyes darted toward the distant embrace. "I'll be okay."

They rolled down the short drive to halt before the mansion. Pallia hopped out at once. She looked back at Stohko, finding him frozen beside the uniloader with his eyes fixed on a large window at the far corner of the mansion, one floor from the top. She looked to the window, following the line of his gaze. "Was that your office?"

He blinked and turned to her. "Yes." He reached behind the driver's seat, pulled out the repeater, and slung it over his shoulder. When he walked around the uniloader he found that Pallia had strayed several steps from the truck, her hands clasped on top of her head, her unzipped sleeves dangling from the shoulders of her bodysuit. She shifted from one foot to the other, her head turning to let her gaze pan over the lawn, the grass wild now and littered with weeds. He wondered what she was thinking, if she was finding herself lost in the ghosts of his past, this secret past that to her was nothing more than trial testimony and scattered images on the news nets, this hidden part of his life that had been lost to her, yet was intimate to her for the way it had impacted her, indirect and inaccurate, but impacted nonetheless.

"Pallia?"

She spun to him, her hands dropping by her waist. She stood there for several moments, and he could feel it, the unease seeping from her, the unease seeping from him, the unspoken *dread* that formed as their unease collided between them, and in its wake, he could hear the ghostly traces of laughter, the laughter of two young girls, lost forever in the silent void of the trees hemming the place.

"It's so *empty*," Pallia said, her voice a whisper.

His eyelids twitched. It was hard to hear her, but he heard the trees. *Elena?* His gaze darted about the woods. *Have you been here all this time?*

Pallia hissed his name as she came before him. She grabbed his arm, her eyes roaming the trees and the gentle sway of their leaves. "Do you hear it again?"

He looked into her eyes.

She squeezed his hands in fascination, in innocent wonder for the whispers in her head, the maddening seduction of the euphoria well at work on her. Soon, though, he knew she would begin to understand. The euphoria was new to her. She would see through it in short order, and then things would change. It always changed, it always became distorted and confused, as in the way he had been. It was the way of Hermium, and fighting it, he knew, was akin to fighting the tides.

With that he took her wrist and led her to the mansion's front door. Taking a deep breath, he grabbed the handles of the heavy doors, gave a tug, and pulled them open on creaking hinges. Long rays of evening light poked into the open doorway, illuminating specks of dust that floated on the disturbed air. The once ordered reception hall was stripped, the chairs and desks that had rimmed its expanse now piled in a corner. There were no spider webs, as there were no spiders on Hermium.

Stohko walked across the room, his boots echoing on the smooth stone tile floor, to come before the main utility closet. The door was unlocked, so he pulled it open to inspect the main breaker board for the building. It was intact, but when he flipped the switches, there was no sign of power to the building, as he had expected. He closed the door and walked over to Pallia, her body outlined in the open doorway. "No power," he said as he walked back to the uniloader.

She watched him go before looking back into the depths of the mansion. The large main stair rose in a fanciful curve to the balcony that surrounded the room and led off to the rest of the mansion's halls and rooms. She sucked in a breath of surprise when Stohko returned to hand her a flashlight.

"Doesn't look promising, does it?" she said with a shrug.

He turned on his flashlight and pointed in the corner to his left. "Basement access is over there." The pale white cone of light was lost in the rays of the setting sun. "Let's go."

He led her across the room, his eyes sweeping across the floor and walls as he half remembered the faces of those who had worked the room. He blinked and fought to stuff their ghosts away as they looked at him in turn and watched him pass. *All in my head*, he told himself as he pulled the knob of a door beside the defunct elevator. After a good thud from his shoulder the door creaked open to reveal a stairwell descending to darkness. With a glance back at Pallia he made his way down the stairs. Small clusters of little rooms spread out to either side, their claustrophobic confines lost to the darkness, but he remembered what they had witnessed well enough: once file rooms, they became interrogation cells, the last stop for many of the HLC members the Fallen Angels had seized.

Teeth clenched, he narrowed his eyes to keep them forward and forget what lay to either side of him. At the end of the hall was the next set of stairs, leading down to the supply dumps of the mansion. He plodded down the stairs, peering about with his flashlight while ignoring the mounting murmur of his memories. *Over there, where a man was beaten until he confessed to everything and anything; against that wall, where two women were shot; behind that door, where he had seen a man hung from a ceiling girder.*

It was too much. His knees wobbled and gave out, dumping him onto the last step. The flashlight clattered to the floor between his feet. He put his hands on his face, shaking his head as he sucked in a tight breath. *Nothing but whispers! Why did I come here? Damn you Siona and your little head games! There's no food here, there's nothing here, nothing but whispers of loss and hurt and betrayal and futility, whispers of ruin and innocence destroyed!*

His head began to pound. His hands groped through his pockets until he found his bottle of pills, tearing them free to clench them against his forehead. *No, fight it, fight it!*

The bolt of agony that tore through his mind snapped his head back as if he had been kicked, his body losing all tension. His hands dropped to his sides, the pill bottle fell to the floor.

Only then did he realize he was alone.

Pallia?

His eyes slid shut as he slumped to the floor.

***

He woke to the glare of the flashlight in his face.

With a gasp he convulsed and shot upright. "Pallia? Pallia!"

There was no reply.

He snatched his flashlight and pills, stuffing the bottle in his pocket as he charged up the stairs and ran back to the reception hall. By the open double doors he halted and turned his flashlight outside the mansion into the dark night. He spun on his feet, coming around to face the stairs spiraling to the upper floors of the mansion. The flashlight clicked off in his hand. It took effort, but then he found himself moving—stiff with hesitation and resistance, but moving—across the room to ascend the stairs. He found it hard to swallow; the tension within was so great it clamped his throat shut. *Why would she go up there?*

He knew the answer. *She was called up there.*

Shaking, he made his way to the top of the stairs. He knew the way, but every cell in his body screamed in protest. He had to go, even as he felt the tremulous silence within his mind for this moment, this long dreaded moment, when the sundered lives of his past would collide.

He walked between several rows of desks. Papers and folders were left on the desks, the whole room having the look of a sudden departure rather than the planned obsolescence evident in the reception hall. But then he remembered this was the one room of the mansion that had to operate, if the mansion was to operate in any fashion as a command and control element. He froze, the last doorway ajar. His eyes were drawn to the desk by the door. For a moment his memories welled up, painting the shadows with visions of a different time, a different life, a different light, and in the midst of it, Ellen sitting at her desk.

She looked at him. Her lips formed a warm, welcoming smile.

"It's been a long time, Stohko."

His eyes widened as he stared at her, but then he calmed as he felt the truth within him.

Ellen, you're gone from me now.

She smiled, looking at him until she gave him the slightest of Hermium shrugs. "It's like fighting the tides," she said. She craned her neck to peer through the slit of the open door. "You have to go the rest of the way."

He followed her gaze to the door. He blinked.

He looked back to her. There was nothing beside him but an abandoned desk.

He pushed the door open and stepped through. The soft light of Hermium's moon cast his old office in a violet glow, the clear sky outside punctuated by twinkling starlight. It reminded him of the view from his portal on the *Solitude*, and in that moment, he felt the tingling paradox of his memories, wondering if this moment existed, or if it had existed so many times all those muddy moments between were being overwhelmed and overwritten in his mind, nullified until his life culminated to one moment, *this* moment, this moment with Pallia amid the depths of murmuring violet shadows.

He looked over his shoulder. As he expected, Pallia stood transfixed before the pictures on the wall. It made no sense to him that they were still there, but then he ignored that inconsistency, and accepted that not all was as it appeared.

"Did you find anything?" she asked, not looking back.

He couldn't answer her.

"I didn't mean to leave you," she said.

"I didn't mean to leave you," he echoed. He walked to his old desk and tapped a finger on the dusty surface. His eyes rose to the starlight in the window before he looked back to her.

She stood there, her back to him, her hands at her sides. In the tomb-like silence of the office her hands rose to one picture in particular, her fingers clasping the frame to take it from the wall. She turned, her eyes settling on him for a moment before returning to the picture. Her arms straightened to hold it out from her, her eyes widening.

He held his silence. There was no need to ask which picture she held.

"The angle," she began, looking back to him. "The angle of this picture. She took it, the girl?"

He opened his mouth, but his voice was lost. He licked his lips. "Elena."

Her lips parted as she studied him, watching him step away from the desk to lean against the window frame, his head still hanging. "It must have been a special moment, that time on the pier," she said with caution.

He squeezed his eyes shut. "They were good people."

"Ellen Fortas," she said under her breath. She turned from him and hung the picture with care. Her gaze held on the image as her hands sank to her sides. "Did you..."

His eyes snapped open. He lifted his head, but she had not turned from the pictures.

"Did you—" she began again, but fell silent. She cleared her throat. "I never told you, but I knew when you took the post planetside. General Keane told me to go, to go to you; he told me what had happened to the man you were replacing, but I was so mad, I was so hurt, I refused, I couldn't. And every day that passed, the harder it was to take it back. Even Owen, puppy that he is, he wouldn't talk to me anymore. All I had was the promise, the promise we made, and the guilt for spiting it, and the hurdle it made, it just kept getting bigger; so big, I couldn't even comprehend mounting it, it just got easier to look away." She turned from the pictures. "We're never leaving this place, are we?"

He stared at her. "No."

She looked back to the picture. "Hopelessness, you know, it doesn't bother me, doesn't bother me at all anymore. After hating this place so long for what it did to us, now I feel like I was always supposed to be here, that if I had, many things would have been different, for both of us, but even as it is, so it is, and maybe, maybe should have been."

He took a step toward her, drawn by her words.

"We both lost our way," she stated, her eyes on the picture. When he held his silence, she looked over her shoulder to find him behind her. Rather than a reply, his eyes lingered on her, his lips trembling. There were so many things he wanted to tell her, so many things he wanted to lay bare, so many things he wanted to put to rest before her, that he didn't know how or where to start; but then, she had said many of them for him, admitted them from her own heart, her own lost way, so like his, so very much like his, that the long distance he felt between them evaporated. In the end, he could think of only one thing, the simplest of things, that which he wanted to say more than anything else, but was still locked deep within by the detritus of his past. When his lips parted, though, she shook her head once. "Nobody's innocent here," she said.

He blinked. "Pallia…"

She closed her eyes. "Take me there."

Such as it was, such as it should have been.

He glanced out the window of the old office. It was dark but for the starlight. The whispers faded from him, Lady Hermium quiet now in her veil of night, for she at last perceived a sense of peace. He looked to the picture and understood. Like all dreams, seductive as they can be, they are poor allusions to what they pursue, to what they seek to imitate, and in imitation, blind themselves to the very things they seek. The meaning of the picture had nothing to do with the image it held. It was the dream it had frozen in his mind, the dream it had unknowingly corrupted, calling to him from that little frame. And he remembered another thought he had once held, his deduction concerning obsession, that any good obsession, any genuine obsession, was blind obsession, blind to the innocence it could unwittingly lead astray.

Hermium in bloom. Why does a planet with no insects flower?

Melogo, please forgive me. I never understood a word you said.

He blinked. It was only a moment, but it seemed he had been lost in himself for hours. He looked to Pallia. He took her hands and gave her a gentle kiss, the way he knew he should have when he left her. He stepped back from her, her wide eyes stunned and locked on him, but he held her hand and led her away from the office, out of the building, and by memory, by starlight, by the dull violet glow of the moon, to the long pier of the mansion. To his disbelief it was still intact. He shed the bulk of the repeater on the sands of the beach and listened to the soft lap of the tiny wavelets on the still bay. Starlight shimmered on its surface in blurred pinpoint reflections.

He looked back to her.

"It's so open," she whispered, her eyes roaming about the bay. "It's so quiet."

He closed his eyes and breathed in the night air. Then he led her down the length of the pier, halting at the end to stand by her side, holding her hand. "As it is, and as it should have been," he muttered.

She looked to him. "It's so empty, but it *aches*, it aches not to be alone."

He sat on the edge of the pier and pulled off his boots to let his feet dangle in the warm water. She sat down beside him and followed suit, laughing at the warmth of the water. "You must have gone swimming here all the time," she said, fanning her toes in the water.

He shook his head. "No. Always too many eyes watching."

She looked across the bay and shrugged. "Just my eyes now."

He stood and stripped off his bodysuit. He gave no thought to his nudity in the open night air, forgetting that since his trial he had hid himself from her in shame. He jumped in the water and swam in a wide arc around the end of the pier before surfacing. The sound of a splash caught his attention. He wiped his eyes to reveal an empty pier. He spun in the water, only for Pallia to surface before him, laughing. She ran her hands over her head to smooth her hair back, its slick dark length a violet halo of the moon's reflected glow.

He stared at her, his nerves tingling as if he were in a dream. "Is this real?"

She smiled. "Does it matter?"

He looked back to the pier. Elena smiled and waved at him. He looked back to Pallia. "No," came his simple reply.

She began to laugh.

He splashed her. She yelped, returning the favor by dunking him. It was silly, he knew, but such was the way it had been between them, and somehow, as if by magic, like the ghosts of the dead around him, this departed soul had returned as well, and not just to him, but to both of them. There was no sense to it, but he hardly cared. The moment was the moment, and he felt as he had not felt for so very long, and saw no point to resisting it, or questioning it, or caring about anything else than the simple existence of that moment. It was *right*, the way he had always envisioned a moment on Hermium should be, he and Pallia and the planet, their Lady Hermium, whispering peace from her trees, banishing guilt and shame to the violet depths of the star laden night, welcoming them into her embrace.

Only one thing remained between them. Unspoken, the promise they had made came to life.

They swam to the beach, but paced to the end of the pier and sat down once again. They laid back on their bodysuits and looked up to the night sky. He closed his eyes, letting the pound of his heart and the tingle of his wet skin in the night air fill his senses, and mingled with that, the sensation of her beside him. She sat up, smoothing her hair back and squeezing the water from its length.

He let his breath go and laced his hands above his head. "Pallia?" he whispered.

She glanced at him from over her shoulder, her lips forming a small grin. The moments passed. Then she straddled him, her fingers meshing with his as she rested her forehead on his. She held her breath as she settled down on him; he could feel every part of her until he felt her pulse as well. Only then did he open his eyes to meet her gaze.

"Just us now?"

"Just us now."

***

Many dreams drifted through his mind, half thoughts that danced about each other and mocked him with a serenade of maddening, muddled messages. The old familiar weight, the inescapable weight of Inevitability, had returned as well to haunt his sleeping mind, eroding the moment of bliss he had shared with his Pallia, his wife. With the weight came other things that had slept within him, and mending his way with Pallia, in a cruel irony, had woke them, and with them, a very unsettling suspicion he had long courted but had refuted with such conviction it struggled to gain consciousness within him.

Until now. Is this my final punishment, not to have my joy without this burden?

He tried to fight the thought that crystallized within him, but it was a futile effort. Hermium, he felt, would have nothing of his denials now.

Chrysopoeia: the art of turning lesser things into gold.

Remnant

His eyes snapped open to the first light of dawn.

He sat up on the edge of the pier and glanced over his shoulder. Pallia, and her clothes, were missing. He dressed, grabbed the repeater, and sprinted to the mansion, only to find her sitting on the front steps, eating from a ration pack. She smiled and waved to him as he approached.

"We have to get back to the *Solitude*," he said, stowing the repeater in the uniloader. "Now."

She looked at him in confusion.

He opened his hands. "Something's wrong," he tried to explain.

She shrugged as she took a bite from a protein bar, but then she stood and pointed over his shoulder. He spun on his feet to see the skimmer racing towards them. It circled the mansion before settling on the lawn, showering them with the morning dew on the grass. Owen clambered down from the skimmer, clutching a repeater in his hands. His eyes were wide and wild, his knuckles white in their grip on the repeater. Pallia stood, but Stohko quickly stepped to his side, placing himself between Pallia and Owen. He called his XO by name, causing the man to blink. "We have to go!" Owen said. "We have to go, we have to get, we have to get out of here, get out of here now!"

Stohko put up a hand to calm Owen. "What—"

Owen lunged, seizing Stohko's arm. "Come on! The crew! The sortie! They went crazy!"

Stohko pulled loose from Owen's grasp, knocked the repeater from the XO's hands, and seized him by the shoulders to still him from his anxiety. Owen looked about, his eyes darting until they settled on Pallia. "Siona!"

Pallia stepped out from behind Stohko to grab Owen's hand. "What happened?"

Owen shook his head, squeezing his eyes shut before they popped open once more. He saw the bottle of water Pallia had left on the steps and pulled free of Stohko to stagger towards the mansion. He slumped down on the steps and drank deeply from the bottle. Only then did they notice the dark stream of blood staining his bodysuit beneath his right shoulder. Pallia and Stohko exchanged a glance before Pallia went to Owen. Stohko picked up Owen's repeater and pulled the magazine loose, only to find it empty. To his dismay the barrel was still warm. He tossed the weapon in the back of the uniloader and took his loaded repeater out of the cab. When he looked back to Pallia and Owen he saw that Owen had slumped against Pallia. The man was trembling, entering shock from blood loss.

"Siona!" he cried out, flailing a hand in the air.

Pallia stilled him as Stohko paced over to them, glancing over his shoulders to the trees. "Owen," he said, trying to get the man's attention. "Owen!"

Owen blinked and dropped his hand to his side. "What did I do...?"

Stohko sat on the steps beside Owen, looking past him to Pallia. "What happened?"

Owen looked to him. "I was sleeping; I was dreaming, nightmares, crazy nightmares—I started dreaming of her, and then she *came* to me," he said, blinking with confusion. "I don't know, I don't know what happened, but then she was there, and then it was just happening..."

Stohko bowed his head.

Owen convulsed. "Starlight and gunfire! It just started! I think, I think it was the sortie, come back while we were sleeping, but it was dark, and I wasn't watching, I was with her instead, and then I was just watching, watching and listening to the slaughter, and she went away; she got dressed and sat there and put her hands on her face, and she was crying..." He closed his eyes, resting a moment to catch his breath. "I could hear the gunfire outside, could hear the screams, not like men screaming, but the way children scream—terrified, but fearsome. I had to shoot, I had to, had to protect..."

Pallia glanced over to Stohko. "What is this?"

Owen coughed. "Bhandhakar," he said. "When it was over, when everyone was dead or gone, he came, he came and shot me, shot me in the back, and they left me, just left me there..."

They grabbed Owen's hands. He coughed and seized, holding that way for a moment before he went limp between them. Pallia's mouth dropped in shock. She pulled her hands away and backed off several steps. Stohko stared down at his XO, frowning before running his hand over Owen's eyes to close them. He sat for a moment before standing and slinging the repeater. He looked about the trees, his thoughts condensing with painful clarity, the sharp cut of a kaleidoscopic glare that fulfilled the suspicions lurking within him. He shook his head and took a deep breath.

"Stohko?"

He looked to Pallia.

She stood there, hands hanging at her sides, her eyes on Owen. "He's dead," she thought aloud. Her eyes rose to Stohko. "He's dead, isn't he?"

He frowned.

She laid her hands on her chest. "Why don't I feel anything? The only thought in me — oh God, forgive me, the only thought in me is—"

"One less distraction," he said for her.

They stared at each other.

He forced himself to swallow before admitting what he knew he could no longer hide. "Before we left the nexus Osler gave me a bomb."

She fell back a step. "I know."

He lost his voice.

She clenched her teeth before she could speak again. "I set it."

His head tipped back.

She opened her hands and looked into her palms before looking back at him. Her eyes wandered to the path leading to the pier before returning to him. "I'm not sorry about it," she said in confusion. "Why is that? How could I do that?"

He stepped toward her and took her hand. He opened his mouth, but he failed to find the words to explain what she was feeling, knowing at the same time it was no longer necessary, as in reality he would only be explaining it to himself. Besides that, he told himself, he knew what Osler had done to her, the argument he had used on her, because it must have been very similar to the one he had used on Stohko: *set the detonator, sink the ship, spite Siona and Bhandhakar for their crimes, let it all pass to Hermium, and finally have your time together, alone, as you know you've always wanted, as you know you must have wished for in these troubled years.*

"Osler," he said. "Elena was his niece."

Pallia shook her head. "But what do Siona and Jason have to do with that?" she asked, but caught herself as the words left her mouth.

"Hermium euphoria," he replied.

They looked at each other. There was no hiding from it anymore. "The *Chrysopoeia*," they said together.

They ran to the skimmer and hopped into its little open cockpit, powering it up and taking to the air. Once above the trees they discerned some pale tendrils of smoke in the direction of the crash site. They raced forward, but not quite as fast as Stohko's thoughts raced, for they were coalescing at a disturbing rate. He knew then with cold certainty that his torture had been carried out nowhere else but on Hermium itself, and that somehow, in some way, it was tied directly to Bhandhakar's Project Chrysopoeia; that Bhandhakar's Project Chrysopoeia and the Hermium euphoria were in fact one in the same, the same disastrous phenomena that was—with insidious and unavoidable means—altering he and Pallia even as they welcomed it in the twists and distortions of their dysfunctional love, even as they in turn altered the euphoria with their reunion—for he came to the final conclusion, with equal certainty, that the euphoria was not fixed; no, it was somehow alive, it breathed, and on a planet of evolutionary primitivism, it was the most alive thing, filling all the empty solitude of the planet with its own energy, enveloping everyone in its embrace, altering everyone in its embrace.

It was the perfect laboratory. Meddling with people, whatever way Bhandhakar managed to do it, there was no better place to do it than here, here where there is no other life except plants, nothing to interfere except our own human flaws and whispers of ruinous inclinations.

His curiosity burned within him. *What is on that ship? What is so despicable even the military wants nothing to do with it, that yet has its own wants, its own inclinations to be held, to be filled, to be loved, and not be alone, to have a home in the warmth and sun—*

He blinked, his heart bucking in disgust and horror. *No—*

Pallia brought the skimmer down beside the *Solitude*. She looked at him, his face having paled. "Stohko?"

"No," he thought aloud, "no, it can't be…"

He heard a shout.

There was a crack of gunfire.

Pallia gasped and crumpled against him.

His eyes bulged as he grabbed her and pressed his hands against the wound in her chest. Blood seeped between his fingers.

"No!" he screamed. "Pallia! No! *No!*"

A woman's cry sounded out. It was Siona.

He looked up to see her running from the trees. Bhandhakar was chasing after her, slow as he was, aiming at Stohko with his handgun. Stohko slumped against the framing of the skimmer's cockpit, cradling Pallia to protect her. Siona came to a stop against the skimmer, bracing her palms against her temples before slapping them on the skimmer. She spun on Bhandhakar, who was pacing towards them now, his handgun still trained on Stohko. "I should kill you Jansing!" he shouted.

Siona turned back to Stohko. "Why didn't you let me go with you? None of this would have happened if I was there, there'd be none of this madness if you hadn't been alone with her! You let your demons loose and the euphoria drove us all insane!"

Stohko struggled to breath. He looked between them in disbelief. The weight of Inevitability had returned with crushing intensity, seeming to strangle the wind from him as he held Pallia's limp form.

Bhandhakar came to a stop behind Siona. "Goddamn the day you were born Jansing! You destroyed my project, you stole my wife; you ruined everything in my life!" He braced himself, leveling his gun at Stohko. Veins bulged on his neck as he fought to squeeze the trigger, but his hand refused to obey. "I can't even kill you now when I want to! See! They won't let me!"

Stohko closed his eyes and pressed his head to Pallia's temple. He was clamping the wound with all his strength, but the seep of blood was fading, and he could feel her pulse weakening.

"Siona, get in the lifeboat," Bhandhakar said with a wave of his gun.

Siona leaned over the edge of the cockpit to grab Pallia's dangling hand. "Don't let her go," she said to Stohko, her eyes locked on him. "Don't let her go!"

"Siona!" Bhandhakar repeated.

"I'm staying," she said without looking at him.

His face fell. "What? You choose this, you choose *ruin* over your life with me?"

She turned to him. "There was never any life with you, there was only serving you! Marrying you made me less in your eyes; it made me your possession!"

Bhandhakar blinked. He lowered his gun with his gaze. He hesitated a moment, but then his eyes snapped back to her, the gun following. He shot her once, in the heart. She flopped against the skimmer before sliding off its hull to the ground. He stared down at her in disbelief. He dropped his gun as if his hand had been stung and looked at Stohko. "Look at me," he said.

Stohko ignored him.

"*Look at me!*"

Stohko opened his eyes to look at the doctor.

"That bullet was not intended for Pallia," Jason said. "It was for you!"

Stohko closed his eyes.

"This place, this forsaken place, it wouldn't *let* me shoot you," Jason continued. He fell silent for several moments. "Of all those who ever came to Hermium, no one was like you. A planet-wide experiment in behavioral control and modification, the likes of which had never been attempted before, and you ruined it, you alone ruined it, with your righteous guilt and misguided shame and all your convoluted denials forcing this place to see its own misguided ways, you ruined my life's work, you ruined an entire *planet*. And when I finally had you, had you alone to dissect you, to dissect you away from what had been attempted here, you *infected* my wife and stole her from me, you infected *me* and reduced me to a mockery of my ambition, and still, even then, I could not remove your contamination from this place, I could only manage to silence certain things within you to stop the suffering of Project Chrysopoeia, and even that failed, because it was bound to you by that point, so infected it was with you!"

Stohko shook his head. "Go away."

"Look at me," Jason demanded. "You owe it to me to look at me when I tell you these things!"

Stohko opened his eyes.

"You must know these things," Jason said, pronouncing each word with care, "because you have caused so much ruin, you have cost so many lives, that you need to know these things to complete the cycle. Hold her," he said, jabbing a finger at Stohko, "hold her tight, because for her sake, you ruined an entire world." He dropped his hand. "I'm going to leave you now, leave you alone here with your Hermium and my

Project Chrysopoeia, your elusive euphoria, that you stole from me. Goodbye, Stohko Jansing," he added and walked away.

Stohko closed his eyes. Some time later he heard the whine of the lifeboat's thrusters as it soared toward space. He looked up, watching the thruster trail until a white streak pierced the sky and the lifeboat disappeared in a ball of light.

The blockade drones were very efficient.

White lines worked their way down from the explosion, descent paths of the lifeboat's wreckage.

He looked down to Pallia. Her head rocked back, her eyes closed. Her lips parted.

"Pallia?" he whispered, cradling her head on his forearm as he held her. "Pallia?" He kissed her forehead. "It's just us now," he said and held her tighter, tighter until there was no denying what he feared.

He looked at her, and he knew. He had lost her.

***

He held her until his strength gave out, leaving him to slump in the cockpit with her body in his lap. The evening grew dark; rain soon drenched him where he sat. Still, he did not move. He had no will to move. When the rains moved off and the stars came out, though, he found himself moving, despite his refusal to budge. He carried her to their cabin and settled her down in their bed. He pulled the sheets up so that she wouldn't be cold, turning her so that she would not wake if he needed to turn on a light to drink his tea.

And then he sat, staring at the floor throughout the night.

***

At sunrise he buried Siona.

Afterwards he sat on a stump, chewing a protein bar as his eyes lingered on the *Chrysopoeia.*

Later he took the skimmer, made his way to the mansion, and took the picture off the wall. He walked down to the pier and sat there for some time, letting his feet dangle in the water. Remembering the bottle of pills in his pocket, he took them out, emptied them into the water, and threw the bottle as far as he could. He did not look to see it plop in the water.

When the rains came he retired to his old office, sat in his old chair, and rested his head on the window to watch the downpour. When the clouds parted he took the skimmer back to the *Solitude* and returned to the stump he had sat on earlier. He chewed a granola bar from the ration pack he had opened in the morning. He thought of seasoned noodles. A throbbing headache grew, but he didn't regret casting his pills away. In some way it made it easier to hear the faint tinkling sound in his ears, but he thought little of that.

At sunset he buried the picture several paces from Siona.

***

He was tired, but in his emotional delirium he had a fitful sleep by the extinguished fire where he had sat with Pallia, Owen, and Siona. Dreams whispered to him, but they were distorted traces again, murmurs of his time with Pallia, his closely guarded memories of when he first met her after getting his captain's license from the Navy.

And then he found himself standing over a small hole he had dug, his eyes closing as that first moment with her drifted through his consciousness. He rubbed his forehead and looked up. The shovel clattered to the ground as he narrowed his eyes against the rising sun. The air was still; there was no breeze, no rustle of leaves, nothing at all.

It's so quiet. Not just quiet, it's more like anticipation. Lady Hermium, she waits for me.

He put his hands on his hips, his eyes settling on the *Chrysopoeia.*

He sat on his stump. His thoughts began to compress, and in his emotional detachment, he began to piece it all together.

First there was Project Chrysopoeia, an effort by the military to control human behavior en masse, headed by Jason Bhandhakar. At some point, Siona Hutchins joined the program, and became his wife.

The Project was moved to Hermium when it was determined that the planet was somewhat of a rare find, a place capable of supporting human life, but had only achieved a basic state of evolution: flora covered the land mass, yet no animal life had evolved far enough to make it out of the water. As such, there was no life on land but the vegetation, so that human life, human inclinations and instinct, were the only behaviors to consider.

Hermium was opened as a vacation planet. That would limit the population; maintain it under the Navy's control, and move test groups—vacationers—on and off the planet at regular intervals, limiting any possible negative exposure. All who came to Hermium raved about the experience, no matter individual inclinations. No one knew the rumor of the so-called Hermium euphoria was in fact the very real effect of Project Chrysopoeia. The Project's flaw was inherent; however, for beneath the beauty and tranquility darker things festered and as well became part of the euphoria. Then came the regressive decay, every turn of negative impulses fed into the euphoria inclined the euphoria in turn to spur more destructive impulses in the planet's residents.

So started the HLC insurrection, and the uncanny way of Hermium to dissolve notions of clarity and organization.

And then I came along, hiding a lonely, wanting tumor of guilt and shame for leaving Pallia. But it must have been that tumor that drew me to the euphoria, that drew the euphoria to me.

He had ached for the dream he held with Pallia. He found himself developing an attachment to Ellen and Elena, only to aggravate that black tumor within him. When he came to his senses and decided to leave, the tumor ruptured. What was the euphoria, what was his lonely Lady Hermium to do? She lashed out through Melogo, but in the typically Byzantine confusion of Hermium's ways, it went all wrong, leaving Stohko alive and Ellen and Elena dead. The ruptured tumor imploded to a greedy black hole. Shame and guilt, guilt and shame, regrets and horrors, dissolution and betrayal, hurt, hurt, *hurt*—the hurting had to stop, it had to stop, it had to lash out, it had to spread the *Hurt*.

Who better to become the agent of retaliation, but he who had bore the tumor?

Melogo and his daughter, they were doomed. And all those others...
Nothing begets hurt like hurt. Any abused child knows that.

He blinked.

With him arrested and the forced evacuation of Hermium, it seemed the euphoria would be done. But somehow Bhandhakar had found a way to work an option through Military Research to possibly redeem Project Chrysopoeia by experimenting on the man Bhandhakar had already decided was most responsible for ruining Hermium. In his ignorance, Stohko took that option. In whatever means at his disposal, Bhandhakar worked to not only remedy the euphoria of Project Chrysopoeia, but to punish Stohko. Yet there was something in Stohko that Bhandhakar could not comprehend, and that was his attachment, his love for Pallia, and the promise they had made, and how these things would seep from him as his mind was picked apart. Infect Siona it did, as she not only perceived what she lacked in her marriage, but that which she craved, until she felt it herself, felt it *in* herself, felt it until her tie to him became inextricable. Likewise Bhandhakar's isolation from Siona became hopeless, and in the increasing emotional strain of his isolated life, lost that one emotion that drove him, his ruthless ambition, so all that remained to him was ruthlessness.

Somehow the Project lingered after Stohko was released. Perhaps there were attempts to implement its effect on other planets, perhaps small labor colonies, where labor insurrections were common, or perhaps it was 'shelved' for lack of a workable solution to its failing. Regardless, it was decided to scrap the whole thing, and where better to scrap such a troublesome failure than the one place so intimately woven with its failure? Then again, perhaps anyone around the Project perceived the euphoria, sensed its desperate loneliness, sensed its longing for the home woven into its existence, the little evolutionary primitive world of Hermium, where the emotional primitivism of the euphoria would be at home, safe behind a screen of Navy blockade drones.

His jaw clenched. *Osler wanted all of it to go away. He must have known something about it. Maybe Ellen wrote to him. Maybe he had run into the Project at some point before coming to the nexus. Then again, maybe he was sent to the nexus because I was there, because Hermium was nearby, and the decision had been made to ditch the whole thing. Who knows, maybe Siona scripted that play of emotions Osler used on Pallia and I to blow up our ship. Siona said they were strapped in before they hit atmosphere, and nobody on our ship had time for that. She knew, she knew, and she just let it happen, she wanted it to happen.*

And so, here we are.

He glanced at the skimmer before settling on the *Chrysopoeia.*

Hesitant at first, but then with increasing ease, he paced toward the little transport, its dark hull growing before him until he stood before the one functioning lock of the wreck, the one Siona and Bhandhakar had used. He cranked it loose and swung the lock open. Cool air washed over him.

The trees rustled. He spun in surprise. He was, of course, alone.

He stepped inside and swung the lock closed to keep the cool air inside the ship. The deck was at a sharp pitch, but he managed to navigate its slope, picking his way through the cramped crew area to the internal lock that interfaced with the transport's cargo pod. He cranked open the inner lock and swung it aside to come face to face with the lock of the pod. Two words were painted in small block letters at the top of the lock: PROJECT CHRYSOPOEIA. Beneath, in larger white letters against a bright red background, there was a caution banner: MAINTAIN CRYOSTASIS.

His throat went dry as the lingering questions returned to him: *What powered, what generated the euphoria? Why does it feel alive?*

He slumped against the lock, unnerved at once. He remembered that one conversation he had with Ellen concerning the rash of missing children on Hermium.

What had she said?

Children who wander off, you just never know.

He clapped his hands over his mouth. Nausea swept over him, but as much as he wanted to run screaming from the transport, he knew there was no hiding from the truth, that he could not evade it as long as he was on Hermium. After all, the truth was with him, the truth had been looking—*searching*—for him all along, had sought him out in his promise with Pallia, had haunted him in the sense of Inevitability that had hung from his shoulders, and yet, had somehow guided him.

He pushed himself up to a stance and cranked the lock release. He took a breath and heaved to pull the lock aside. It clanged against the bulkhead of the lock assembly, but he paid no heed, his eyes locked in the depths of the cargo pod. The transport, he realized, was larger than he thought.

Reaching into the depth of the pod were two long rows of transparent tanks, filled with fluid and dotted with various tube ports. Banks of monitors with intricate displays were nestled about the tanks; cables and power feeds snaked about the tanks like black sinews, only to disappear behind them. At the far end of the single narrow walkway that led down the pod there hung a small light illuminating a cramped workstation before a tight cluster of monitors. The sound of the place reached his ears, the low hum of air circulators, the occasional clicking of pumps to move the fluid in the tanks, but above all, and forming an almost hypnotic lull, was the gentle tinkle from the steady aeration of tank fluid.

He fought to swallow over his dry throat. His eyes were wide. The tanks were dark, but he didn't need any light to know what they held. He had found them, found them at last, *all* of them, the lost children of Hermium, stolen away by agents of the Project, harvested by Bhandhakar for the Project, locked in stasis, frozen in their innocence, and with them, the purity and innocence of their immature emotions, there subject to whatever technology minds like Bhandhakar embraced with the intent to manipulate and project them.

Chrysopoeia, the art of turning lesser things into gold.

Madness, came a single thought.

And yet, insanely successful.

He couldn't bear to look any further beyond the neat rows of cylinders. They reminded him of Choykin's refuse pod.

His head began to shake. He clamped his hands over his temples as the pain he had known from his torture returned with a vengeance. Groaning, he staggered from the transport, thinking only of his pills, and the warning Siona had given him when he had been released, that without the pills he could suffer serious side effects. Dropping to his knees by his cabin in the *Solitude*, he knew what the real risk was, that whatever they had done to him, some blood vessel in his brain was swelling and ready to burst. It was a consideration at the periphery of his mind, though, the piercing pain of pressure between his temples too intense for him to form any coherent thought.

He rocked forward, wrapping his arms around his head.

The agony was unbearable.

He sucked in a breath.

"Pallia!"

The agony erupted.

He convulsed. His body went limp. His hands dropped to the dirt, and shortly after, he flopped on his side. He laid there, his eyes wide and blank. There was some sense that remained to him, but it faded in a hurry.

Time for one more thought...

His vision blurred away as the bleed in his head let his brain die piece by piece. From the darkness something new took shape, and he felt a sense of lightness to his body, but then that too began to fade, and soon, all he knew was the last conscious whisper of his mind.

...Pallia...

***

"Ah, my good friend, any bites?"

Stohko turned to see Melogo standing behind him with a chilled drink in his hand. Stohko looked down to notice he was sitting on a bucket at the end of the pier, his boots off and the legs of his uniform rolled up. He fought to swallow and looked back to Melogo.

His old friend clapped him on the back. "I thought we lost you. There you were fishing, and then you were gone, and now you're back."

His eyes dropped to the pier, his gaze darting about in confusion.

"Melogo! *Thermae et vitae!*"

He spun on his bucket in shock. "Ellen? Is that you?"

She looked at him with a curious smile as she walked to him. "Of course it's me," she said and waved a hand at the apparent silliness of his question. "Elena was asking for her cake. I think Melogo and his little lady set the thought in her head. I was going to get the candles ready; I could use some help with the plates. Where—oh, there she is."

Stohko looked past her. At first he couldn't move, but then he rose from his bucket and stared. When he moved he almost knocked Melogo into the water, Ellen laughing as she caught Melogo's arm and sent his drink pouring down his shirt. Stohko noticed none of it, his wide gaze locked in grateful befuddlement.

She came to him and took his hands.

"Pallia," he gasped, his eyes welling up. Without thinking he smothered her in a crushing embrace, holding her so tight she wheezed against him as her arms circled him.

"Easy," she said. "It's okay, I'm here; we're here."

Ellen walked by them, patting Stohko on the back as she passed. "So where were you off to?"

"A better lure, a better bait," Melogo joked as he passed by on Stohko's other side.

Pallia leaned back from him to catch his gaze. "Yes, where were you? I turned for a moment, and you were gone."

He blinked. "I just—" he started, but then closed his mouth. He looked back to the end of the pier before meeting her gaze. He laid a hand on her cheek. "I thought I lost you," he said in a whisper.

She tipped her head. "Lost me where?"

He sucked in a breath. "Am I dreaming?"

She shrugged and gave him a knowing smile. "You know what? It is as it is. That's all there is to know. Do you really want to know more?"

"It is as it is," he said and nodded. He wiped his eyes. "Where was I?" He looked back to the end of the pier. "I don't know. I guess I just drifted away for a moment; I guess I was lost. No bother, now I'm here." He turned to her. "You know I couldn't leave without saying goodbye."

She frowned and poked his nose with a finger. "That would have been totally unacceptable," she said with mock propriety. "Besides, where would you go?"

He blinked and stepped back, but she took his hand. He looked at her, speechless.

She squeezed his hand. "Don't tell me you forgot our promise?"

He took a deep breath. "Never."

Ellen called them.

"Cake time," Pallia said with good cheer, and, holding his hand, led him off the pier. He could see the mansion in the distance. The lawn was a lush, manicured green. The evening sky, the evening breeze of Hermium, it was beautiful, just as Pallia had once said to him.

He stopped behind a tall bank of shrubs when he saw Melogo's daughter run by with Elena. Pallia turned to him, but he shook his head. "I can't," he said, his guilt welling up.

Pallia smiled. "She wants you there." She took his hands. "They *all* want us there. They've been waiting for us, for the two of us, together."

He blinked, his mind racing. "They've all been waiting..."

A breeze rustled the leaves of the tall trees. Between it, he heard the old familiar murmurs.

His face went pale.

Pallia shook her head and gave his hands a tug. "It's not in your head anymore. Come, and see for yourself. You can't believe how beautiful it is."

He stepped from behind the bank of shrubs and froze. Ellen and Melogo turned to smile on him as Pallia put her arm around him. Melogo's daughter and Elena stood on either side of the cake. But what caught his gaze, what stilled his heart and yet at last set Hermium in bloom around him, was the gathering of children before him, all of them clad in white, a joyous throng arrayed behind the cake and clapping their hands for Elena to blow out the candles.

They're all here, no longer lost, but found, found at last.

"See," Pallia said to him, "look at them. It's just like we had promised each other."

He stood and stared, remembering the promise. It was all he could do.

A piece of heaven for our little angels.

He wept, but held Pallia's hand, and between his tears, found his voice, and joined them in song.

Enemy, I Know You Not

I

The dying fires of Tropico smoldered in the night, peering like little red eyes from the darkened face of the planet.

Sergeant Ellister frowned as he stood in the viewing lounge of his troopship. His gaze lingered on the planet, his mood sinking as the planet's sun began to illuminate an arc of daylight across its rim. He blew out his breath and shook his head before thumping a fist on the bulkhead next to him. "So after everything, you're telling me it's a matter of trust?" He tipped his head. "All right, I trust him," he said, his frown resuming its hold on his face. He looked to his side. "You know, this whole thing with Hovland, I thought it was Security's business. It's not up to me to clear him, so why bring me down here?"

Training Officer Sheffield, slouched against a bulkhead across the lounge from Ellister, shrugged. "This is the only quiet place to talk. Don't forget, it's celebration time." He glanced at the planet beneath them. "The campaign's over. This insurgency—this part of the rebellion—it's over. We won. Time to cut loose."

Ellister's frown did not relent. "Then leave my platoon alone."

Sheffield smiled. "As it happens, I've got replacements for your platoon." He looked to Ellister. "Security says everybody's a green light. You too, by the way—you're officially cleared, even though the papers haven't gone through all their channels just yet. I wanted to let you know. That was some little show you pulled down there," he reminded the sergeant as he nodded his head to the planet.

Ellister looked away. "I was justified."

Sheffield waved a hand. "We can justify anything if we try hard enough, but that's a threat to our standards, and in those messy gray areas, that's where questions and doubt live. Order—to maintain order—things have to be black or white. Clear lines, distinctive boundaries; it's the only way to keep things sane. Remember that." He leaned off the bulkhead. "I'll go talk to Hovland. Now do yourself a favor and get drunk like everybody else."

***

Lieutenant Hovland stared at the tasteless food on the resin meal tray. About him, the troopship's cafeteria was crowded and loud with shouts of drunken triumph. Food took flight over his head; an occasional body would jar his table. His ribs still ached where he had been clubbed with a crowbar, but he was more upset that his medications barred him from joining the drunken rowdiness. Yet the thought of that sent a sense of relief through him, and it wasn't a bad feeling, for it reminded him that he was still among the living. It was no small claim, considering the campaign had ended with eight men lost from his platoon.

A pale hand came out of the confusion and swept away his tray. He looked up, only to sigh at the disheveled creature before him. "Sheffield," he called out across the noise.

The TO put his hand on the table and dumped himself on a seat across from Hovland, his typical smile of mischievous glee pulling at his lips. "I got you new meat," Sheffield said with a tip of his head.

Hovland put a hand to his ear, Sheffield's words lost in the noise. "What?"

Sheffield leaned forward. "I said, new meat. They're a bunch of losers off Tropico's spaceport—sentries with nothing to watch over now. They'll fill out your complement; get your squads filled again." He slapped Hovland on the shoulder. "What's the matter?"

"I could use a few days to heal up," Hovland said over a ragged chorus of shouts rising up from the far corner of the cafeteria. "I'm in no condition to start training recruits."

Sheffield waved him off. "You got the new meat, old boy. I already talked to Ellister. It's all set."

Hovland blinked. "Ellister? It's *my* platoon."

Sheffield put a hand to his ear. "What?" He waited, but when Hovland opened his mouth Sheffield stood and patted Hovland's shoulder. "Catch you tomorrow," he said and pushed off into the jostling mob of the cafeteria.

Somebody bumped into Hovland's back, driving his ribs against the table. Pain sparked through his torso. Across the cafeteria a chair was thrown in the air. Bodies collapsed under its weight when it came down. The crowd started to focus on the area; Hovland focused on the exit.

Fights broke out. It was going to be a long night for Security.

***

Private Lippett sat on his bunk, still wet from his shower, his white trunks clinging to his skin. He looked around the cramped squad room—more a hallway than a room; it was one of three adjoining rooms to form the platoon's home aboard the troopship. As his bunk creaked under his weight, a handgun slid out from under his pillow. Across from him Lieutenant Hovland's sleeping form shifted a bit, the man's hands in a constrictive grip on his little pillow.

Lippett leaned forward to peer down the length of the squad rooms, drawn by a sudden swell of voices. Some of the new soldiers had filed in, sheepishly protesting the insults thrown at them from established members of the platoon. Lippett glanced at Hovland before waving the recruits to silence, the gun in his relaxed hand forcing the issue. He stared at them before looking down at the weapon to dismantle it for a meticulous cleaning. No sooner had he started than Ellister loomed over him and shoved his shoulder. Lippett looked up, and even he could see the annoyance in Ellister's gaze before Ellister let it vent. "What are you doing?"

Hovland groaned as he realized sleep had become a lost cause. He loosened his grip on his pillow and rolled flat on his back. He grumbled, sniffed, and coughed. The pain in his side forced his eyes open, just in time to see Ellister shove the side of Lippett's head with a heavy hand. "Sergeant Ellister," Hovland said through a dry throat.

"Lieutenant," Ellister gave as a crisp reply, but the formality ended there. He grabbed Hovland's shoulders and pulled him to a stance. "New meat," he said and turned to their recruits, steadying Hovland with a hand on his chest. "Lieutenant Hovland," Ellister said to the recruits.

The recruits stared at Hovland. "He doesn't look so good," one of them said.

Ellister bared his teeth. "Hey! You're not sentries anymore! You earn your right to talk! You don't even have a name around here yet, meat!"

"The Lieutenant was captured," Lippett said, his plodding monotone almost lost beneath Ellister's shouting.

Ellister's eyes darted down to Lippett. "You can shut up too," he ordered.

Lippett nodded to himself. "They caught him, smashed him with a crowbar, and plugged him with them neural darts—"

"I said, shut up," Ellister repeated and shoved Lippett to silence him.

"Yeah, but you took care of it Ellis," a voice said from behind the recruits.

Ellister nodded. "That's right Miller, and don't forget it." He looked past the recruits, down the length of the squad room. "Army already paid for the bullet, right Messina?"

Hovland looked to the recruits. They shifted until they looked to the stolid gaze of Sergeant Messina to realize the truth of Ellister's implication. Hovland wondered what the recruits were thinking, but came to the conclusion that he really didn't care. Disgusted with them, he pushed Ellister's hand away and barked for everyone to separate. More than once he and his men had run into problems with civilian disapproval while planetside on Tropico. The military had kept residents insulated from the ferocity of the rebellion, but in their pampered existence the people had grown critical of a campaign of which they knew nothing.

Did they think it was some game?

He vented his frustration by snatching his handgun from Lippett's grasp and stuffing it under his little pillow. He turned to the recruits. "Stow your gear," he said and shoved past them. As far as he was concerned Ellister could have them.

He didn't have to wait. Before he left the room, Ellister was already shouting.

***

An hour later Hovland found himself sitting in the cafeteria, staring at something the food packers called 'mid-meal'. He'd have given a week's worth of his military stipend for a genuine, home cooked dinner.

He frowned, wondering if they could have forced the rebellion into submission had they bombed the planet with the troopship's food.

He shook his head. Sarcasm and cynicism go nowhere, he thought with a sigh.

About him, in the quiet emptiness of the cafeteria, hung-over deckhands were busy cleaning the mess from the previous night's celebration. The white walls of the room were splattered with crusted food; several tables had been torn free of their mounts and left in a haphazard pile. Food waste crunched and squished under his feet whenever he moved them. To him it was a disgrace, fostering the hostility within him. He had the urge to push, an aimless *push* against a reality to which he no longer felt fully connected.

Sheffield's short, pale, disheveled figure approached him. Of all the people on the troopship, the TO was the last person he wanted to see at the moment. The training officer sat across from him. "So what do you think of your new meat?"

Hovland shrugged. "Ask Ellister," he said and put a forkful of food in his mouth.

Sheffield nodded and started to poke his finger through Hovland's meal, but then grinned and leaned on his elbows. "I know they're a sorry lot. Won't stand a chance when we hit dirt again." He scratched the stubble on his chin, scrutinizing Hovland. "You know how it is, this thing with the rebellion, these insurgents, these so-called 'Military Pacifists', 'mips' as they call themselves, they just seem to be dug in deeper and tighter with each planet we hit."

Hovland looked up to Sheffield's dark, puffy eyes. The training officer needed a shave. Hovland sucked in a breath, the darker side of his mood emerging. "No, no they won't stand a chance," he said. "They'll get wiped out. Maybe I should just do it myself, and save them some suffering. What do you say?"

Sheffield laughed. "I'd say you're right."

"I am right," Hovland said, but bit his tongue.

Sheffield grinned. "You guessed it Hov. I've scheduled you to take them on a run in the simulator. Harden them up a bit; give them a little real life experience."

Hovland dumped his fork in his food. "No."

Sheffield opened his hands. "The decision's been made."

Hovland shook his head. "What about Security? Far as I know, those greeners haven't been cleared. Hell, as far as I know, *I* haven't been cleared since being captured."

"Your clearance came through last night, and Ellister was cleared from that bogus murder charge for murdering the bastard that was holding you. Security doesn't party, you should know that," Sheffield said, gazing about the cafeteria.

Hovland shifted in his seat. "My ribs are aching. How can I manage a training sim if I can't carry myself?"

"Double up on your meds," came Sheffield's careless response, signaling the end of the discussion. The TO stood, but then turned back. "You can make something of these recruits, Hovland. You've done it before. Besides, you've got one of the best in Ellister. Hell, you two took that idiot Lippett and managed to keep him alive all this time."

Hovland stared at Sheffield, trying to dismiss the authority the man held by defining him as nothing more than a little slob. In the end he shrugged, worn down by another exercise in what he saw as the mounting futility of his life. "It's not Lippett's fault the way he was born."

"Brain-less," Sheffield said, enunciating to drive his point home.

"He's made it this far. Some of the new meat won't be as lucky."

Sheffield looked at Hovland, a humorous glint in the TO's eyes. "All the more reason for the sim run, old boy. Make them something more than Lippett, okay?" he said over his shoulder as he left.

Hovland opened his hands. He sighed and looked at his medications. He debated a moment before heeding the better wisdom of Sheffield's advice and doubling up on the pills. He groaned. "On three," he said, and closing his eyes, swallowed the pills.

***

He wandered about the corridors of the troopship's lower levels, feeling dazed and weak as the drugs went to work. The corridors were busy, but no one paid much attention to him. It was easy to get lost in the mass crowd of the troopship's human complement.

He had to press himself against the corridor wall so a remote service monitor could roll by, its little wheels squeaking under the weight of the garbage container riding on its frame. It struck him how narrow the corridor was; he found it ironic when he thought of the troopship's immensity, the vastness of its hull. Over the time of the rebellion and repeated insurrection suppression campaigns, the hull's volume had been partitioned and repartitioned until the only open rooms of impressive size were the cafeteria and landing bay. Perhaps it was claustrophobia, perhaps it was some lingering trauma from being captured and tortured on Tropico, but he felt a desperate need to have space around him, volume, distance—a *buffer*.

Buffer, he scoffed. There was no place to run in the confines of the troopship, he knew. The burden of the simulator run weighed on him. His thoughts drifted to that claustrophobic virtual world within the troopship, the simulator and its inescapable, endless landscapes of hostility. The technology was nothing remarkable, common enough in consumer entertainment consoles, only bent to the military's requirements: grid lines became terrain, pixel palettes became the night sky and the color of mud and rocks, various replicated subroutines became artillery shells and enemy combatants. Velocity and impact kinetics became bullet wounds, and with them, facsimiles of pain and mortality, all to instill that most priceless possession of an infantryman, combat experience.

Although he could rationalize the advantages, Hovland despised sim runs. Within the construct of the military and the rebellion he felt manipulated enough as it was; the paradoxical concept of immersing himself in an endless terrain of inexhaustible foes within a fist-sized portion of a computer supplied by the lowest bidder buried within a troopship in the midst of space and its pitiless vacuum... It was too much to bear for a mind of pragmatic concerns.

Nothing more than a fancy game of pretend, he told himself, but it did little to ease him. The memory of his capture and torture were too near for him to erase the conclusion he had reached after Ellister and the platoon had rescued him, the stark conclusion that trust required a forfeiture of control, and so was a precarious thing, whether to man or machine.

***

The new recruits stood in one clump in the squad room, nervous faces peering at one another. Ellister looked from the fully geared recruits to the experienced members of the platoon, who were lounging on the tiered cots of the squad rooms, chuckling to themselves.

Ellister shook his head. "That's it, laugh it up boys," he said, silencing the platoon. He turned back to the recruits with forced patience. "Look, it's a simulator run, not a combat run. You don't need any of your crap with you; it'll be programmed in the immersion. Don't you people play video games on Tropico?"

Embarrassed, the recruits looked at one another until Ellister pulled at their gear. It only took a moment before they caught on. Ellister turned away, shaking his head, cursing beneath his breath. "Just wear your shorts. It's always hot in the simulator rooms. Understood?"

Hovland entered the room. Standing there, staring at the hapless recruits, he shook his head, any encouraging words fading from him. His orders fell from his mouth with little sign of vitality. "Prep room, one hour. Sergeants, get your squads ready." He looked to the recruits. "We have a saying around here to get us to do all the things we don't want to do, and it goes like this: *on three*. Count to three and just do it, short and sweet." He studied the recruits. "On three! Move!"

Ellister frowned with Hovland's tone, but turned on the platoon to slap them into action.

***

"Now the way I see it," Sergeant Webb said, holding up a finger, "we lost eight long timers on Tropico, right? So that leaves us with twenty-two in the platoon out of three squads of ten, standard set up."

Sergeant Messina shrugged as he sat with Webb at a prep table, watching the platoon file into the stark white simulator annex. "So?"

Webb held up a hand. "Just follow me. Now of that twenty-two, me, you, and Ellister each have a squad. Patrone's the medic, so he always hangs on Hovland's side. Lippett hangs on his other side. Garnett's got the squawk, so he hangs behind Hovland. So tell me, how many able bodies does that leave us on the line the next time we hit dirt?" He shook his head and looked around the room. "Sim or no sim, mips are going to kick our ass next time. This is a waste of our downtime, with all the mess we just went through. Ellister cleared of murder, Hovland cleared by Security, eight meats off Tropico's sentry squads for replacements, and we have to go do a sim run? We should be slumming in our bunks."

Messina shook his head and leaned toward Webb to rest a hand on his shoulder. "I'll tell you what I'm worried about. Got a friend in Fourth Army, he said a mip agent got into the simulator with a platoon, fried the bunch of them. Had a virus coded into his subconscious, subliminal executables or some crap Security called it, but this thing gets into the network running the sim, and that's *it*. Whole platoon wasted. Brain dead."

"Ah man," Webb hissed.

Ellister clamped a hand on Messina's shoulder. "Put a lid on that," he said and kept walking, heading for a clipboard on the far wall. It hung next to the lock that led into the simulator room, and served as a roster to check off all personnel entering the simulator. It was part of the new Security protocol, adapted after the 'mishap' with Fourth Army that, officially, had nothing to do with infiltration or sabotage. A few steps from the lock Ellister passed the recruits, driving them back with a glare until he found Miller hovering behind Webb and Messina. He snapped at Miller and jabbed a finger for him to step into open view. Ellister took the clipboard from the wall, keyed his security code into the lock, and waited for the lock to slide open. Then, one by one, he called out the platoon's roster and watched them file into the simulator room.

In a few minutes the annex was empty and Ellister leaned against the open lock. By the book, he had to wait until all personnel were checked off before he and Hovland secured the lock. He stared down at the clipboard, drumming his pen as he stood in his shorts, and noted the names that were left to check: Hovland, Miller, Lippett, Boden... Boden? *Who the hell?* He ground his teeth, but then remembered Boden as one of the recruits.

"Damn," he said to himself and looked up, at once pointing with his pen. "Hovland! Where the hell were you Hov? You left me some load of crap to deal with."

"I know," Hovland said as a simple apology and looked down to his ribs, which were bound with gauze and tape. "I had to get myself wrapped up. I was hurting."

"Yeah, well," Ellister started, but then lost his temper and hung the clipboard. He put a hand on Hovland's shoulder. "Don't you go to pieces on me in there, got that?"

Hovland nodded. "It's just the ribs, Ellis. Hurts when I breathe, hurts to laugh; everything hurts. Takes all the zip out of you. Sheffield came by; he gave me a last minute briefing."

Ellister handed him the pen and gave Hovland another pat on the shoulder. He was about to step into the lock when he saw Lippett stroll into the annex. A handgun clip hung from his neck. "What the hell is that?" Ellister began, but looked past Lippett as Miller hurried by.

"Had to piss," Miller said with a shrug as he ducked behind Lippett. "Boden's in there too."

Lippett stopped short, looking down at his clip for a moment. "Good luck charm, Sergeant." He hooked a thumb over his shoulder. "Forgot it; went back for it."

Ellister shook his head. "Hey, genius, you know it won't be with you in the sim, right?"

Lippett looked down at the clip again and scratched his forehead.

Ellister gave Lippett a shove. "Figured as much," he said and walked into the simulator room. Most of the men were already unconscious, stretched out on the firm bunks that ran down either side of the room. He keyed his security code into the lock's access panel and glanced at the operations console on the wall by the first bunk. All lights were green, telling him that all present had their immersion caps fitted, with all interface leads of each cap contacting a close shaven head. He glanced at the simulator immersion settings, configured by the engineers maintaining the simulator, guided by dictates of the resident training officer—Sheffield, in their case. All that remained was for Hovland to lock the settings.

Ellister looked over his shoulder.

"We're still missing one," Hovland said as he reached past Ellister to key in his security code for the immersion settings.

"Boden," Ellister said, but then turned as the recruit walked into the room. Ellister watched him pass as he sealed the simulator lock. "Nice of you to join us."

"Sergeant," Boden said, standing with his arms wrapped about his chest. "Had to, had to go. Nervous, you know."

Ellister shook his head, but Hovland shoved Boden towards a bunk. "I'll hook him up," Hovland said with a sigh.

Satisfied, Ellister walked to his bunk and sat down, frowning when he squirted contact cream on his head. He spread out the cold cream before settling his immersion cap. He looked to find Hovland fitting Boden's cap.

Ellister tipped his chin up. "Ready?"

Hovland looked over the platoon. "On three."

II

Hovland came to the slow conclusion that immersing in the simulator was like sinking to the bottom of an ocean. There was the sensation of a great pressure weighing down on him, and yet the stranger sensation of weightlessness, as if he was floating within his body. It was an eerie reminder of the neural darts—before the torture had started.

So dark...

He felt air in his lungs. He held his breath before letting it out and opening his eyes. From the darkness an inhospitable terrain came into view. The sky was black, the perfect black of the simulator, yet the landscape was illuminated with a dull twilight. The ambient temperature was comfortable and there were no discernable weather attributes. He was huddled in a small crater; about him the rocky ground swept away in all directions. To the east its broken surface rose to a low ridge. To the south there appeared to be a dip, perhaps a small valley. To the west and spreading to the north to meet the ridge ran a chain of small hills. Thirty meters dead north a massive boulder sat on the open plain.

He sank down in the crater and clapped his hand against his chest plate. The armor deadened the blow, but it was enough for him to be certain there were no pains in his chest. Sheffield had kept his promise, blocking sensory feedback from Hovland's ribs. With a sigh of relief,

Hovland performed a quick inventory of his gear and flipped down his radio mike.

Confused voices sounded out, among them the voices of his squad leaders reigning in the platoon. From what Hovland could gather the simulator had dropped each of them in isolated craters. He frowned. By now, he was sure the recruits were close to panic.

"Listen up," he said over the radio, returning to his old self. He rolled his shoulders, satisfied, despite his displeasure at being immersed in the simulator. "Listen up," he said louder, the babble silencing. "We've been dropped all over, so just keep calm. If you look around there's a large boulder out in the open. Everybody head for it. You new meat out there, just take it slow, and keep low."

He took a deep breath and settled his hands on his repeater. With a quick glance about he scrambled out of the crater and headed for the boulder. The landscape, in its peculiar way, held a certain metallic sheen, as well as his clothes. His skin held the same tone, an unusual artifact for the simulator, seen only during times of heavy network traffic. No rest for the simulator today, he decided as he flipped off the safety of his repeater.

He hustled forward, catching the silhouettes of the platoon as they converged on the boulder. Soon enough he was huddled next to the cold monstrosity, supervising Webb, Messina, and Ellister as they organized their respective squads. Only then did they recall that all the recruits were assigned to Webb's short-handed squad. Webb protested that fact, but Hovland settled the matter by deciding they would shuffle squads once they had their bearings within the simulation. With that done he called over Garnett, the little com-tech unpacking his one vital piece of equipment: the uplink, a small terminal representing the simulator's download subroutine. Through it the platoon could uplink to the simulator for two-way communication with the observing training officer. Sheffield was the scheduled TO for their immersion, which gave Hovland little comfort. The TO had been caught sleeping more than once during simulator immersions he was charged with monitoring, situations that had almost cost him his post. But like most things in a military straining to keep up with increasing demands levied upon its personnel, 'almost' was a long, gray expanse.

Hovland turned to Garnett. The man was typing status codes into the uplink, his fingers moving with nimble grace over the keyboard, halting only to accommodate the brief pauses between communication prompts.

One of the recruits pointed to the uplink. "Hey, what if that gets blown up?"

Garnett's eyes did not move from the uplink. "Can't be destroyed," he said. "The simulator voids all damage to certain specific equipment."

Ellister settled down behind Garnett. He reached over to rest a hand on Boden's neck cowl, securing the man's attention. "The uplink can't get blown up. It's in a library of protected equipment within the simulator." He stared at Boden and tapped a finger to his temple. "Just remember, we're not."

"We're clear," Garnett said to Hovland and packed his gear.

Hovland nodded and looked to his sergeants. "Weapon status?"

Ellister pushed his helmet back to rub his forehead. "Sticks and stones. Standard issue repeaters, one heavy repeater, one shoulder launcher—but it's butch, direct line of fire, simple thermal sighting system. I have three grenades and a sidearm; Webb's got a rangefinder. That's it."

"My grandfather had better stuff than this," Webb said with a sigh.

"Weaponry wasn't the goal here," Hovland reminded Webb. "We're supposed to break in the recruits, that's all."

Messina looked about their position. "So what's the story?"

Hovland took another survey of the area before turning back to his sergeants and waving them close. Miller tried to crowd in, but Webb and Ellister glared him away. "If we had an objective Sheffield would have given it to us," Hovland began, trying to guess at the TO's game. "It's got to be a survival session."

Webb cursed. "A run and gun. I hate these. Being a duck in a barrel sucks."

Ellister was already looking over his shoulder. "We should get up on that ridge."

Hovland nodded. "That's exactly what I had in mind." He checked the light meter on his repeater's scope. "The twilight's fading. Ellister, take your squad on radial nine-oh, dead east for the ridge. Webb, Messina, take your squads and cover our flanks." He stood up and snapped his fingers. "Let's make it hasty," he said to the platoon. "I want us on high ground before deep night."

With assorted grunts, grumbles and curses the platoon fell in order. Using Webb's rangefinder they figured the distance to their objective and with that an approximate time to reach the heights. Two and a half hours, Hovland thought with a sigh. He looked to Webb. "We'll never make it before we lose the light, and the new meat probably don't know anything about night fighting," he said, but Webb only tipped his head.

Lippett patted his chest plate where his lucky clip would have dangled.

***

Time faded in the monotonous plod of the march. The platoon was quiet except for curious chatter between the recruits, spiced by Miller's occasional retorts. They passed over the plain without incident, their eyes alert as they scanned the landscape. When the light dropped below the mean optical breakpoint on Hovland's meter he ordered everyone to infrared. The platoon slid their visors down in response. With the passing of each quiet moment, Hovland's anxiety grew as he waited for the inevitable attack, wondering how hard Sheffield would go at them. He didn't have to wonder for very long.

Hauser, of Messina's squad, picked it up first, his eyes narrowing as his hands tightened on his heavy repeater. "Movement, radial three-oh-oh," he said and unlocked the repeater's ammo spool in his backpack. "Image faint."

Messina and Ellister each raised a fist, the platoon halting and sinking to a crouch. Webb snapped his fingers, prompting Wilkins and Stone to ready the platoon's rocket launcher. Webb looked down radial 300, concentrating for a moment before he saw movement.

"Confirmed," he said over his radio, "multiple targets on line. They've got the height on us."

"Movement!" Miller's voice erupted. "Boss! Radial one-two-oh! Flank! Flank!"

"Shut up Miller," Hovland said. "Ellister, you got movement up the ridge?"

"Negative on that," came Ellister's reply. "Nine-oh is all clear."

Hovland looked to either side. The three squads of the platoon formed the corners of a triangle. "Webb, Messina, hold your squads and cover Ellister as he moves up the ridge. Hold fire until my call." The crunching of gravel sounded out as Ellister brought his squad up the ridge. Hovland grabbed Garnett's shoulder to pull the com-tech close. "Get on the line and get me a confirmation. Don't know, could be friendlies out there in a parallel immersion," he said and patted Garnett's shoulder. Garnet nodded and headed up to Ellister's squad. Hovland looked about. "Lippett! Get up with Garnett. You too, Patrone. Move!"

Rising to a half stance, he scurried over to Webb's squad, settling himself in the midst of the recruits. They seemed pale, even for the waxen hue of simulator skin. "Listen up. Just hold your ground. You're sentries, you have that experience. You've sat on walls and watched for movement before. This is no different. When the word comes, just fire at anything that moves out there," he said, extending an arm to make sure they understood. "Our people are behind us. Whatever you do, don't get up, don't run; don't do anything stupid. Just keep your heads." He looked them over, waiting until they nodded one by one. Only then did he realize he had yet to learn their names.

Gunfire rattled from Messina's squad, Messina responding with measured orders to direct their fire. Garnett's voice crackled over the radio; Hovland pressed the side of his helmet to his head to hear the com-tech's acknowledgement of enemy troops.

"They're not on infrared," a voice said nearby. "Where do I shoot?"

"Simulator trick," Hovland said, turning to the recruit. "No thermal signa—"

The recruit jumped to his feet to run.

Hovland lunged to drag the man down, but the firefight erupted about them, the recruit picked apart in a hail of bullets. Hovland looked up the slope. "Ellister! Get on that ridge!"

Wilkins slapped Stone on the shoulder and ducked, Stone rising to a crouch as the rest of the squad opened fire. With a screech the launcher fired, the projectile leaving a brilliant exhaust trail as it lanced across the broken ground and detonated. Bodies flew in the explosion. Stone turned to Wilkins, the man's eyes narrowing against spent repeater casings bouncing off the rocks. "Load me!"

Behind them, Messina shot up a flare to illuminate the ridge in a rosy glow. Out of the shadows black armored figures came into view, caught in the open. Hauser cut them to pieces with the heavy repeater, the rest of the squad picking off the stragglers that ducked away. From behind a boulder a pair of grenades flew up and landed within Messina's position. "Down, down, *down!*" Messina ordered, but one man was shredded between the two clouds of shrapnel, another stumbling armless until he went down in the crossfire.

Hovland clenched his teeth. "Ellister!"

"Flanking fire," Ellister said over the general frequency.

There was a puff of smoke and a screech; Stone dropped to the ground after his rocket took flight. Above, at the ridge's crest, Ellister's squad opened fire, their repeaters pounding down the ridge from their height to slaughter the enemy troops. Bodies spun and crumpled, others went down under Ellister's precise shots. Down on the ridge, rallied by Ellister's success, the rest of the platoon began to advance along the bank of the ridge, pressing the simulator's troops from their few safe positions to kill them in the crossfire.

Hovland tackled another recruit, one of the surviving few who had not died by running in panic. Cursing, Hovland slapped the man's chest before leaning across the man to keep him down. "Ellister! Status?"

"Hold fire," Ellister's calm voice said over the radio. "We're good; it's good, ease up."

The platoon's fire came to an abrupt end, a few stray shots sounding out before silence settled. Hovland called around the platoon to check for any activity, but all was quiet. He sighed with relief, ignoring the recruit beneath him. He stood, slung his repeater, and looked over to Messina's squad where several men were milling around their casualties. His eyes trailed across Webb's squad to find most of the recruits dead.

Webb came up before him. "You all right?"

Hovland snorted and opened his hands at the dead recruits around them. "What a waste. I should have paired them off with long-timers right from the start."

Webb nodded. "Yeah," he said and pushed up his radio mike. "Makes you wonder."

Hovland held up a hand to silence the sergeant. "I know, but we're still stuck here." He looked up to the featureless simulator sky and nodded to himself. "Right, we're still stuck here." He looked to Webb and waved Messina over. "Gather supplies from the dead. I want us on top of that ridge. Let's go."

***

Garnett took a pull from his water bottle, wishing it contained something more potent as Patrone bandaged the assorted shrapnel wounds Messina's squad had suffered. Somewhat ignoring the wound Patrone was cleaning, Garnett closed his bottle and pointed in the squad's general direction. "So is it bad?"

Patrone glanced at him before patting the shoulder of the man he was tending to send him on his way. He shrugged and packed up his gear. "Looks like they're going easy on me this time," he said. "The trauma subroutine isn't running much detail. It seems we either have minor wounds or fatality. Not much between."

"Just a survival run," Garnett thought aloud. "You know, I've never bought it in here."

Patrone closed his pack and gave Garnett a curious glance. "I got stuff to do," he said and walked off towards the rest of Messina's men.

Garnett shrugged and took another sip of water, waving as he saw Hovland emerge from the darkness, the lieutenant walking about the position the platoon was fortifying. "What's up?"

Hovland sat next to the com-tech. He took off his helmet and set it between his feet before rubbing his face. "New protocol. Sheffield told me Security wants all simulator events confirmed through the uplink, including our casualties." He looked at his watch to check the time, and after some estimation, figured their casualties should be back in their bodies, lounging around the simulator room wondering what to do with themselves. He blew out a breath. "Start checking on our men; make sure they've been backed out of the simulator. Then send a call to Sheffield on our engagement and our number of KIA's." He stood, catching Ellister's eye and waving him over. The sergeant looked impatient, angered, but then Hovland expected that, given they were left to finish the simulator run with hardly a recruit to show for the effort. As Ellister neared he could hear the sergeant's curses grow in volume.

Garnett said nothing, losing track of Ellister's grumbling as his attention focused on the timer at the corner of the uplink's screen. His gaze dropped to his watch. He checked the uplink again, only to realize there was a marked discrepancy between his calculations and the elapsed time on the uplink. He blinked and looked to Hovland. "Boss?"

"Damn new meat," Ellister hissed, his hand wrapped over his radio mike to talk in private with Hovland. "Former sentries my ass. I don't think Sheffield got any training for them."

Hovland tipped his head before patting Ellister's shoulder. "Exactly. That's why what's left are up here with you."

"Screw it," Ellister said. "They'll be wishing they never left Tropico."

Garnett cleared his throat. "Boss—"

"What?" Hovland and Ellister said at once, both of them turning on Garnett.

Garnett pointed to the uplink. "It's our feed speed. It's way off."

Hovland shook his head in confusion. He turned to Ellister before the two of them shifted around Garnett to peer over the com-tech's shoulders at the uplink's screen. From the shadow of a boulder Webb's head popped up to stare at them. "The speed's way off," Garnett said again, glancing between Hovland and Ellister. He put his finger by the timer. "The time compression is cranked all the way up. Our sim is running way off. The time factor's been set to twenty. We're going to be in here for a *long* time."

Ellister glared at Garnett. "Can't be. I checked it myself before hooking up."

Garnett turned on Ellister, emboldened with wounded pride.

Hovland had a more immediate concern. "Did our people get across?"

Garnett raised his hands. "It's too soon. Back-up time depends on system traffic loads."

Hovland frowned. "And you're sure about this, about the feed speed?"

Ellister lowered his head. "Yeah, he's right. Look at the time."

Hovland rubbed his forehead before dropping his hand and looking down the ridge. He hesitated a moment before waving Webb and Messina over. "Keep the perimeter patrols close," he said. "Rotating shifts of four, just outside our position. Looks like we have a problem with our speed setting, so minimal risk until it's straightened out."

Webb shrugged. "Just a glitch."

Messina shook his head, suspicious at once. "No it isn't. How many sim runs have we done? The feed speed has never been off."

Webb looked to Messina, but it was Ellister who spoke. "I told you before—you need to shut up with that."

Messina continued to shake his head, his stubbornness getting the better of him. "Hey, you *know* what I'm talking about. It's like what happened in Fourth Army, to that other platoon."

Hovland turned to Messina, but before another word was spoken, their eyes lifted skyward as flash-fire shells lit the black night. Shadows swirled about the ridge in a ghostly dance.

Hovland looked over his sergeants. "Webb, you better get us some ammo counts."

***

Hovland shook his head. "Are you sure?"

Garnett shrugged. "Sure as I can be. Flash-fires, you know, they simulate interference, so even though the uplink isn't a radio, it cuts in and out."

Webb stared at the uplink. "Goddamn Sheffield. Can't give us modern weaponry, but still manages to screw around with signal technicalities for something that isn't even real."

Garnett looked to Hovland. "I need higher ground; I can uplink better from height."

"Out of the question," Hovland said at once. "You stay here, protected."

Garnett threw his hands up. "Then what the hell good am I?"

Ellister frowned. "He's right."

Hovland ignored the agreements of Webb and Messina. From the moment Garnett had confirmed that their casualties backed out of the simulator flat-lined their worst suspicion seemed true: somehow, the simulator had become lethal. Yet without a viable uplink, they were left blind to whatever larger problem had effected their simulator immersion, and with their feed speed off, time would be a heavy weight against them. He took a deep breath and pinched the bridge of his nose as he tried to concentrate, but in the end, he knew he had no choice. "Okay Garnett," he said. He looked about before pointing behind them, where the ridge's backbone rose to a low peak. "Head up to that perch. Keep in radio contact. Take Cricket with you."

Garnett's eyes narrowed. "That twitchy freak? He can't sit still."

"Exactly why he'll be good as your extra eyes," Hovland said before turning to Ellister. "Okay, let's start the patrols."

He watched as his sergeants departed to pull four men from the platoon for the first patrol. The rest of the platoon shuffled a bit, settling themselves into secure positions behind the channels of rocks they had found on the ridge's crest. Beneath them, to either side, the barren plain stretched out to the horizon, emerging from darkness in the intermittent twilight from flash-fire rounds. He took a sip of water from his bottle as another flash-fire went off above their position. A blast of static sounded over his radio. He raised his bottle for another sip, but caught himself. If the simulator had been sabotaged, there was no telling how much trouble they were in. It was all in Sheffield's hands: only help from outside the immersion could get them out intact, and if that took a day of effort, it would translate to twenty days of survival in the immersion with no support, no supplies, against an inexhaustible enemy.

He cursed to himself as he screwed the bottle shut and secured it in his belt pouch. It was paranoid crap, all of it, he argued against his suspicions. Sheffield, being the obnoxious slob that he was, screwed up the feed speed—or changed it, just to mess around with the platoon—and that, and only that, was why it appeared—just appeared—that their casualties were flat-lined by the simulator. They're not actually dead, his thought ran. Nothing was wrong. They would be out of the immersion in no time, and he'd sit with Ellister and gripe about it over some beer, just like the old days.

The thought trailed away as he considered the one thing that mocked all those comfortable, convenient conclusions, the fact that he had been captured and tapped with neural darts. He had no memory of the entire episode. He couldn't trust Sheffield, because deep down, he wasn't sure he trusted himself.

***

Garnett held his repeater before him, peering through his infrared under the lip of his helmet. The ridge tapered to either side, the peak only a short distance away. He dropped to one knee and looked around, ignoring Cricket as the man crowded beside him. The landscape was empty except for the scattered quartet of the first patrol circling the platoon's position. He licked his lips, radioed to Hovland, and made for the peak.

He scrambled to its top and found a cup-shaped hollow ideal for cover. He wasted little time, settling himself in the peak's hollow before pulling the uplink from his pack. He looked to Cricket. "You can go now."

"Boss said to stay," Cricket said, his eyes darting about the plain.

Garnett turned. "Listen private, as your corporal, I'm telling you to get lost, understand?" he said, already annoyed with Cricket. "I'll smooth it out with Hovland."

Cricket hesitated, looking several times between Garnett and the platoon's position. "Yeah, it'll be good," he said under his breath. "Yeah, right, okay. Okay, see you later," he added and made off from the peak.

Garnett rubbed his hands together. "Peace at last," he said and flipped on the uplink.

***

Ellister sat next to Hovland and took a slow survey of the plain through his repeater sight. "It's still very quiet out there," he thought aloud. A flash-fire went off overhead, as if in protest. "Hear any word from Garnett?"

Hovland hooked a thumb behind him, toward the peak. "He's been working through the uplink. Sheffield ordered us to stay put. Other than that, nothing yet."

"What about getting us out of here?"

Hovland shook his head. "No word."

Ellister shifted to rest his back against a rock. He rubbed his chin, looking at his hand when he realized the simulator had not mapped the stubble of his chin. He blinked the thought away and pushed up his radio mike before leaning close to Hovland. "What are we going to—"

"We'll do what we have to do," Hovland interrupted with a listless monotone.

Ellister tipped his head. "That doesn't sound very convincing."

Hovland shrugged. "I'm just tired, tired of all this. We're supposed to be doing this for the recruits, and we lost almost all of them because they hardly had basic before being dumped on us. We're doing this to suppress a rebellion, but the planets we go to, people don't seem all that happy to see us. We're supposed to be winning, but we're skipping around space, stomping out one insurgency only for another to spring up. We're supposed to be safe within our ranks, but we know the mips have excelled at infiltrating our ranks at every turn—whether it's intelligence or combat or even our networks. But *this,* if this is what we think it is, then they can get us even *here,*" he said and tapped a finger to his forehead.

Ellister studied him for several moments before he said anything. "If I didn't know better—"

"It's got nothing to do with what happened to me," Hovland said, but then frowned. "I don't know, maybe it has everything to do with what happened to me." He looked to Ellister. "The way things have been going—in general, I mean—it's just… I don't want to be paranoid, but it seems hard to know our purpose, our way, when I'm not so sure who the so-called enemy is anymore."

"Well that's easy," Ellister said. "The enemy is the son-of-a-bitch firing at you."

Hovland couldn't help but grin. "Ah yes, the clarity of good old pragmatism."

"News," Garnett's voice said over the radio.

Hovland glanced to Ellister and tapped the side of his helmet. Ellister lowered his mike and switched to command frequency. Hovland looked to the peak. "What's up?"

The com-tech's breath hissed as he inhaled. "Ah, I'm still collecting information. Apparently Sheffield logged in a fairly complex survival scenario for us; but with the feed speed off, it's being rammed into the simulator routine several times over. It's way more traffic load than Sheffield's protocol had anticipated."

Hovland rubbed his forehead. "And that leaves us where?"

"Well," Garnett began, but fell silent. "Ah, well, I can tell you this, the feed speed is a definite malfunction at the simulator level, which means we're going to be stuck here for a way long time, way longer than Sheffield had figured when he set up our logistics files for the sim. It looks like our guys are still stuck in backup because of the system traffic load created by our simulator malfunction, so it's actually too early yet to tell if the immersion feedback is lethal."

Hovland looked to Ellister, but Ellister shrugged, leaving Hovland at a loss. "Right," he said. "Anything else, keep it on the command line." He pushed up his radio mike. He turned to Ellister, but the sergeant had nothing to say, his eyes lifeless with the simulator's metallic sheen.

***

There was no solace in sleep.

Hovland may have sat still, but his eyes darted about beneath his lids, probing the shadows of his memories to make some greater sense of his situation. Things connect, in some way or another, that's the way life goes, he thought. He had been a practical man in his term of service; an efficient officer, he believed, and his men respected him, gave him what he asked of them. He had believed in the cause against the insurrection, against the rebellion, *any* rebellion, titles be damned: for him, there was order, order to existence, and it had to be maintained, because of all things he had learned one thing, and that was the subversive, insidious trend of humanity to sink into dissension, conflict, and anarchy.

Or so I believed. I never should have gone out alone, never should have been captured—what was I thinking? A moment of carelessness, but that's it, isn't it?

One moment, that's all it takes, and the subversion comes in; it's out there, always waiting, always hungry.

It had been another humid evening, that night he was captured. He had left the base, checked off with Ellister and took a night's leave in the city outside the base while the platoon was off rotation. He had gone to a woman's apartment, a woman he had met, one of the base's local support personnel. She had invited him, welcomed him several times before, gave him a home cooked meal, just stood there with her back to the kitchen sink as she watched him eat, the evening sun a warm glow on the curve of her cheek. He looked at her, and standing there in that long yellow light, she formed an alluring vision. He never suspected, never once, never for a moment, and when the drugs she had put in the food knocked him out he found he would be jarred from more than his consciousness. Before he collapsed, someone came from behind and cracked him in the ribs with a crowbar—*why do that?* The stupid, careless, confident senility of his security had fled, leaving him to wake in some hellish basement, tied to a chair, the sensory cap for the neural darts strapped to his head. *Like hot pokers through the brain*, Security had warned them before they had hit dirt on Tropico. The description paled beside reality.

And that's all it takes, just one careless moment. Meet her for dinner, no problem. Take the platoon with some unknown recruits into the sim, no problem.

He blinked. He didn't know what to think anymore.

"Got the counts," Webb whispered, startling him. His eyes snapped toward Webb, but the sergeant was looking to his repeater to check his clip. "If we conserve, keep the fire tight, I think we can hold out pretty well." He rested his repeater in his lap and tipped his chin. "Second patrol's back."

Hovland followed Webb's lead to watch the four men of the patrol emerge from the darkness. They swung their legs over the rocks that formed the platoon's defensive perimeter and settled down, shaking awake four men for the next patrol. Hovland watched them, the idea of being able to focus on something other than his own thoughts and suspicions a welcome distraction, even if it defied all sense for him to leave the platoon's position and join the patrol.

But why not? It's my platoon, and it's just a simulation.

He frowned as the thought gained momentum. *Go on the patrol...*
His eyes narrowed. *Why so motivated to go?*

He shook his head, annoyed by the debate. He stood and waved one of the men down to take his place in the patrol.

Webb looked up in surprise and hissed to Hovland before grabbing the lieutenant's arm. "Hey, you're supposed to stay here. Get some sleep."

Hovland shrugged. "Can't sleep. Besides, I'm bored."

A ripple of flash-fires lit the ridge, revealing the other three men of the patrol: Miller, Lippett, and Boden. Webb shook his head. "You've got to be joking," he said and looked back to Hovland. "You know, maybe it is better you go."

Hovland glanced at Webb before his eyes trailed away to Boden. He took a breath and tipped his head before walking off with the patrol.

***

Webb woke from a light sleep to the sound of hushed voices coming over his radio, but it was Garnett's nervous stammer that caught his ear.

"Hovland, you there? Hovland?"

Hovland responded without delay. "What?"

"We're in deep shit boss, I mean deep—"

"What happened to our men?"

Garnett's shaky breath rasped like a storm over the radio. "It's confirmed! They came back flat-line! They're gone! This goddamn thing is killing us off!"

"Are you sure it's not the uplink?"

"It's working and I know what I'm doing!" Garnett paused, muttering something lost in the static of the radio before he raised his voice. "That's not all. Sheffield says Security can't get into our simulator room!"

"They have the wrong code," Hovland said. "Calm down."

"It's not the code! Somebody screwed with the lock!"

Webb sat up straight, his eyes wide until a chain of flash-fires rippled overhead and sent a wash of static over the radio.

"Said a couple of hours to cut through the lock," Garnett's voice crackled over the radio. "Boss, we're trapped."

"Keep on the uplink," Hovland said. "Tell Sheffield we need a recommendation as to our course of action. Until then, keep your mouth shut."

Webb nodded, but his heart quickened. If Garnett's information was correct, they were stuck in the simulator for hours, in real time—days in simulator time, given their feed speed. He flipped down his helmet mike and peered about to locate Ellister and Messina before waking them. Several voices hissed behind him. Curious, he turned to see Cricket settle down among his squad. Webb grabbed the man's neck cowl. "Hey! What the hell are you doing here? You were supposed to watch Garnett!"

Cricket shifted, his eyes going wide. "Sergeant! I, I mean, he—"

Across from them another member of the squad rose to his knees and put his hands on his lower back to stretch. The reckless danger of the act was typical of the subconscious dismissal of the simulator's threat. Webb pursed his lips and jabbed a finger towards the man for him to sit. No sooner did the man look at him than his head snapped to the side. A distant crack sounded from the plain below. The man fell, unstrung.

"Sniper!" Webb called, the single word erupting from him as he dropped to the ground. Out on the plain a flare streaked up into the night sky and burst to cast a rosy light over the platoon. Gunfire rattled below, followed by confused shouts.

"On watch!" Ellister's voice scratched over the radio. Rounds began to ricochet off the rocks of their position. "Patrol! Patrol! Fall in on our perimeter!"

Someone screamed as another round found its mark in the platoon. Messina cursed as he looked about to narrow the source of the shot. "Everybody down!"

The radio crowded with several voices calling the same word: "Movement!"

"Get some firepower on the plain!" Webb said, waving men about. "And keep down!" He crawled over to Ellister, who had made his way to the two men who had been shot. One was dead, the other lay trembling in a messy pool of blood before going limp. Cursing, Ellister pulled a grenade and tossed it down the ridge. "Where's Hovland?"

Webb jabbed a finger to his side. "Patrol!"

Ellister's eyes bulged. "What?" He grabbed his helmet mike and pressed it to his mouth. "Hovland! Get your ass back here!"

A loud thump sounded. A mortar shell detonated in a cloud of rock fragments short of their position, the blast a brilliant flash on the platoon's infrared. Ellister scrambled over to Stone and Wilkins, the two men already loading a rocket. Ellister pushed between them and pointed down to the plain. "Wait 'til they pop the next one, and target the heat bloom!"

Stone nodded as Wilkins pulled the launch tube to full extension. Ellister rolled away, shouting for Hovland until he came to a stop beside Hauser, the man's heavy repeater letting out a deafening roar as he fired down the ridge. Ellister peered over the man's shoulder to see shadows spin about the rocks below as more flares made their way skyward. "Watch your fire!" he said, shouting directly into Hauser's ear. "We still have a patrol out there!"

Hauser shot him a glare before looking back down the ridge and drowning his comments with the heavy repeater's fire. Despite the weapon's reassuring roar another mortar shell exploded within their perimeter. Ellister lifted his head to see a ragged body rebound off a boulder with a wet slap before flopping to the ground. He pointed to Wilkins and Stone. "They ranged us! Rocket! Now!"

Stone slapped Wilkins' shoulder and ducked, yelling when he noticed a man rise up behind Wilkins. The rocket screamed away; exhaust flashed back into the soldier's face, propellant scorching a cavernous hole in the man's head. Down the ridge, shadowy figures scrambled and then vanished in the rocket's detonation. In the next moment, a ripple of fireballs blew out as mortar shells erupted in the blast.

On the opposite side of their position Messina's eyes widened as he looked down the slope. "Support, support! Overrun on my line!"

Ellister slapped Webb's shoulder. "Go!"

Webb scrambled off and rallied his squad to Messina's aid as Ellister kept his men in place to hold the other side of the perimeter. He called Garnett over the radio, his eyes darting to the ridge's peak as Hauser lugged the heavy repeater past him toward Messina's squad. When

Garnett failed to respond, Ellister tapped his helmet to jar his radio and called again. "Garnett! What's your status?"

Webb returned to Ellister's side. "Hey!" he said and grabbed Ellister's arm to get his attention. "He's up there alone! Cricket's back here with us!"

"Ah shit!" Ellister ground his teeth and turned back to the ridge's peak. "Garnett!"

As if on cue Garnett's broken signal came through. "Is anyone hearing this? Lethal feedback on all channels! Hovland? Anybody?"

Webb and Ellister locked eyes before yelling into their mikes.

"Oh man," Garnett said with relief. "I thought you guys forgot about me! Listen, Sheffield had Security try to replay the surveillance feed from our room, but the cameras were disabled. He—"

"Not now! Hold your position!" Ellister ordered. "Messina! Get us ready to move!"

The flash-fires subsided, the darkening sky allowing Garnett's voice to come through strong and clear. "Wait," he said, "listen up. Sheffield repeats: he wants us to hold position. He's having trouble fixing our location in the immersion."

Ellister ducked his head at the incessant gunfire from Messina's squad. "The simulator isn't having any trouble!" He looked over his shoulder. "Messina!"

Messina dropped a clip and popped in a fresh one, grinding his teeth as the platoon's guns hammered away around him. The simulator's troopers were rushing without any concern or effort to conceal themselves. The platoon's guns devoured them, cutting them down in groups.

"Hey!" Garnett said. "What the hell are you doing up here?"

Webb and Ellister turned away and looked up to the ridge peak. There was a flash of repeater fire, echoed by a rattle over their radio. Shocked for a moment, they gathered their wits and called Garnett's name in unison.

The platoon's guns came to a ragged halt.

Messina's breath rasped over the radio. "All clear."

The last flash-fires traced away. The endless black emptiness above them returned. The plain faded away to shadow just as the static faded from their radios.

"All clear," Hovland's voice echoed over the radio.

Ellister's eyes bulged. "Hovland! Where the hell are you?"

"On the ridge! I ordered the patrol to find cover and lay low before the flash-fires wiped out our radio. I'm coming up for a situation report."

Webb flipped up his radio mike. "He doesn't know?"

Ellister ground his teeth. "Meet us at the peak. And get Cricket."

***

They found Garnet sprawled in the bowl of the peak with several bloody holes in his chest. His eyes were open wide, and his repeater lay at his side. The uplink was still in his lap.

Hovland looked around the peak, knowing that no one could have come on the com-tech without being seen. Despite that, he struggled to calm his natural inclination to agree with the conclusion of his sergeants that someone in the patrol had murdered Garnett. The grounds of their suspicion were convincing enough: based on Garnett's last words, the obvious fact that he had taken no measure to protect himself, and the presence of spent repeater casings, as the simulator didn't code for spent casings from the weapons of its troopers.

Ellister looked up at Hovland, his eyes boring into Hovland from across the peak's crest. His hand had not left the trigger guard of his repeater since Hovland's patrol had returned. "Still think we've lost our minds, Hov?"

Hovland rubbed his jaw, considering the suspects already in the minds of his sergeants.

"Our people are dying for real," Ellister said. "*Our* men, flat-line. And now we're stuck here, trapped by the same mip that killed Garnett."

Hovland tipped his head. "Come on Ellis, that's jumping to all sorts of conclusions." He shifted on his feet, his words ringing hollow even to his ears. "You can't say it was a mip," he said, intent on proving his point. "What about Cricket?"

Messina shook his head. "Garnett sent Cricket off. He was up here alone."

"Why'd he do that?" Hovland asked, but his empty question fell on deaf ears. "Even if he sent Cricket off that doesn't mean we have some renegade mip running around in here with us!"

"Then what the hell else?" Messina said and spat on the ground. "I'm telling you, it's the same thing that happened to that platoon in Fourth Army."

Webb nodded. "I think he's right."

Messina thumped a fist on Webb's shoulder. He and Webb moved to either side of Hovland.

"Mip or not Hov, we got a rat," Ellister said. "You have to see that."

Hovland knew the next step. Ellister would hunt for suspects. The list was short, and Hovland was on the wrong side. His chest grew tight. *The patrol! Miller, Lippett, Boden, me. Why did I go on the patrol? What was I thinking? Shit, what must they be thinking —?*

Ellister's eyes narrowed. "You have to understand, Hov."

Hovland blinked, and then it happened. Webb and Messina grabbed his arms from either side. Hovland tensed, but froze when Ellister loomed before him. Ellister said nothing, his gaze steady on his old friend before taking his repeater.

III

Miller stared with definite fear at Ellister, and more directly, the repeater in the sergeant's hands. "This is crazy!" he cried out in the silence that had settled over the platoon. "I ain't no mip!" He looked around, his eyes wide with his shattered nerves. Boden, Lippett and Hovland stood in a line to his left.

Messina rubbed his forehead. "Nobody's accusing you in particular, Miller."

"Screw you!"

Webb grunted with frustration. "Enough of this," he said and walked up to Miller. The private leaned away until Webb grabbed him and forced him to kneel. "All of you! On your knees!" he said, forcing each of the patrol in turn to the ground. When he came to Hovland, he stared at him for a moment, his eyes narrowing. "You volunteered for the patrol!" He grabbed Hovland's neck cowl. "You pulled Weaver from the patrol and put yourself in!" His hand recoiled as if stung, but then he backed off, shaking his head as an uneasy chatter rose from the platoon.

Ellister turned to the patrol. "Let's think this through, step by step."

Hovland sucked in a breath, his stomach dropping away. It wouldn't take much to pin him as the one. And then, he knew, Ellister wouldn't think twice. The surreal nightmare of his situation numbed his mind. He refused to accept it, but it was undeniable.

No, this can't be happening. Not to me.

He remembered that strange urge, that strange thought that had compelled him to join the patrol, and it woke a desperate fear, a desperate doubt within him—*did the mips turn me into a mole, and Security missed it? No, no, can't be, can't be!*

Messina caught Hovland's unease and stared at him. "Hey, listen, Garnett said someone tampered with the simulator. For that to follow, someone had to be alone in the simulator room before or after we were all hooked up, right?"

Ellister's eyes narrowed. "I checked everything before I hooked myself up. Everything was good. Green lights all the way. Nothing was touched."

"Then it had to happen after you hooked up," Webb said. "Who hooked up after you?"

Ellister tipped his chin to the patrol. "Right here."

Curses sounded out from the platoon. Messina waved them to silence. "Then that's it," he said with relief, gesturing at the patrol with an open hand. "We can just hold their weapons, keep them under guard, keep an—"

"No," Ellister interrupted. "One man shot Garnett, not four. We still have the sim to deal with. We can use three extra bodies on the line." He looked at each man of the patrol, the gears of his mind grinding away.

Webb shrugged. "Then we go through them, one by one."

They turned to Miller. Half the platoon spoke out on his behalf: too scared, no backbone, no outside contact from the army, a troopship rat. Miller shouted agreements with each one, but lost his bravado as he got the gist of their words. With sunken pride and a slack jaw he listened until Messina pulled him to his feet and returned his repeater. "That's more like it," Miller said, trying to make himself imposing as he clutched his repeater. "I ain't no mip," he said again, more to himself than anyone in particular.

Next they turned to Lippett. He was heckled as being too stupid over the time they had known him to sabotage anything as complicated as the simulator. He was a simpleton, and had the puppy-dog loyalty of an uncomplicated mind. Messina pulled him to his feet after a few moments and handed him his repeater. Lippett nodded, his face down, as he was shoved back to seclusion behind the ring of the platoon's anxious faces.

They moved to Boden, no one speaking out in his defense. He was a recruit, a nobody, an unknown out of a city recently overrun by the rebellion and riddled by infiltration agents. He was one of many locals that had been recruited as spaceport security after a cursory background check and then assigned to a regular unit to fill empty spaces. Yet Webb and Messina agreed that there was little opportunity available to Boden, and had that opportunity presented itself, he would have been seen by either Ellister or Hovland before they had hooked up. And right there lurked a problem, because Ellister had hooked up before both Hovland and Boden, while Hovland—

Ellister's eyes narrowed as he stared at his lieutenant. "Come on Hov, give me something," he said. "You were the last one to go under, that would have left you alone in the simulator room. You would have had access to the lock, to the feed speed, to everything. Webb said you volunteered for the patrol. Garnett would have trusted you more than anyone, and next to Garnett, you know the most about the simulator."

"I didn't do this," Hovland said, but then pointed at Ellister. "Where's the uplink? Get Sheffield on the line. Security has video feeds of the sim rooms; have them replay—"

"Yeah, right." Ellister's eyes narrowed. "Someone disabled the cameras."

Hovland shook his head, a chill running through him as he sensed the platoon's eyes boring into him. "I didn't do anything," he said, opening his hands. When only blank stares met him he took his helmet off and threw it down in frustration. "No, no! I didn't do anything!"

"That he knows of," Patrone said. Ellister turned on the medic. Patrone pointed to Hovland's head. "Neural darts. They had him for *hours* before we found him."

"That's it, that's it!" Stone said. "Who knows what the hell they put in his head!"

Wilkins shoved Stone. "Security cleared him. This is crap."

"To hell with Security!" Miller said, pushing between the platoon's ranks. "Where the hell is Security now?"

Ellister glared at him. "Miller, you need to shut up."

Miller, despite his fear, refused to relent. "Well?" he said, looking over the platoon. "Where are they? So what if Security claims they probed him! Like they never screw up?"

"Shut up!" Ellister said and shoved Miller back into the platoon's ranks. He turned to Hovland. "Goddamn it Hov, give me something!"

Hovland opened his mouth, but despite his fear and indignation over the accusation, his paranoia seized him and saw the thread of credibility against him. *I don't know what they did to me in that basement. Who knows what's in my head? How do I defend myself if I don't even know myself anymore?* His gaze shot to Patrone for the medic's cancerous insinuation. It was the worst thing Hovland could have done, confirming Patrone's assumption in the eyes of the platoon.

Ellister stared at his lieutenant in the imploding silence.

"Goddamn Hovland," someone said in disbelief.

"Our own lieutenant," another voice spoke out.

Hovland's eyes darted over his men. Voices welled up around him. The collapse had started; there was no stopping it—

"What are we gonna do?"

"Kill the bastard!"

"He's the friggin' lieutenant. We can't just shoot him!"

"Goddamn mip is what he is."

"Kill him!"

"Shut up!" Messina ordered, stilling the platoon as their uneasy ring began to close about Hovland. He repeated the order, shoving several men away from Hovland when no one moved, but he could sense in the air what they felt: they wanted blood, they wanted retribution. They had been fighting too long, too hard on Tropico and with only a few hours rest had been thrown in the simulator, only to be stranded. The flurry of shouts rose up once more, festering with the platoon's collective rage. Helpless, Messina stared at the paranoia that erupted before him.

For no apparent reason, the tumult ceased. The platoon was speechless. Messina spun and froze.

"Hey, Ellis," Webb whispered, his hands open before him. "Come on, ease up..."

Ellister's eyes narrowed as he pressed his handgun against Hovland's forehead. Hovland was on his knees, silent, fists clenched at his sides. He squeezed his eyes shut as he waited for the final shot.

Flares lit the sky with a series of soft pops before Lippett's voice rose up.

"Ambush!"

Gunfire erupted around them, the thump of mortars following. Explosions tore into the ridge as they worked their range onto the platoon's perimeter. The platoon scrambled to their positions with confused shouts. Hovland's eyes opened to tight slits as the pressure of the handgun's snout left his temple. He looked up, only to find Ellister hovering over him. The sergeant frowned and swung his handgun, cracking the butt over Hovland's head.

Hovland flopped on his side. The world shattered in a kaleidoscopic blur of phosphor shadows.

***

Miller looked down the ridge. "Hey," he said to Patrone, "what the hell is that?"

"I don't know. Weaver spotted it after the mortars stopped. Have you seen Webb or Ellister?"

"What's it doing to the ground?"

"Looks like pixilation," Patrone guessed. "Loss of resolution in the sim, I think."

Hovland groaned and strained to lift his head, crusted blood flaking from his eyes as he opened them. Pain sparked through his skull. He peered down the ridge, his mouth dropping when his eyes focused. At the base of the ridge a black cylinder, a meter or so in height, hung in a low hover. It emitted a rhythmic thud, like the beat of a heart, and with each beat a growing circle of ground lost focus and dimmed to an empty black.

He looked about to find Miller and Patrone staring down the ridge at the cylinder. Hauser settled down beside them, his eyes locking on Hovland for a moment before he looked away and headed back up the ridge. Hovland was not sure what he saw there: a trace of guilt, or worse, anger. Hovland opened his mouth, but found he had nothing to say. Despite his desperate situation, his pragmatism mocked him, leaving his objective sense no other conclusion but that which Ellister and the platoon had reached.

He looked back to the cylinder. *Have to think; thinking is all I have left.* One thing was clear to him, and that was the nature of the cylinder—it was nothing more than the representation of the sabotage program within their immersion. If it had a representation, that meant someone had to encode it as part of the sabotage program, and if someone had gone to the length to encode a representation, it followed that it must serve some kind of purpose to be visible within the immersion. At the same time, all those things erased any doubt that the immersion's malfunction was the result of anything *but* sabotage.

Patrone flipped up his radio mike. He looked to Miller and pointed at Hovland. "Messina wants me on the uplink. Keep an eye on him," he said and moved up the ridge.

Miller looked at Hovland. Miller opened his mouth, but then closed it, his lips pressing into a tight line. He rested his hands on his repeater.

***

Patrone stared at the uplink nestled in his lap. Behind him one of their wounded groaned in pain before going quiet. Patrone glanced over his shoulder. Of the platoon's original strength, only twelve actives were left, not including three wounded. The last round of mortar attacks had been brief but brutal, the simulator's troops having nailed the platoon's position from their previous assault. With no other choice but to disobey Sheffield and move before the next strike, Ellister and Webb had gone out to scout the surrounding area for a suitable place to hide. With supplies and manpower running low, it was obvious to everyone that they could not risk going head to head with the simulator's endless pool of troopers.

Patrone's radio crackled with Ellister's voice. "Any headway?"

Patrone dropped his hand in his lap. "Nothing."

"Come on Patrone! Stop jerking around and give me something!"

Patrone rolled his eyes at Ellister's impatience, but held his silence.

Messina leaned over Patrone's shoulder, pointing to the screen as Patrone scratched his temple. Messina read the displayed message. "Sheffield's on the link."

"Give it to us on the command line if it's sensitive," Webb said.

Messina looked to the gathering platoon and knew it was too late. The platoon, already demoralized by their situation in the simulator, sank in despair among the rocks. Messina pursed his lips, shocked as he read the entirety of Sheffield's message. He looked up to the black simulator sky, a low moan slipping from his throat before he could silence himself.

Hovland looked back to the platoon as they slumped to the ground. His eyes darted about as Miller walked away to find out what was going on. His helmet lay out of reach. His hands were bound behind him. He looked out to the vast emptiness of the plain.

An hour's march out from the ridge, Webb and Ellister hid in the shadow of a boulder, looking back to the ridge. Webb lowered his helmet mike, anticipating Messina's message. Ellister's fingers constricted around his repeater. "Come on Messina," he said.

After a short pause Messina's voice came over the radio. "Engineering is working through the simulator lock by cutting it open. The ship's systems are shutting down one by one with corrupted network traffic coming out of the simulator's servers, all from our immersion. Navigation has completely failed. Our orbit is decaying."

Webb closed his eyes. "How long until they get us out?"

"Looks like four hours."

Ellister looked to Webb. "How long until we crash into Tropico?"

Messina hesitated. "If fleet tugs can't stabilize our orbit, three hours."

Webb cursed, but Ellister smacked his shoulder to silence him. "Listen to me Messina. Get a message out to Sheffield. Orbital decay and all that shit is meaningless to us if he can't get some help in here and soon. Supplies—water, food, ammo, anything they can program into our immersion."

There was a pause, but then Messina let a single word slip over the radio: "Idiot."

Ellister turned on him. "What?"

"Not you—there's one more thing," Messina said and shook his head. "Sheffield says 'good luck.'"

Hovland set his teeth. He overheard part of what Messina had said, but the reaction of the platoon was more telling. He began to rock against a small stone behind him in an effort to cut loose the belt binding his wrists. He froze when he heard Miller cursing about the good luck comment, but then went back to his task, taking effort to make his work less noticeable.

Miller snapped his fingers, causing Hovland to go still. He looked up to watch Miller scramble past him along the ridge. Miller snapped his fingers again before pointing past Hovland to Lippett. "Hey, Lip-putz, I got a job for you. Yeah you, get over here."

Hovland rolled onto his belly, craning his neck to spot Lippett's shoulder lamp bobbing toward him. "I don't like the looks of that thing down there," Lippett said.

Miller grabbed Lippett's arm to pull Lippett down next to him. He flipped off Lippett's shoulder lamp before smacking the back of Lippett's helmet. "Stupid ass!" Miller said and jerked Lippett's neck cowl to get his full attention. "It's bad enough they've got our position nailed and you go walking around with a big hello sign on your shoulder. Keep that thing off!"

Lippett blinked. "Didn't want to trip, you know."

"Like it would do anything to the rocks in your head," Miller said and smacked the back of Lippett's helmet once more. "Look, just watch Hovland, okay? He's bound up so all you have to do is sit there, understand? I want to talk to Patrone, so just watch him for me."

"Okay," Lippett said and watched Miller go up the ridge. He folded his shoulder lamp shut before working his way over to the same boulder Miller had been using for cover. He stared at the mysterious cylinder, watching as it continued to pound away. With a scratch of his nose he settled behind the rock, almost lost in the simulator's shadows.

Across the darkness he locked eyes with Hovland. They studied each other, but said nothing. Hovland put his head back to stare at the sky.

Lippett's gaze mirrored Hovland's before he looked to his lieutenant. He took off his helmet.

***

"Well that settles it," Patrone said and set his helmet down. He waved Messina over, tapping the side of his mouth so Messina wouldn't talk into his helmet mike. The sergeant hesitated, annoyed by Patrone's direction, but then flipped up his mike. When he saw Patrone nod his head at the uplink Messina frowned. "What now?"

"Take a look," Patrone said, shifting so Messina could get in front of the screen.

FLEET TUGS UNSUCCESSFUL
NO OTHER PLAN TO EXECUTE
FLEET PREPARING EMER EVAC MEASURES FOR CREW
SIM INTERVENTION UNSUCCESSFUL
RECOMMENDATION: ON SITE CALL – FREE HAND

Messina stared at the message. It only took a moment for him to reach a decision. He rested a hand on Patrone's shoulder. "Erase it."

Patrone turned to him. "Should Ellister—"

"No, he shouldn't," Messina said and hit the erase key to wipe the message. He looked to Patrone. "If Ellister gets a free hand we're going to have four dead bodies here, understand? I'll tell him the rest and we'll take it from there. If he has that on-site call, he'll do it the only way to be sure, and I don't know about you, but him shooting that mip on Tropico that had Hovland, it was murder, plain and simple. I've had enough with executions. Besides, what the hell good would it do us now anyway? We're in this mess, and that's it, and if we're going to die, I don't want wasted blood on my hands. Got it?"

Patrone's gaze fell as his head sank.

Miller walked up behind them, the two men turning to glare at him. He stopped and waved his hand about. "Where's Ellister? I want to talk to him." He grew uneasy beneath Messina's scrutiny, shrugging several times. "I could, uh, I could talk to you…"

Messina glanced down the ridge to where Hovland had been bound. "Aren't you supposed to be watching the lieutenant?"

Miller nodded, but pointed down the ridge. "I asked Lippett to do it for me."

"I bet you did," Patrone said under his breath, but fell silent under a glare from Messina.

"Hey, I ain't no mip," Miller said, guessing at Patrone's comment, but he gathered himself and shook it off. "You know, I was thinking about who might have planted that cylinder thing. We all accounted for each other except Boden and Lippett, and Hovland was out the whole time. So you tell me who we should be tying up—I say it's the greener."

Messina tipped his head back, surprised that Miller could apply his mind to anything besides the two minutes in front of his face. After some thought, though, Messina shook his head. "Hovland was out the whole time during the last bombardment, and his hands are bound, but that cylinder thing, I'm not sure. But whoever messed with the simulator, that could be part of their program, so they wouldn't have to bring it in here and deploy it."

"Maybe Hovland night-crawled," Patrone said. "Sometimes when soldiers sleep in high stress situations they crawl as a subconscious effort to escape."

Miller's eyes narrowed on Patrone. "Why you so quick to sell the boss out?"

Patrone opened his hands. "You started this; don't accuse *me*. Whatever the case, there is one thing, and that is for a man who was bound, a man who was unconscious, we found him ten paces from where Ellister left him after knocking him out. That's why Ellister told *you* to keep an eye on him, not that idiot Lippett."

"Knock it off," Messina said, glancing between the two men, but then his eyes widened. "Unless, unless someone moved him to cover their own actions, moved him during the confusion of the bombardment when everyone was running around." He shook his head. "You know, I've been thinking, and maybe this mess we're in, all this, it's just some game cooked up by Security to test us."

Patrone tipped his head. "Now *that's* paranoid."

Miller looked to Messina. "What the hell would they do that for?"

"Security," Patrone said, but then shrugged. "They do whatever they want to do."

Messina rubbed his forehead. "Some kind of experiment, maybe?" He frowned. "I don't know. A mip sabotage, a mip infiltration, up here on the troopship? I have to tell you, I'm having trouble buying into that, the more I think about it."

"They've managed to hack and infiltrate just about everything else," Patrone said, opening his hands. "I mean, that's what the whole mip psychology is about, right? Infiltration, betrayal, double talk, undermine anything that forms any foundation of trust or security?"

Miller shook his head. "Forget it. No way our own guys would do this to us."

Messina leaned towards them. "I got a friend in Security, and one time he told me they were working on ways to infiltrate a mind hooked up to the simulator, instead of using neural darts. He said they could make you do things in an immersion, they could control you, even over-write your will, and you just watch."

Patrone's eyes narrowed. "That's wrong. I mean, really wrong."

Miller blew out a breath. "That's crap, is what it is. What's the point of doing that to us, of doing it to your own people?"

Messina's eyes widened. "Behavioral studies? Loyalty or discipline challenges?" He looked to Patrone and Miller. "Who knows?"

"If you think about, I mean really *think* about it," Patrone began, "you could take all of society, all authority, and just say it's one big game of lies and deception to keep people in check. People only believe you're in control if you manufacture enough of an image to convince them you're in control."

Messina nodded. "The illusory reality of authority. I read that somewhere."

Patrone shrugged. "Maybe, maybe more than that. Consider this," he said, his voice dropping to a whisper. "You know, I've been thinking, taking a more philosophical look at things. Think of society as a body, a body that fights infection. These worlds we go to, these suppression campaigns, you would think that we're the immune system of that body, putting down the infection of insurrection. But wherever we go, things get worse. So in some way, you could almost say *we* were the infection, and maybe all this, all this going on, is just some way for society to get rid of the current order, that the current order, the order we impose, is not an infection, but a tumor, a part of the body turned against itself. Evolution or revolution; if you're in the middle of something, can you really tell them apart?"

Messina stared at Patrone before shaking his head. "Hell, that's right out of the mip handbook on rebellion, taking right and wrong and turning them inside out. But then, maybe that's why Security would do this, to see how we'd question the reality of it."

Miller looked to Patrone. "You're an idiot," he said as a flat denial of Patrone's thoughts, but before the medic could reply, Miller turned to Messina. "And you, you know what? I can't believe you're listening to this crap. Ellister's right. You and your little 'friends', it's like chat-time at the old women's home."

Messina punched Miller in the chest. "Piss off!"

Patrone hooked Messina's arm, cursing at Miller.

Repeater fire tore the silence, all eyes turning down the ridge where a chain of muzzle flashes arced into the sky. Messina grabbed his repeater and scrambled away. Confused shouts sounded out as the platoon's fatigue broke out in automatic fire. Messina ran down the ridge to Lippett, only to find the man stretched out unconscious. The belt that had bound Hovland's wrists lay cut on the ground and with it any reservations Messina held about Hovland's complicity in their situation. He looked up the ridge and jabbed a finger toward the plain. "Hovland's escaped!"

Turning back to the plain, he rested his cheek on the stock of his repeater to sweep the area with his infrared sight. It didn't take long to find Hovland's distant heat shadow running across the cold landscape. Messina shouted to Hovland before firing a shot in the air, but Hovland kept running, cutting a curve to place the cylinder between him and the platoon. Messina shouted again, but Hovland continued to run.

"Cut him down!" Ellister said over the radio.

There was no need to listen. There was no choice in the matter.

Messina ordered the platoon to hold their fire when he noticed the platoon raising their guns in his peripheral vision. Instead, he settled his cheek against his weapon, took aim, and fired a dead shot.

Nothing happened.

Cursing, Messina flipped to full automatic and let off a chain of rounds. Again, nothing happened—no hits on Hovland, no ricochets off the rocks around him, not a single trace of evidence that the rounds had left Messina's gun. He picked up a small stone and threw it in the direction of Hovland's shrinking form. The stone spun through the air, but when it passed over the cylinder, it pixilated and disappeared. "Damn you Hov," he said and glared at Miller as the private came up beside him. Messina waved the platoon over and pointed at them in turn. "Pair and pursue! Dead or alive, I want Hovland accounted for!" he said, and the crisp order, a definitive order to do *something,* served to motivate the platoon double-quick.

"Hovland escaped?" Webb said over the radio. A wave of static washed over the command frequency and in its wake Ellister's voice rose up. "Who was watching him?"

"Miller," Messina said, "but he blew it off on Lippett."

Webb muttered something over the radio, but Ellister's reply came through crystal clear. "Bind up that bastard until I get there!"

Messina pointed to his men. "Lippett! Patrone! Get over here!" He turned as gunfire erupted on the plain. Panicked cries rang out over the radio, several voices screaming for cover fire that no one was left to provide. Messina's eyes darted about before he realized his error. He ordered the platoon to fall back, but it was too late. He looked back up the ridge, cursing under his breath. On the plain, they had no height advantage, but on the ridge, the simulator's troops had their position nailed; it was the frying pan or the fire.

Ellister's voice came over the radio, calling for Messina.

Messina scrambled to bring the platoon back in some form of covered retreat. They were breaking, firing wild, as they ran for the ridge.

"Messina!" Ellister and Webb said together.

"What, *what?*" Messina cried out in frustration. "I need you two over here! Get back here!" But it was only then that he understood the urgency in their voices. Flashes of mortar launches bloomed in a long line across the plain, the whoosh of incoming shells already sounding out. "Run!" was all Messina managed to get out of his mouth, the futility of their situation overwhelming his years of experience. "Scatter! Mortars! Run! *Run!*" He spun and looked back up the ridge. *The uplink!*

Out on the plain, Hovland dove behind a boulder, wincing when he hit the ground. Had he known the troopers had snuck up to the ridge he would have run in a different direction; as it was he was amazed he hadn't been shot. With a curse he pulled himself up to see explosions light the length of the ridge.

Messina charged to the crest, rock flakes pelting him as mortar rounds went off around him. He grabbed the uplink and sprinted for the backside of the ridge, his heart pounding with the mindless need to escape.

Down on the plain Ellister and Webb came to a halt behind a boulder, watching a line of mortar explosions tear across the ridge. Barrage after barrage erupted, shattering the entire position the platoon had held as their defensive ground, obliterating the site. After the eighth barrage the explosions ended, and the eerie silence of the simulator returned to them.

Webb blinked, tapping the side of his helmet as he called Messina's name into his helmet mike. "Anyone?" he whispered in desperation, but sank to the ground in the empty static that came as the only reply. He looked up. "Ellister, man, we're alone..."

Ellister stood stock still, his eyes locked on the ridge, Webb's words not seeming to register. After several moments Ellister took off his helmet and dumped it on the ground to run his hands over the close cropped stubble of his hair. Then he wiped his face and dropped his hands on his repeater before looking back to Webb.

He frowned. "Webb old boy, I guess it's just us now."

IV

Hovland pulled himself up to peer about the plain, wary of any troopers that remained. He stared up the ridge to spot survivors, but there was only a lingering cloud of dust. He began to pick out the dark silhouettes of troopers combing the ridge for survivors, and as he listened, he heard the pitiful moans and yelps of those too wounded to escape, too alive to slip into the bliss of unconsciousness. They were silenced one by one beneath the rattle of a trooper's gun.

It was too much for him, to listen to his platoon, his men, suffer a systematic slaughter. The immediate past fell away from him, leaving him not with faces of accusation but the trusting faces he had known. Doomed or not, he had to act.

He set his teeth and headed for the ridge.

***

Messina gasped, struggling to keep hold of his senses. He shoved the uplink before him and pulled himself forward, dragging his shattered legs across the ground. His repeater lost, his life fading, he knew there was only one positive thing he could do, and that was to get the uplink to Webb and Ellister before the simulator's troopers captured the device. Knowing full well the troopers were finishing off the wounded remnants of the platoon on the other side of the ridge, he realized his end was soon in the coming, either from his wounds or a trooper's muzzle flash. It mattered little, allowing him to focus on his task.

He gasped Webb's name into his helmet mike before slipping off his elbows to lay face down on the backside of the ridge.

A little more, he urged himself.

A boot crunched before him.

He sighed. At least it was over. He looked up, but then blinked, for what stood over him was not the black shape of a simulator trooper, but the shadowed outline of someone from the platoon. He struggled to raise his hand as he sucked in a breath, but he only managed a single desperate plea for help.

The shadow shifted. A repeater barrel swung toward him. He cursed and let his head sink to the ground. The barrel pushed his helmet off before he felt its cold circle press against his temple.

"Screw you," he said, and then he knew no more.

***

Webb and Ellister worked their way to the ridge, wary of an ambush. The area was being swept by troopers, but they knew the uplink was somewhere on the ridge, and if they were to have any chance of survival, they had to retrieve the device. Fatigue weighed down their feet and hunger gnawed at their stomachs; thirst was kept at bay by their dwindling water supply. Despite those distractions they didn't fail to perceive the report of a single repeater round.

They ducked, startled by the sudden sound. Ellister flipped down his infrared but the shadow he glimpsed disappeared before he could get a good fix. He clenched his repeater and turned to Webb. "That was a repeater," he said, his eyes wide and wild.

Webb nodded. "It has to be the rat!"

Ellister studied Webb. "Are we clear on this, or are you going to get lame on me like Messina?"

Webb pursed his lips before he spoke. "This isn't like Tropico, not like anything we've done. If we have to die, then hell, we take out this rat-bastard first."

Ellister thumped a fist on Webb's shoulder. They kept low and covered each other as they worked their way up the ridge.

***

Miller cowered under the hollow of a blasted boulder as he watched the last of the troopers march away from the ridge. Patrone, Hauser, Wilkins, Stone, Weaver; all of them gone, *gone!* He wiped his face and shook his head to gather his wits. *Think,* he yelled through his mind. He checked through the platoon's roster to account for everyone. After several moments of confused sorting he came to a list: Webb and Ellister, off on the plain, Messina, who bolted with the uplink—*bastard!* And then there was Hovland—*goddamn Hovland!*

He looked around and kept a tight grip on his repeater as he crawled to the crest of the ridge, hissing Messina's name as he went. Before he reached the crest he heard a single repeater report from the other side of the ridge. He slumped down and lay still, squeezing his eyes shut. After several nervous moments he opened his eyes and peered past his shaking hands to look over the ridge. For a single heartbeat he thought somebody moved on the other side, but he blinked, looked again, and saw nothing but the perfect black of the simulator's sky.

"Messina," he said again, but his anxiety gained the best of him, and he bolted, scrambling on all fours across the broken rocks, bouncing off boulders in haste. He slipped on a sheet of loose gravel and tumbled forward to crash against a boulder. His helmet rolled away, clunking against the rocky ground as it disappeared down the ridge. He groaned and wiped the grit from his face before waving a hand in frustration for losing his helmet. Only then did he become aware of something poking into his side. He turned, and with muted elation, he found he was laying on the uplink. What little glee filled him evaporated when he noticed Messina drawn out beside him, his temple collapsed in the bloody havoc of a repeater round impact.

Miller gasped, his hands resuming their clutch of his repeater, his eyes darting about. Over the pound of his heart he picked up the sound of footfalls below. Without hesitation he spun and opened fire, glimpsing two figures as they dove for cover between the rounds of his repeater. He dropped to a crouch and scurried down the ridge through a channel of boulders. Nervous laughter bubbled from his lips. *That's it! I ain't no mip! All the rest of them, screw them! I'm gonna live! I'm—*

Caught blind in his surge, it was a short way from Messina's body when Ellister ambushed him. Miller never saw it coming, only felt the gun butt as it swung out from behind a rock into his gut. With a wheeze he doubled over and toppled in a confused pile. Before he realized he had even hit the ground Webb was on him. The sergeant yanked away his repeater and jerked Miller to attention by his neck cowl. "Where are you going?"

Miller gasped. "Ah man, you guys are alive! I thought I was it!"

"Shut up," Ellister said, crouching beside Webb to pin Miller with a knee across the throat. "Check up that ridge," Ellister said to Webb and looked down to Miller, whose eyes shifted as Webb made off toward Messina's body. "Hey, Ellister," Miller said, going hoarse with the knee on his throat, "I didn't kill Messina, I—"

Ellister's eyes narrowed. "Who said you did?"

Miller tried to push at Ellister's leg. "Come on, get off! Look, I didn't know it was you guys coming up!"

Ellister extended a finger from his grip on the barrel guard of his repeater. "I bet," he said. "So where's your helmet?"

Miller blinked. "What? I tripped," he said, pushing once more at Ellister's leg as Ellister glared at him. "I fell and I lost it, I'm telling you!"

"You couldn't pick it up?"

Miller sucked in a breath. "Come on man!"

"He's dead," Webb's disembodied voice called over Ellister's radio. "Messina's gone."

Ellister swung his repeater around to point the barrel at Miller's face.

Miller squeezed his eyes shut, his feet scraping for purchase on the ground. "I ain't no mip!"

Webb stepped out from behind a boulder, his eyes shifting between Miller and Ellister.

Miller's eyes darted to Webb. "Help me!"

Webb frowned, but held silent.

Miller cursed and looked back to Ellister. "Please! Don't!"

"I'll do what I need to do to protect the platoon," Ellister said.

Miller clawed at Ellister's leg. "Come on! They're all dead!"

Ellister leaned forward to push Miller's head back with the repeater muzzle until the ground bit into Miller's scalp. "We're not," the sergeant reminded him.

Miller clenched his teeth, staring at Ellister before his mouth burst open. "Then just do it already! Come on! Come on you piece of garbage!"

Ellister drew a deep breath.

Webb forced himself to swallow. He could barely find his voice. "Stop..."

Miller punched at Ellister's leg. "Just do it!"

"No!"

Ellister's eyes snapped to Webb. It was Hovland.

They turned to the direction of Hovland's voice and shouted his name in unison. Miller took advantage of the distraction, shoving at Ellister's leg to topple the sergeant. The moment Miller was free he rolled over and bolted. Ellister whipped around and let off a burst. Miller staggered, his innards spilling out of his belly before he flopped dead on his face. Webb gasped and slipped back against a boulder, but Ellister hadn't finished. He paced over to Miller's prone form and fired a single round into the back of his head.

Ellister nodded over Miller's body. Then he dropped his clip and slapped a fresh one home. He pulled back on the repeater's bolt, ignoring Webb as Webb sank down, agape as he stared at Miller. Ellister shifted on his feet and drew a deep breath to shout once more for Hovland.

He didn't have to wait for Hovland to reply.

"You can't murder my men!"

Ellister blinked, his eyelids twitching. He shook his head, but the twitches returned. He closed his eyes, took another deep breath, and held it before letting it go. When his eyes opened the twitches were gone. He turned to Webb.

Webb stared in disbelief. "Oh no," he said, shaking his head, "no, can't be—"

He grabbed his repeater, but Ellister had him beat. In a rattle of rounds it was over. Webb slumped beside Miller in a pool of blood.

"Ellister!"

Ellister tipped his head. "Lippett!" he called out. "Hey Lippett! We have a lieutenant to kill! Let's go!"

Hovland dropped as if he had been shot, his limbs unstrung as his mind labored to digest the reality imploding around him. *Lippett, Ellister—both of them?* Despite the seeming insanity of it, the preposterous audacity of it, the pieces somehow fit—a crowning achievement for insurrection, for subversion, for paranoia and insecurity, not to infiltrate a simulator immersion down on a planet, but up on a troopship, where safety and security seemed given, a warm blanket to hide from the harsh cold reality of being planetside on campaign. Two agents planted in a platoon, played off each other to divert suspicion. In the simulator, in the immersion, have the two of them in different areas at all times: Lippett on patrol, so he could murder Garnett, and Ellister with the platoon, to focus wrath on Hovland. Later, Lippett to set Hovland free, chase him away with his repeater under the guise of mercy. Hovland saw what he had first thought an act of Lippett's mercy for what it was, a way to confuse the platoon, distract their vigilance to allow the simulator to wipe them out. In the meantime, Ellister was tucked away from the scene with Webb, under the pretense of finding a new refuge for the platoon. It all fit, it was insane, and it surged through him on a wave of desperation heightened by the simulator's twenty-fold rush of time.

All those years in the platoon — it can't be! Ellister killed the mip that was holding me prisoner —

— had to murder him to cover his own tracks, in case that man somehow revealed Ellister's duplicitous nature during Security's interrogation.

No, this is Ellister, this is my friend, this is a man I sat with many times, shared laughs with, shared five years with, and all this time, just waiting? Can't be!

He put his hands on his head. He knew he had to think past sentiment and the illusions of what he thought he knew. That was the game of subversion; those were the veils of infiltration and trust that hid insurrection agents. *In the end, they don't fool us, we fool ourselves with trust; it is trust that's the liar, it is Trust itself that forms its own worst enemy.*

He remembered those last moments before hooking up to the simulator, with Lippett wandering into the annex with his new good luck charm dangling from his neck. *A handgun clip. He could have had a datacube and patch cord in there, could have hacked the sim right from the room, just after the rest of us went under. All the years I protected him!*

Hovland dropped his hands. His eyes darted about. He had to arm himself.

He went on all fours and peered from behind a boulder, right into the sight of Lippett's repeater. With a curse he threw himself, repeater rounds pounding the space he had just occupied. He scurried off in the opposite direction, fighting to keep his balance as Ellister joined in with Lippett and both men sent showers of repeater fire about him. He wondered then where all the simulator's troopers had disappeared too, but in a rotten turn of luck, figured the simulator was no longer capable of generating the artificial troopers. He ducked between several channels of boulders, the repeater fire fading from his vicinity as Ellister and Lippett lost track of him. He halted to catch his breath and strained to hear any footfall or voice that could aid him.

It was Ellister who broke the silence. "Give it up Hovland!"

"Put your head up!" Lippett said. "No more pain! Ask Messina!"

Hovland rolled over and picked up a small rock. Gazing past the boulder he was using for cover, he whipped his arm across the ground, sending the rock on a low arc to crack against another boulder.

Ellister pointed. "Get him!"

Hovland took advantage of the misdirection to sprint down the ridge toward the platoon's last position. He made it to cover just as Ellister realized the rouse and sent bursts of repeater fire cascading around him. He dove and came to a halt against the ragged remains of a corpse. Ignoring his disgust he shoved the body aside in search of a weapon, only to find the rocket launcher, with a rocket in the tube. He grabbed the launcher, pulled the tube to its full extension and rose to his knees.

Lippett stood atop a boulder a short way off, sweeping the surroundings with his repeater. When the rocket launched he spun, his eyes going wide the moment before the rocket impacted the boulder and tore him to shreds.

Hovland dropped to the ground. He looked over his shoulder to see pieces of Lippett spin through the air. He turned and froze.

Ellister stood before him, repeater trained square on his face. "Put the launcher down," Ellister said, motioning with a tip of his head.

Hovland debated, but Ellister was too far away to swing with the tube. He dropped the launcher and opened his hands. He sucked in a breath. He felt numb, trapped in an amoral void between the empty exhaustion of futility and the pointed rage of betrayal. But those things lost their meaning to him, dissolving from focus, pixilated to a gray nothing, before the simple yet surreal reality of the weapon trained on him, and more so the *thing* that held it steady. He pictured his body, his body far away in the simulator room, bare but for a pair of white shorts, exposed, defenseless, and seeming at peace, even as he stood trapped in a nightmare.

I'm not going to die here, not like this.

And then he heard its maddening dovetail: *There is no 'here'…*

His mind cleared. He found himself feeling quite calm.

He blinked. "I guess you have me now," he said.

Ellister stared at him.

Hovland raised his hands. "Well? Why wait?"

Ellister frowned. "Couldn't shoot you in the back. Old times' sake."

Hovland looked at him in disbelief, but knew better than to directly challenge Ellister's statement. "So who were you originally?"

Ellister blinked. "It's not important."

Hovland shook his head. "It's the *only* important thing left."

Ellister held his silence.

"Because I need to know who it is that's going to kill me," Hovland continued, "some stranger, or the man I knew, because he wouldn't put up with any of this, he couldn't stand the presence of himself right now." He took a slow step toward Ellister, keeping his hands open to keep Ellister at ease. "Come on, give me your handgun, we'll go out together. Nice and tidy, for old times' sake. Nobody gets the last laugh, nobody's left standing. The Ellister I knew, he'd take a draw over a loss to a mip any day, just to keep the balance, keep the order, keep it all right."

Ellister stood for some time, but then lowered his repeater and gave Hovland a small tip of his head. "Yeah, I guess we kicked some ass in our run," he said, his empty gaze sinking to the ground. He pulled his handgun and glanced at it before looking back to Hovland, his eyes narrowing in suspicion.

Hovland shrugged. "You know after I'm dead you'll be stuck here by yourself," he said, straining to keep Ellister's teetering intellect off course. "There's no way out, no way to hide from yourself anymore, and then you'll have to choose. With me gone, the subversion wins either way — either you kill yourself with your platoon lost, or you sit and wait for the troopship to disintegrate around you, so the mip still gets you." He shook his head. "It's not a good deal."

Ellister looked down at the handgun. He held still, but then tossed it to Hovland.

Hovland caught it, almost dropping it in surprise. He fought to maintain his composure, maintain his calm demeanor, convinced that the mutual ambivalence of those two facades, blanketing their mutual madness, was the only thing keeping him alive.

Ellister pointed to the gun. "Put it to your head."

Hovland swallowed over a dry throat and put the handgun to his temple. It was tough to do as if he had no care for his life, but he knew the irony of it — the path he sought to save himself was only open if he showed no interest in saving himself. When the cold circle of the handgun came against his temple Ellister turned the repeater to put the barrel under his chin.

"On three," Ellister said.

Hovland swallowed. "That's it?"

Ellister shrugged. "I trust you."

Hovland blew out a breath.

Ellister blinked. "One—"

Hovland turned his hand and fired. The awkward angle almost snapped his wrist, but he couldn't miss at such short range. Ellister's head kicked back before lolling forward. He stood there for a moment, eyes no more blank than they had been, even as blood streamed from the hole in his forehead. He fell, collapsing in a pile.

Hovland slumped against the boulder behind him, his hands dropping to his sides. The gun dangled from his fingers as his ear buzzed with the blast of the round. He stared at Ellister for some time before his head began a slow nod. "It worked," he said to himself, but any comfort he hoped to feel faded as the sight before him registered in his consciousness. The strange blur of it flashed through his mind, draining him with its implications.

He walked up the ridge and crossed over its crest to find the uplink. He ignored Webb and Miller as the men he had known, instead marginalizing them as more victims of that greedy beast he cursed as trust. He walked away and found a large boulder. He set the handgun beside him and opened the uplink on his lap, but then reconsidered and set it down on his other side. He looked across the empty plain.

"Okay then," he thought aloud, "what now?"

He rested his head in his hands and closed his eyes.

V

He sat for what seemed to be hours, the feed speed a forgotten reality. Nothing threatened him within the simulator. The mysterious cylinder remained, pursuing its erasure of the immersion's virtual substance. He wondered what would happen if the troopship lasted long enough for the cylinder's work to reach him; if it would kill him, or if he would blur and fade like the rest of the landscape. The symbolism of it drew a little mocking laugh from him, but then the thought drifted away, and he was alone again.

His thoughts wandered to the abstract, pondering the point of the sabotage. All the effort of the rebellion to manipulate things to get Ellister and Lippett into the platoon… Was it a stroke of luck that it worked, or had it been tried innumerable times before Ellister and Lippett managed to succeed? And even aside from that, even aside from what the mips must consider a success, what was there to show for it? The military's campaign against localized insurrections wouldn't stop. All the effort, even there, there in the nowhere of the immersion, all the arguing and fighting and death over who was a rat and who wasn't, it was for nothing. There seemed no point to it, only wasted effort.

And that's why it never ends, he deduced. If there was order, there had to be anarchy as well; the oxymoronic 'military pacifists' were just another weight in that convoluted balance. The wary weariness of futility, mused a dissolute thought. It echoed through the immersion's emptiness, at home among the abstraction of the simulation. Could that thought be the goal, though? Not necessarily to win, but to break people, whittle them down, erode them, let them lay down to sleep, and then, no more? Could that even be considered a victory?

He thought of the rumor, the rumor of that other platoon that had fallen victim to a sabotaged simulator. He wondered what those men had done, what their last moments had been, if they had even known what was happening.

Immersions, simulators; not so abstract after all.

The uplink beeped, startling him. He rubbed his eyes and looked to the terminal's screen.

HOVLAND
HAVE TO TALK
SHEFFIELD

He shook his head, unsure if he was hallucinating, but the words remained on the screen. He set the terminal in his lap, typed a response, and hit the send key. His eyes rose to the featureless black sky as he waited for an answer to come down.

NO TIME TO WASTE
ORDERED TO RETRIEVE YOU
ARE YOU ARMED?

His back stiffened with suspicion. Moments passed, but he realized he had no choice except to follow Sheffield's prompts on nothing but trust. Cursing under his breath, he picked up the handgun and checked the clip before remembering he was surrounded by weapons. With a shake of his head he typed his response and hit the send key.

GOOD- TIME TO STICK A FORK IN THE TURKEY
RAISING YOU FROM SIM SLEEP WITH MEDS
DO YOU FEEL THIS?

His face sank at Sheffield's message until his left arm contorted against his side. With a grunt he shook his hand to loosen his arm, his heart pounding with the anticipation of escaping the simulator. For a moment he imagined two windows opening in the sky to reveal the world without through his physical eyes, but the detached whimsy of that notion only served to remind him of his dilemma. His eyes sank to the uplink as he typed his acknowledgment.

GOOD- YOU HAVE TO SEVER FROM INSIDE
PUT GUN TO HEAD
PULL TRIGGER
SEE YOU ON OTHER SIDE

He snorted at Sheffield's instructions. He had an idea what the TO's plan entailed; it wasn't all that different from what he had done with Ellister. Only this time he had to hope that the drugs Sheffield pumped into him could rouse him from the immersion before the simulator's feedback killed him. It was a sloppy plan, but at least it was *a* plan.

He put the terminal beside him and took the gun in his hand. It was not the plan that bothered him, or the greater odds of it not working, but the odds if it *did* work. *And what then?* With every moment the question weighed on him he felt his anger welling up, anger and frustration and resentment that by passing up a risky plan for survival he would have to accept some aimless notion of futility as the summation of his life. *Because that's what subversion wants. Subversion wants you to give in, subversion wants you to be listless and apathetic, subversion wants you to roll over and just take it. I've taken enough. If blowing my brains out is the only way to keep my sanity, then so be it!*

He put the gun to his head, mumbling a stream of epithets.

He squeezed his eyes shut and screwed up his nerves. "Oh hell! On three!"

Yet for some reason—some reason he would never understand—he fired on two.

***

"...and that's when I pulled the trigger, and now I'm here," he said and shook his head. He sipped his beer and set it down on the table, peering in turn at Webb, Messina, and Ellister. The troopship's retreat, the Bunker, was cramped and confined like every other place on the troopship, but with its lights dimmed the nearness of the walls did not seem quite so near, and with the ceiling painted an even black, the stifling darkness felt uncorked above them. Nevertheless, they sat shoulder to shoulder around their cramped little table, close to the point of claustrophobic confinement after the vacuous, yet paranoia filled, immersion.

Hovland shrugged; his comrades were quiet around him. He had arranged the meeting, arranged permission to get them into the Bunker. It was reserved for officers, but in the fallout of their immersion, he had been given some latitude.

Webb shifted in his seat, his gaze on the table. "So what about Sheffield? No problems with that?"

Hovland shook his head.

"I wish I could've been there when you beat the piss out of him," Webb said.

Messina nodded. "I would have liked to add a few shots to the mix."

"He had his orders," Hovland said, his old even temper evident. "He was just the end of the chain."

Webb looked to Hovland. "Did he at least say anything?"

Hovland hooked a thumb over his shoulder to the decorative crest hanging on the wall behind him, emblazoned with the unit banners for their troopship. Surrounding the banners ran the military's motto, adopted since the inception of the rebellion campaigns: THAT WHICH DOES NOT BREAK US SHALL MAKE US STRONGER. "He said it was just part of the military's program, part of the program against the corruptive thoughts of rebellion. It's all about testing the periphery of order, the illusion of control, and they used us as a test-bed for whatever paranoid fantasy their psychologists wanted to play out. A veteran platoon, a mix of unknown replacements, a lieutenant who had been captured, an immersion fresh off a tough campaign; murder, mistrust, and the suspicions and accusations to go with it—they hit us with both barrels, just to see how we, as a sample of the military, would respond."

"They over-wrote my will," Ellister said, his eyes narrowing as he looked up from his mug. "You have no idea what that felt like, what it still feels like."

Hovland took a sip of beer. "They did that to most of us, to various degrees," he said, sympathizing with Ellister. "With me, they planted the thought in my head to go on the patrol—the very thing that set me up, that sent us down the spiral of paranoia and suspicion."

Ellister gulped his beer and let his gaze fall to the table. "But it *killed* Lippett," he whispered, refusing to look up. "Simpleton that he was, his subconscious rejected the over-write, fought it until a blood vessel blew in his head. What did I do? I *twitched.* I can't stop thinking about that. I'm not slow like he was. Why didn't it kill me, why didn't I fight it like he did, why *couldn't* I fight like he did?"

Webb waved a hand. "Forget it. It doesn't mean anything."

Ellister's eyes locked on Webb. "It means everything," he corrected. "Worst part... You know what the worst part is? Somehow, some way, looking back on it, the things they made me do, those things make some kind of sense to me."

"That's it," Messina said and pushed his beer away. "I'm done. I'm putting in for a transfer."

Hovland looked to Messina. "You didn't do anything wrong," he said before opening his hands on the table. "None of us did. That's what I wanted to tell the three of you, force you to sit down so that we can put this thing behind us. The military did this to us; we didn't do it to each other. The things we did in that immersion, that wasn't us," he added, looking to Ellister.

Ellister burped.

"I've got nothing to be ashamed of," Messina decided. He propped an elbow on the table and pointed at Ellister. "But you," he said, jabbing his extended finger at Ellister, "I'm *done* with you."

"Eat that," Webb said and glared at Messina. "It wasn't really him."

Messina turned a hard glare on Webb. "Don't forget what he did to that mip on Tropico when we found Hovland. You know what? I'm not afraid to say it anymore: it was *murder*, plain and simple, and all that shit he pulled in the simulator, it was just more of the same. I don't care if some prick wrote it in, hacked his mind to make him do those things, he *did* them, and that had to come from somewhere *in* him. That's why it killed Lippett, but didn't kill *you*," he said, jabbing his finger once more at Ellister before looking to Hovland. "And what about Patrone? Did Sheffield tell you anything about him?"

Hovland shook his head. "I asked, and I was told not to ask."

Messina slapped a hand on the table. "And what is that supposed to mean? One of our guys, one of our long time guys, they just take him away, no explanation, and that's it? He just disappears into Security, and we sit here and suck on it?"

Webb's eyes narrowed on Messina. "What are you saying?"

"Patrone said some things to me in the immersion," Messina began, "some stuff about society and authority and insurrection, and at the time, I thought it was just talk, but now, now that he's gone, I don't know. He fingered you, Hov, and he wanted me to give Ellister that on-site call the moment we had it, and he said stuff to make Miller and Lippett look like they were helping Hov try to escape—it's like he was fueling the fire any way he could. It stinks, and I just can't figure it right, and with him sucked away to Security for whatever reason, it just makes it stink all the more."

Hovland sipped his beer. "You're putting the cart in front of the horse. You don't even know if that was him, or if some Security operative was writing in those things."

Webb turned to Hovland. "But if Security did it, why take him away? They did it to all of us; at least that's what they told us during debriefing."

Ellister forced a swallow. "Yeah, but they refused to tell us where we stopped and their over-writing began. They claimed it was classified."

Webb shook his head. "So what are we saying? You think Patrone was a mole for Security all along? Or," he dropped his voice to a whisper, "do you think he was a *mip* mole that by some crazy coincidence got revealed?"

The question hung over the table between them. None of them knew what to say.

Messina stood, opening his hands before his chest. "That's it. I didn't sign up for crap like this, to deal with this kind of garbage, or play these kinds of guessing games. I'm done," he said and walked away.

Webb moved, but Ellister shook his head. "Let him go."

Webb leaned forward to look into Ellister's eyes. "What do you mean, let him go? He's been with us from the beginning! You'd just let him walk?" He turned to Hovland. "You can't agree with this Hov…Or do you?"

Hovland hesitated. "Give it time," he said. "We're up here until we hit dirt again, and nobody's hinting when that might happen. He'll get over it. He'll see."

"See what?"

Hovland opened his hands. "What's the point of being pissed about it? It's done. Fighting it, whatever that 'it' may be, that's just wasted effort. There's no getting away from that."

Webb opened his hands. "Then what's the point? That's mip thinking, making your brain into jelly, wondering what's the right or wrong of things."

Hovland shrugged. "But that question remains, and you have to answer that for yourself," he said, not happy with the vague nature of the thought. "Messina has his answer. Lippett had an answer too. I thought I had an answer, but I'm not so sure anymore."

"And that was?" Ellister asked without looking up.

Hovland sighed. "A faceless sense of order, I guess, so I put myself against an equally faceless sense of disorder. I thought I knew where the difference was, and that was the border, the front, for me." Webb stared at him, but he looked to Ellister. "Do you remember what you said to me in the immersion? That the enemy is the SOB firing at you?"

Ellister tipped his head. "Yeah, I remember that."

"It's as simple as that," Hovland said with a nod, "because thinking is nothing but trouble. Putting a bullet in my own head to escape the paranoid hell of that immersion, Security anticipated that, looked for it, wanted it. They made a point of telling me that. And that—that alone— says a lot."

Webb looked at Hovland in disbelief. "That's it? Be stupid, and be led by the nose?"

Remnant

Hovland eased back in his chair as his eyes settled on Webb. "You have to believe first, so that you can let go, *before* you can be led by the nose. You could call it trust, if you want to." He shrugged. "It's a sweet, soothing delusion."

Webb rubbed his jaw before dropping his hand on the table. He studied Hovland, then Ellister, and without a word, walked away.

It was quiet at the table. For the moment, it felt fine.

Hovland took a breath. He wanted some word on the state of his men, but with Webb and Messina gone, he found his opportunity diminishing. Sheffield had whisked him away from the simulator room for debriefing, which had turned into a several day ordeal after he had assaulted the TO upon learning Security's ploy in the immersion.

Considering it, Hovland couldn't help but sigh before looking to Ellister. "How's the platoon?"

Ellister shrugged, his eyes resting on his beer. "It was all messed up after the immersion, all confused. There was a lot of pushing and shoving, a lot of finger pointing and accusations. Couple of fights until we realized Lippett was dead. Security was all over us; they split us up for debriefing. That's when Patrone disappeared. Later they just sent the rest of them back to the squad room. They kept me for a while longer," he admitted with a frown.

"Lippett's dead," Hovland said, his gaze distant.

"Dead and gone." Ellister looked at him. "What are you thinking?"

"I tried so hard to protect the simple bastard," Hovland said, looking back to Ellister, "and I blew him to pieces without a second thought. It never even occurred to me until now. Why is that?"

Ellister shook his head. "That gets left on Security's doormat, nowhere else. Besides, like you said, what happened in the sim, we can't hold ourselves accountable." He fell silent for a moment before he found a way to convince himself of that thought. "It doesn't mean anything, Hov."

"You know, Ellis—"

"Messina's right," Ellister interrupted, but then frowned. He hesitated before clearing his throat to find his voice. "But you're right, too." He shifted in his seat, his eyes never leaving the dark depths of his beer. "I think that's what it comes down to, and that's why it's all screwed up. I still feel it; I have this feeling like I'm clinging to the top of that ridge, but the slopes on either side are steep, like cliff steep, and they just drop away to blackness. It's there every time I close my eyes. I think I'm going to be there for a long time."

Hovland nudged Ellister with his elbow and picked up his beer. "You know what? Forget it. Come on, I have open vouchers for the bar. Let's get good old, stupid drunk."

"Right… Yeah, right," Ellister thought aloud. He blinked and looked at Hovland before raising his beer. He waited until Hovland raised his as well.

They stared at each other, but it was Ellister who spoke.

"On three?"

Remnant

Once upon a dream I had a life, and even though that dream came to an end, my life did not. My life simply changed, began anew, and as what, I have yet to decide, for in the absence of all that was, in the absence of all restraint, I may be something that was only a whisper in me before the change. And the change was the passing of the world, the passing of the world under the shadow of a nameless thief in the night, and it cared not for what waste it sowed in the lives of those it left.

Anyone reading this will know of what I speak: 'it' is the plague, the nameless plague, and nobody knows what it is, or where it came from, but in the end, these things matter little. Whatever it is, it came upon us as swiftly and with all the vacant pity of the harvester's scythe.

One in fifty thousand: that was the last approximate incidence of natural immunity in the human population. For the rest there was only death, regardless of age, gender, race, or prosperity. After all the generations of human strife, we had finally met our equality.

This is the only logic that remains in this empty world.

And for some reason, I remain as well.

***

A branch snapped in the night.

Peter slumped down behind the tree where he had been sitting, cursing his carelessness. The notebook that held his writing must have stood out like a beacon under the stark moonlight. Clenching his jaw he pulled down his black ski mask and rolled onto his belly, taking care to be quiet. His eyes darted about the shadows of the forest as he tucked his little notebook into a thigh pocket.

Nothing moved.

After a brief mental debate, his eyes shifted from his rifle to his slingshot. He snatched it at once, grabbed a rock, and taking aim at a tree some distance away, let the rock fly. It hit the tree with a pop. To his dismay the rustle of leaves broke the following silence. Something was out there, something big—

"Hello!" a voice called. Male. "Anyone there?"

Peter frowned and kept his silence. A handful of people left in the entirety of New England, and someone has to bother him?

"Hello!" the voice called again. "My name's Jim MacPherson! I'm from Boston!"

Peter took his rifle in hand, flipped off the safety, and peered through the night scope. He wasn't sure why, perhaps it was the societal nature of the human mind, perhaps it was the looming fear of insanity through loneliness, but he found his voice and spoke. "Don't move! I have a sight on you!" He scanned the woods with the scope, searching the darkness. "Are you alone?"

The stranger let out a low laugh. "Aren't we all?"

Peter froze. He had the stranger in sight. The man was standing by a tree, his hands open at his sides.

"Hey! I told you my name. What's yours?"

"Are you alone?"

The man looked about. "Yes, I'm alone. Look, I don't want any trouble. Just passing through; heading south as fast as I can. Nights are getting real cold. Am I still in Connecticut?"

"Keep on walking."

"I'd appreciate it if you could point me some place where I can get canned foods. They last the best, you know. I finished my last can for dinner. Tuna." The stranger waved. "My name is Jim MacPherson," he said again. "Come on, man! I haven't talked to somebody in weeks. I'm tired of talking to myself. You know it's real bad when you can't even have a decent conversation with yourself," he added with a laugh.

"Peter Lowry."

"What?"

Peter stood and lowered his rifle. "Over here," he said and raised his arm. He pulled up his ski mask. "My name is Peter Lowry."

Jim looked to him and smiled, but he kept his hands in the open. "Nice to meet you, Peter Lowry," he said with good nature. When he made out the rifle he lowered his hands. "Hey, uh, you're not gonna shoot me, are you?"

Peter stared at him. "Only if you need to be shot."

The humor fled Jim's face. "Look, sorry to bother you. If it's fine by you, I'll be on my way. No trouble. You can keep all of Connecticut for yourself. No problem." He backed off several paces before lowering his head and turning away.

Peter frowned, his gaze roaming the dark woods as he debated with himself. Before he lost sight of Jim he stifled his reservations and opened his mouth. "Wait. I'll show you in the morning. But tonight we stay out here."

Jim sighed with relief. "Works for me," he said with a clap of his hands. He hurried over to Peter and sat on the ground. He wore a large hiker's pack, which he promptly shrugged off, only to dig out a water bottle. "Nice rifle," he noted as Peter sat down across from him. "Have you had to use it?"

Peter ignored the question. "You're from Boston?" he asked and waited until Jim nodded. "Then you should know not everyone is so pleasant. Some of those who are left, they're not all there. Scavengers. Wild. You understand?"

Jim frowned before tipping his head. "Oh yeah, I hear you on that one. I saw some of the riots on the news. That's when I left the city. My uncle had this cabin, so I took a load of food and batteries and water and headed out there." He stopped short, pressing his lips together as he stared at Peter. "Hey, do you mind if I talk? I haven't talked to anyone in a while. I know some people don't like to talk, but I like to talk. Chatty, my uncle said. My girlfriend, too. Boy, I miss her, you know?"

Peter blinked.

Jim clenched his fists. "Sorry. Too much, right?"

Peter couldn't suppress the grin that tugged at his lips. Despite his suspicious nature, his instincts told him he had nothing to fear from this stranger.

Jim looked down, seeming to assume the worst from Peter's silence. "Okay, I know, talking too much." He drank some water. "It's just, I forget, you know? I've always been what you'd call a people person. Could sell snowballs to an Eskimo," he added with a laugh, but then caught himself. "Strangers, first meeting and all, too much to say. Have to learn, I guess. The way things are, people who like to talk, I guess we're kind of the odd lot out. That's all right. I'll be quiet now."

Peter shook his head. "No, no, go ahead," he said, trusting his appraisal of Jim. He wasn't sure how long he would entertain Jim's intrusion on his solitude, but for the moment, he figured it was harmless enough to listen to someone babble after hearing nothing but birds for more days than he cared to count.

Jim tipped his head. "Great! Well, as I was saying, I was up at my uncle's cabin. I didn't know I was immune. One night some people broke in, beat me up, took the food, everything. A couple of them were coughing. When I came to, I found them all dead. After I buried them, a few days passed, and then the power went out. That's when I started to hear explosions from the direction of the city."

"Untended industrial facilities," Peter guessed.

Jim opened his hands. "I guess so. That's when I took off. I tried to drive, but the roads were all blocked. Piles of cars and trucks smashed into each other; you know, people, they just dropped dead while they were driving. So I walked from then on." He drank some water before rubbing his hands together. "Getting cold early this year," he said before tipping his chin to Peter. "Mind if I start a fire?"

Peter looked about the woods before his eyes settled on Jim. "You are alone, aren't you?"

Jim held up his hand, two fingers extended. "On my honor."

Peter rested his hands on his rifle, making it clear that if the fire was some kind of signal, there was no doubt where the first shot would go. "A fire would be fine."

Jim blew out a breath as he dug through his pockets. In short order he had scraped together some small branches, kindling, and with some patience, got a flame going with a match. He opened his hands over the little fire and looked back to Peter. "So where you from, Peter Lowry?"

Peter hesitated before answering. "New York."

Jim let out a low whistle. "The city? No wonder you're out here. Heard some bad things on my radio. Gangs going wild. Bodies all over the place."

"No," Peter corrected. "I'm from Long Island. Things were no different. I managed to get a rowboat and I rowed across the Sound to Connecticut. I thought my arms were going to fall off." He rubbed his forehead. "I left everything behind."

Jim frowned and bobbed his head. "I hear you on that one," he said with a sigh. Then he laughed, sitting up straight as his mood changed. "Hey, you know, I look at it this way. Before, there was more people than stuff. Now there's way more stuff than people. It's all just sitting there. That's always been the problem, right, people wanting stuff they couldn't have? Well Pete, the meek have inherited the earth, and it's an endless clearance sale, you know?" He laughed again, looking off to the depths of the woods before rubbing his chin. "So we wait 'til morning, huh? Problems around here?"

"Rat swarms." Peter looked to the black sky. "They come out at night."

"Yeah, I heard about that, too," Jim replied. "Back before I left Boston, there was this group of holdouts in some radio station that I was listening to. The rats swarmed them while they were on the air calling for help. It was horrible. Kind of sucks, if you think about it. Survive the plague, only to be eaten alive by a swarm of rats." He shrugged and then leaned back against his pack. "Mind if I sleep?" he asked, but began snoring before Peter could answer.

Peter studied his new companion. He sat for several moments before reaching in his pocket for a blister pack of caffeine pills. He swallowed one dry, but then reconsidered as he studied this stranger sleeping in total trust across from him and swallowed a second pill. It was going to be a long night, he knew. Sleep would have to wait.

***

Restless with caution and caffeine, he couldn't relax until he probed a wide perimeter about their resting spot. Part of him felt he could trust Jim, but the rest of him knew better than to trust anyone left in the world. Rather than disarm people of their hostility and aggression, he felt the vast emptiness and loneliness of the plague had, for some, only amplified those negative aspects of human nature.

It was a thought that nagged him as he sat after walking the perimeter, only somewhat satisfied that nothing had emerged on his night scope. After laying the rifle across his lap he took his little notebook in hand and returned to his writing.

The plague moved with stunning speed. New York was no different than any other place in that the deaths didn't start in a localized trickle, but rather by virtue of the plague's insidious nature, people who were seemingly healthy would start dropping by scores in several places at once. By the time it came to New York we knew well enough what would happen next—quarantine, that is, seal off the area and let it take its course. The first twenty-four hours were the worst. The anarchic spasms of panic, looting, and pillaging ended as abruptly as they began, but when they were over, the finality of silence was beyond imagination.

I remember when it came upon us. It was a sunny, clear day. I hid with my family in our house. People came looting that night, setting fires, and we nearly burned with the house. We hid in the woods in the abandoned state mental hospital grounds by our neighborhood, but it was too late. We huddled down under a picnic table in the rain to sleep together. I was the only one to wake up in the morning.

I had nothing to bury them with. That's when I realized they were the lucky ones, because it was over for them. But for me, things had just started; and leaving them was the hardest thing I ever had to do. I don't consider myself one of the 'blessed few' like the Pope said before he died. A cursed remnant in the wreckage of our world; this is what I am. For what sins I have to answer, I don't know, but in the aftermath, I know that sin has become a meaningless word.

There is only the amoral dictate of pragmatism in a life without any external bounds, any sense of guarantee for a future. Why I answer to that dictate, I do not know, but I know it will eventually decide who—or I should say what—I will be in this new world.

***

He woke with a start.

Jim clapped his hands and opened them before his chest. "Hey, check it out: coffee."

Peter blinked, but then his hands swarmed about in a quick inventory. He clutched the rifle to his chest and glared with wide eyes at Jim.

Jim rolled his eyes. "Dude, I'm not gonna steal your stuff, and I'm not gonna take your rifle. Hell, if I wanted to, I could be back here in a few days with a friggin' tank. This is the beauty of it now! Why would I want your stuff?" he asked in disbelief. "Embrace our paradise, man. We can have anything we want; there's no need to take anything from anyone!"

Peter stared at him, unsure what to say.

Jim threw his hands up. "Oh, hey, I'm sorry. Coffee, I already had a few cups. Guess the rush got to me. Look, you want some?"

Peter hesitated a moment before he shrugged. He reached into his backpack and handed Jim a tin mug. Jim filled it and then filled his own. Peter held his mug, pretending to enjoy the steam while he waited for Jim to take the first sip. Only then did he drink.

Jim grinned. "So what did you do, before?"

Peter frowned. "I worked in a hospital."

"Didn't like it, huh?"

"No, it's just it didn't do me any good when the plague came."

Jim nodded. "Yeah, I hear that. I worked in a deli. I was living with my uncle, saving up so I could take legal aid courses at night with my girlfriend. Talk about a waste of time! I would've been better off joining the Boy Scouts. At least I'd have been a little better prepared for all this." He tipped his chin to the fire under his coffee pot. "You don't appreciate what a pain it is to start a fire when your lighter runs dry. You know, matches, they kind of suck. Too temperamental."

Peter tipped his head to the side. "The store I'll take you to has plenty of lighters. It's one of those mega-mart places. Somehow it was hardly touched. Most of the people around here, I think they died in their sleep."

"I heard about that. Some small towns, by day they were okay, but overnight the plague does its thing and the whole place is wiped out."

"All of this, it's unreal," Peter sighed.

Jim's eyes narrowed. "Hey, do you think it's one of those engineered plagues? Some bio-weapon that got out, or was let out?"

Peter opened his hands. "I don't know. Does it really matter?"

Jim shook his head. "You know some of those government types are probably hiding out in secret bunkers. They should have to pay for this."

"They're already paying for it." Peter sipped his coffee. "Would you want that, locked up somewhere? Think about it—they can't come out; they're stuck like rats underground. Their supplies will run out, but I think they'll all go nuts before that. No, the only survival is immunity. Either you have it, or you're dead."

"I guess you have a point on that," Jim said with a shrug. "Ah hell, it's our world now, right? No one telling us what to do, and no one to judge. It is what we make of it, right?"

Peter sipped his coffee, his stomach knotting around the familiarity of Jim's thought. "I guess." He stared into the dark brew he held until his eyes rose at the sound of Jim rustling in his pack. "If you're thinking of eating, just wait. We'll have the coffee, walk down to the store, and eat there."

Jim gave an eager nod, poured out the rest of the coffee into their mugs, and packed away his gear. "What do you say we walk and drink?"

Together they slung their packs and made off through the woods, cresting several small hills until Peter motioned for Jim to stop before the crest of one last hill. He finished his coffee and stuffed his mug into his pack before slinging it back on his shoulder. Rifle in hand, he ducked from tree to tree until he raised his rifle and surveyed below with his scope. After a few moments he eased and waved Jim on, but held a finger to his lips to signal that they should be quiet.

Jim came up beside him and stared down the hill into a large parking lot. It was one of those typical shopping amalgams that had replicated across the country, stripping communities of their local identities by making any place seem like a familiar place. Nevertheless it was an impressive site, the large tan cement block buildings set one after another like a buffet of unrestricted materialism. The only distraction was the scene of the parking lot, a picture of chaos frozen in mortality's stillness.

Peter pointed to some of the storefronts, their windows smashed. "There was some looting," he whispered, "but they must have been sick. I found the bodies in the stores and had to pull them out to keep the rat swarms out of the buildings."

Jim squinted and pointed to a charred area of pavement behind one of the stores.

Peter hesitated. "There was a fire."

"Why are we whispering?"

Peter tipped his head to the stores. "Look at this place. There's a lot to take. Some people come and then go, and those I just watch. But some think they can stay. I keep the lights off in the store to discourage people, make them think the place is already ransacked." He shook his head. "It's always the bad ones who think they can stay."

Jim gave him a sidelong glance.

"They don't like it when they see me," Peter added. "I'd rather find them before they know I'm here." He turned to Jim. "I'll lead. You parallel me, off to my right. We should be fine."

Jim nodded, but to his dismay Peter slung his rifle and pulled out a handgun from inside his jacket and flipped off the safety. Then he reached under the hem of his coat, pulling another handgun from a hip holster. A third handgun came out from under the leg of his baggy cargo pants, strapped to his hiking boot. With that done he took his rifle in hand and waved Jim on, his lips pulling to a small grin when Jim produced a tiny fan knife from the pocket of his coat.

They made their way down the hill, to the edge of the parking lot. A small cluster of cars sat at one corner, some of them smashed together. Peter tipped his chin to show Jim the ragged skeletons that sat in the vehicles. Pressing forward under the growing light of a cloudless, crisp autumn day they went from car to car until Peter stopped to survey the mega-mart through his scope. After a quick nod he waved Jim on and they entered the store. Peter waited for Jim to head along the aisles to the right so he could survey the aisles on the left.

When Peter was done he glanced over his shoulder to see Jim give him a thumbs-up. Peter pointed down the aisle he stood before and waited until Jim caught up with him. It was the frozen aisle of the store's supermarket section, and the freezers still hummed with power. Jim stared in awe before looking to Peter, who swept an open hand of invitation before the freezers.

Thirty minutes later they sat in the manager's office to a breakfast of microwave sausage and egg sandwiches and orange juice from frozen concentrate.

"Easy does it," Peter said when Jim put a third sandwich in the microwave. "Too many of these things will kill your stomach. Most of the time I have cereal for breakfast."

Jim nodded, but then shrugged and cooked the sandwich anyway. "I've been eating canned tuna, canned tuna, and more canned tuna. This is like a friggin' gourmet meal. You're a good man, Pete, sharing this with me. I wish there was something I could do in return."

"You already have."

Jim turned. "What?"

"You've behaved like a human being," Peter said with a straight face.

Jim stared at Peter until the microwave beeped, startling him. He took out his sandwich and sat down before the manager's desk, behind which Peter sat. "You know, I've been thinking," Jim said between bites of his sandwich. "Those cars out there, one of them has to be in running condition. We could load up on supplies, and what do you say, you and me, we head south together?"

Peter took a slow sip of his orange juice and put his glass down.

Jim waited, but then wiped his mouth on a paper towel and shrugged. "I mean, yeah, you got a great thing going here—right now. But you gotta be realistic, Pete. Winter's coming in a hurry. Couple of weeks; it's gonna be ass-biting cold out there. And you don't know how long the power's going to last. I found some places on the way down here that had power, but no sooner would I settle a bit and then it was lights out."

"The south won't be any different," Peter said with certainty.

"But it's warm. I'm thinking that'll draw some people, maybe there's a little community down there or something—what?"

Peter blinked, realizing too late the pained expression that had seized him. "I don't think so. Besides, what happened to what you said about making your own way, and no one to pass rules or judgment on you?"

"Yeah, but you have to be realistic," Jim insisted. "I mean, what are you gonna do? You're gonna stay here alone? What kind of future is that?" He shook his head. "Come on, you said you worked in a hospital; that's a good practical skill people could use. What were you, a nurse, a pharmacist? Doctor?"

Peter's eyes narrowed. "I worked in the lab."

Jim's head bobbed back. "Okay, whatever, no offense intended, but you still have a professional skill. Now look at me. What kind of weight does a deli-guy with half a legal aid degree rate? Nothing but grunt work. But you, you could be *some*body. The world's being remade, Pete, and we can all have a part in it this time. It's gonna be great this time around—society, I mean. A few months ago, we would have passed each other without a word. But here we are now, and people being such social animals, hell, it's like we're old buddies. I mean, look how easy we're talking to each other. Every word, every word you trade with someone now, it's worth its weight in gold. There's so few of us left, it makes us all mean a whole lot more, you know. Supply and demand, Pete. Supply and demand."

"Right, supply and demand," Peter said, his voice heavy with cynicism. "And the minute you become part of some little community, society will do what society always does: you can't be yourself anymore. They're going to impose their rule on you, control what you can have, argue about what you can or can't do, expect you to do this or that, and if you don't you're an outcast, and the very people who will relegate you to obscurity will tell you about their community values while they take all that's good in the world for themselves. What remains of the world is not all this garbage we're living on top of like flies on dung, the remains of the world *are* the dung piles, and it's us, it's what's in us, this disgusting thing in us that's glorified as 'humanity' rather than being demonized for what it is."

Jim sat in silence, somewhat stunned by Peter's lecture. He forced himself to swallow before he could speak. "So what is it?"

"It's—" Peter began, but fell silent at the sound of breaking glass.

Jim spun in his seat, only for Peter to still him by grabbing his shoulder. Jim turned his head, but Peter had already let go of him to draw his handgun. He looked down to Jim, holding a finger to his lips, and gestured to the office door with his eyes. Together they crept from the office, Peter glancing back to make sure Jim was keeping pace as they emerged from a hallway at the back of the store.

They could make out two voices. There was a man's voice, full of anger, and a woman's voice, filled with a desperate mix of defiance and fear. A deep scowl came over Peter, and then he was up and moving, scurrying down the frozen aisle to the front of the store where he stopped and crouched at the aisle's mouth. Jim came up beside him, the two of them looking toward the registers to find the source of the disturbance. A man and woman grappled there, the woman pinned on the floor and the man pulling at her clothes. His hands came free; one clamped her neck while the other whipped a gun from the back of his pants.

"Get off her!" Peter shouted and stood, leveling his handgun.

Surprised, the man and woman both froze.

Jim's eyes bulged as he looked to Peter. "What are you doing?"

"Put the gun down!"

"All right, it's down," the man replied and set the gun on the floor.

Peter kept his eyes on the man. The woman on the floor scrambled toward Peter and Jim as Jim waved her over. She crouched behind Jim, trembling.

Peter tipped his chin to the gun. "Kick it away!"

The woman shifted, but Jim put his arm out to bar her. She peered over his shoulder to get a look at Peter, her hands grasping Jim's arm.

"Keep your hands up!" Peter said and halted, only a few paces from the stranger.

"Easy, easy, let's talk it out," the stranger said. "She's the only piece around for miles. Tell you what. You can go first, no hard feelings—deal, man to man, all right?"

Jim looked to the woman as her hands tightened on his arm. "Hey, we're not going to hurt you, okay?"

The stranger looked to Jim. A crooked grin spread across his lips before he looked back to Peter. "Oh, hey, if you're queer, whatever, fine by me, I'll just take her and go," he said, trying to read into Peter's lack of response.

The woman lunged against Jim's arm, her strength surprising him as he fought to hold her back. "Two days you chased me!" she shouted. "Two days! You goddamn animal!"

"Shut up," the stranger snapped before looking back to Peter. "Look, she's crazy, all right? Isolation dementia, understand? I'm not the bad guy here. Watch." He motioned with his eyes to a small gold cross dangling from his hand by a delicate necklace, which he tossed to the woman before looking back to Peter. "Okay boss, so you have the gun. I got that. I'm a cop. I've had people draw down on me before. If you were gonna shoot, you'd have done it already, so stop jerking around before you start something we're both gonna regret. Put it away before someone gets hurt."

Peter studied the man, his eyes narrowing. "You were a policeman?"

The stranger's mouth opened.

Peter fired.

Jim and the woman hit the floor. The stranger staggered as the bullet blew through his forehead and tore out the rear of his skull. He fell back a step before crashing onto the magazine rack behind him and slumping to the floor.

Peter lowered his gun, but kept it trained. To be sure, he nudged the man with his boot, but it was obvious by the streaming splatter of gore on the magazine rack that the stranger was indeed dead. Satisfied, he turned to look at the woman huddled behind Jim. "Who are you?"

She trembled, her eyes wide on the dead man.

Peter prodded the body with his boot. "He can't hurt you now."

"I can't believe you just shot that guy," Jim said, his eyes wide.

Ignoring him, Peter kept his eyes on the woman. "What's your name?"

Jim stood, numb with disbelief. "You just killed that guy!" He looked to Peter. "What the hell was that?"

The woman's senses sprang back, unleashed by Jim's apparent defense of the dead man. "Two days that bastard chased me!" she said and popped to her feet. She reached down and snatched the necklace on the floor before her. "Son-of-a-bitch! You had my trust! You were supposed to protect me!"

Jim opened a hand to Peter. "Why did you have to kill him?"

"What would you have preferred I do?" Peter asked, relaxing his firing arm to point the gun at the floor.

The woman nodded. "There was nothing else to do."

"He was armed," Peter said. "Once a person is armed they don't give it up so easily. He'd have been back."

"Son-of-a-bitch," the woman repeated and looked up from the corpse. "He *would* have been back," she echoed.

"He'd have killed us," Peter said with dire certainty.

"You don't know that!"

Peter leveled a harsh gaze on Jim. "Do you remember what I told you when you asked me not to shoot you in the woods last night?" He looked to the woman as he stepped before the corpse to block it from her sight. "Peter Lowry," he said and swung the handgun behind him.

The woman blinked, but then looked to him. "Emily Lewis."

"I'm Jim MacPherson," Jim said from behind her, drawing her gaze.

"What are you doing out here, Emily Lewis?" Peter asked.

She looked back to Peter, hesitating before she shook her head to gain her senses. "I work for the government—"

Jim clapped his hands. "I knew it!" He pointed to Peter. "See! There is a community to go to!"

Emily nodded and ran her hand over her head to push back her brown hair. "Yes, I work for the government. Some of it still remains— people that ran into shelters, mostly, and they communicate from there— but others like me, who have immunity, we gathered at Camp David. We're going out to try to secure various sites; you know, power plants, industrial sites, nuclear plants, military installations, and to sequester vital supplies, like medical gear and pharmaceuticals, particularly antibiotics. More importantly, we also scout around for survivors." She glanced back at the dead man. "He was my escort. He was supposed to protect me. There were four of us on a helicopter, and we had to land. Engine problems. He killed the other two with us and started chasing after me. Like a goddamn bloodhound the way he tracked me." She looked to Peter. "If you hadn't come when you did…"

Peter shook his head. "Enough of that. It's over now."

"We have food," Jim said, ignoring Peter's glare at the use of the word 'we'.

"Does the plumbing work? I'd like to wash up a little."

"I'll show you," Peter said and pointed towards the hall that led to the manager's office. He started to walk with her, but stopped and called over his shoulder for Jim to get a mop and floor cleaner from the house-wares aisle. Then he continued on, pacing ahead of her and leading her on with a tip of his head. She hesitated, but when he stopped and held up his hands she hurried to catch him. "There's a lot of clothes in the woman's section. It's in the middle of the store," he said, hooking a thumb over his shoulder. "You can change out of that jumpsuit, if you want to."

"Ah, no, that's okay." She stopped, wrapping her arms about her chest, her shoulders hunched in a defensive posture. He turned, waiting as she scrutinized him, her indecision to trust him clear in the tight pressed line of her lips. She took a deep breath, gave him a small nod, and followed him up the stairs to the manager's area. "So you and Jim live around here?"

"I do," he replied. "Jim's passing through. I came here from New York. Long Island."

"Oh," came her simple reply.

He looked back to her with a frown. "Right, 'oh'. I guess you know some of the things that went on. That's why I'm out here in the woods." He stopped, fished in his pocket for a set of keys, and unlocked a door. She peered over his shoulder into a bathroom. "It all works," he said and pointed to the far corner. "I rigged up a little shower from parts I found in the homeowner store down the way. Not much water pressure, but if you really want to clean up, it's there. Clean towels on the stool in the corner." He looked to her, not failing to notice the uneasy look on her face at the thought of being defenseless in the shower. He shook his head and offered her the keys. "It's the only set. The door has a manual deadbolt that locks from the inside. I'm not going to hurt you. I'm not like that."

She forced a smile and nodded before closing her hand on the keys. "Look, I—"

He waved a hand to ease her. "Take your time. You can eat after, if you want. I'm going to help Jim clean up." He left her, making his way to the office to sling his rifle before heading downstairs to find Jim sitting on the floor a few paces from the dead man. When Peter approached Jim glared at him. "There had to be another way, Pete."

Peter sighed. "It's not up for discussion."

Jim pursed his lips. "No, I mean there has to be a better way. If this is what we do, if we just start killing each other, what hope do we have?"

Peter crouched across from Jim, the body between them. Peter ground his teeth to check his growing anger. "Listen to me. You want a better way? A better way is a way without the psychos, murderers, molesters and rapists that we used to coddle with excuses while they victimized the rest of us. A better way is a way without fear for the person next to you."

"So then who decides?" Jim asked, but shook his head. "That's vigilante crap. That's the friggin' wild west all over again."

Peter pointed outside the store. "Do you see any other law enforcement around here? Do you think anyone will answer if you call nine-one-one? Remember you told me this is my Connecticut? That's not a joke to me, you should know. Now help me."

Jim shifted, but he acquiesced, and they set about cleaning up the mess, first carrying the man from the store and laying him outside. Then they went back in the store, dumped floor cleaner over the area, and mopped it up. The menial labor seemed to lighten the mood, more so with the corpse out of sight, and Jim paused to lean on his mop, waiting for Peter to look at him. "So what do you think of her, Emy-lou?"

Peter looked up from his mop. "You already have a nickname for her?"

"I think it's kind of clever," Jim congratulated himself. "And I think she's okay."

Peter studied him.

"Oh come on man, you know, she's cute, don't you think?" Jim said with a wink.

Peter frowned. "But for the dumb luck of us being here she'd be getting raped right now by that animal out there," he said, pointing out the front of the store. "You're giving me crap because I shot the bastard, only to turn around and start sizing her up? And I'm the bad guy?"

Jim blinked. "Hey, relax, Pete. Just an observation, okay? Didn't mean anything by it."

Peter pushed his mop. "Leave her alone."

"So you can make a move?" Jim asked, but held up his hands at once. "Forget it. I'm sorry. It's just, you know, it's been a long time, and, well, we are human, and it's what we do, right?"

"Let's just clean up," Peter said as he mopped.

With the mopping done they went outside, and with Jim taking the man's feet, and Peter taking his hands, they carried the body around the store to the scorched area Jim had spotted in the morning. They set the body down where Peter indicated with a tip of his head before Peter walked to a nearby dumpster to pull out a small can of gasoline. Jim fell back a step, wiping his hands on his thighs. "You know, that's what brought me here," Jim said with care, "the smoke from the fire."

"I only burn at night," Peter replied as he opened the can, but froze when he realized how Jim had caught him. He looked up, annoyed.

Jim held his gaze on Peter. "So you've done this before."

"Set a fire?" came Peter's obtuse reply as he looked back to the can. "Sure."

"No," Jim corrected, "I mean you've done *this* before."

Peter looked up at him again. "What was I supposed to do with the bodies around here? Let them rot and make a breeding ground for flies, mosquitoes and a banquet for every little scavenger around, not to mention the nauseating stench of the rot?"

Jim stared at him.

"I don't have to answer to you," Peter said and doused the body with gasoline before returning the can. He came back with a stubborn glance at Jim, lit a match, and set the body to burn. The stink drove Jim back to the store with Peter close on his heels. Once inside Peter came up next to Jim and waited until Jim looked at him. "I've done some things out here, things I had to do to survive," he explained. "I'm not proud of those things, not a single one. And while most of them would be considered crimes in the world-that-was, in the world-that-is they were acts of necessity. I'm not an animal, Jim. I told you before—I *thanked* you—for behaving like a human being. That's all I ask of anyone, and as long as that's the way it is, there won't be any problems in my Connecticut. Okay?"

Jim hesitated before nodding.

"Good." Peter put his hands on his hips. "I'm going to get myself a little meal."

"I think I'll get some canned food for my pack," Jim said and walked off into the store.

Peter returned to the frozen aisle, grabbed a microwave dinner, and walked to the manager's office. He paused by the bathroom, long enough to hear the water turn off. With a nod he paced to the office, cooked the meal, and sat down at the table. He was hungry, yet when he looked at the meal all he could see was the messy splatter of the man's head on the magazine rack. He cursed under his breath and pushed the meal away before slumping in his chair.

There was a knock on the office door.

"Can I?"

His eyes snapped open to find Emily standing in the doorway.

He stared at her for a moment before sitting up and waving at the chair before his desk. "Ah, sure, have a seat. Are you hungry?"

She sat down before his desk, a towel around her neck as she pressed her hair to dry its wavy length. "Peter, I want to thank you, for what you did, I—"

He shook his head. "Don't."

She looked at him in surprise, her mouth open as she sat lost in her sentence. Then she pressed her lips closed and eased back in the chair. "Look, there's little enough left in this world," she began, her face settling as she studied him while his eyes darted about the blank wall to their side, "but there's still room for us to look out for each other, for common decency, yes?"

"Perhaps," he said and glanced at her before looking down to his food. It was one of those 'healthy' brand microwave meals, which to him meant too little to eat with too little taste. He frowned when he realized his gaze at the meal had caused her to look at it and realize he hadn't eaten. Annoyed with himself he pushed the plastic plate away and looked back to her. Jim was right, a thought whispered: she was cute, and it reminded him how alone he had been. And with that thought guilt welled up from his marital oaths, oaths that had not died within him, even though his wife had been taken from him. "Jim's right," he said, the declaration causing her eyes to snap to his. "I killed a man. There should've been something else I could've done. There must have been something else I could have done."

She shook her head. "We both know where that was going. No matter what, that was coming to a bad end."

"Still, I wish you wouldn't thank me," he said, holding up a hand. "When you thank someone, it implies something," he thought aloud, his eyes narrowing on the wall. He looked back to her, deciding what he wanted to say. "When you thank someone it lends some goodness, some credibility to the act the person performed."

"You saved my life. In my book, that rates pretty well. Like it or not, you have my thanks."

He rubbed his forehead as he fumbled to convey his thoughts. "Emily, I don't regret protecting you from that man. I most certainly regret handling it as I did."

She held a steady gaze on him as he sat with a hand on his forehead, concealing his eyes from her. His other hand fidgeted with the plastic fork on his desk.

She looked at the wall behind him. A picture hung there, one of those generic frame fillers of a sunset beach. She tipped her head as she ran a hand over her hair to push back its wet, wavy mass. "Well, I guess it's an odd way to meet someone," she said.

He lowered his hand from his forehead. "What?"

She shrugged. "The way we met."

He looked to his meal. It was cooling, but a few tendrils of steam still rose from the tangled mass of noodles. He found himself at a loss for words.

"Hey, you know what?" she asked, the sudden lightness of her tone almost startling him. "This is the world we live in. Pragmatic morality. We'd have it different if we could."

He thought of his life, his life before the plague, and sank away before he could stop himself. "Yes, yes. Maybe, maybe I'd have it different."

"Peter?"

He blinked, his eyes focusing on Emily. He cleared his throat. "Jim joked to me last night that the meek had inherited the world. I know the Pope called those of us who survived 'blessed'. But there is no sense left in this world," he said with a shake of his head. "If there was any sense I'd be dead and my family would be alive; the good among us would've survived, rather than the dysfunctional remnants."

She stared at him. "You're educated. That's good."

He blinked.

She patted a finger on her lips. "I can tell by the way you talk."

"So?"

She tipped her head as a lock of dark hair slid across her face. "Well, it's just that certain diction, grammar, vocabulary, they require some thinking when thoughts are framed and vocalized." She grinned. "See, that's just a thought, too."

She leaned forward in her seat, propping her elbows on the table as she straightened her neck to hold her head high. "You're not a bad man, Peter, you're just trying to find your way in a world that's a mess. But you're not alone. I want you to know that, and those of us that are left, when we talk about immunity, we're not just talking about the plague. The slate's been cleaned, so to speak. We need people like you, Peter, good people who can make difficult choices. Look at what you've secured here for yourself: clearly you see some kind of future, some kind of purpose for order in the world. You can put that purpose to good use. The world needs to be rebuilt, and we need good people, resilient people—people like you, who can do hard things and not cave to them."

He leaned forward and stared at her. "Is that the recruitment speech?"

She smiled before letting out a soft laugh. "I know how it might sound, but it's more than just some speech."

"You believe it?"

She nodded, holding her smile. "I believe it."

He could see by her eyes that she was being truthful. It only made his conviction to maintain his isolation all the more resolute. "You don't want to recruit me. I won't be good for any community you bring me back to." He leaned on the desk, mimicking her pose to force his point. "You need to understand something, Miss Lewis. I *despised* the world-that-was. Even as I feared for my family when the plague came, part of me welcomed the anarchy with open arms, part of me relished the idea of having it all come crashing down, part of me had always longed for the time after it all fell apart and the twisted adventure of survival without any external check. My wife was my compass, but she's just a memory now, and I promise you this, there's only one thing that really remains in this world, and it's the seduction of power, and the madness of power without external check. Out here, I can do *anything,* and I have no one to answer to."

His words washed around her, but she didn't flinch. "Okay."

He pointed a finger at her. "You think I'm a good person, because I helped you."

She took a breath. "I'd like to think so."

He frowned as he stared at her. "Then you should know the truth. I'm so helpful because the more helpful I am the easier it will be to make you and Jim leave."

She let her breath go. "So that's the plan?"

He gave her a single nod. "That's the plan. No offense, no criticism, no judgment. It's just the way it's going to be."

"Okay." She stood. "Did you hang that picture?" she asked, tipping her chin to the wall behind him.

He stared at her until her calm, unblinking gaze forced his eyes down to the cold, congealed mass of his noodles. "I'd like to be alone now," he said and waved her off.

"It's a nice picture," she said. "Probably would be nice, being there."

He sat for several moments, growing uncomfortable with her lingering presence. She was reading him, analyzing him, dissecting him in an exchange too subtle for him to understand, and knowing that, he found himself unnerved, desperate for her to leave him in fear she might ask a more probing question. On the other hand, part of him would have welcomed the exchange, thrilled by the uncertainty of disclosing his crimes, and how she might respond. In the end, he realized, he would never know, and perhaps he didn't want to know.

He laid his hand on his forehead and closed his eyes.

Her chair squeaked on the floor. He froze. In his little fit, he forgot she was still in the office. But then she did something that befuddled him; something that—despite what he had said to Jim—in his in-dwelling projections of a little encounter with her never figured into his consciousness, but something as well that stilled his heart in his chest.

She lingered there, standing over him. Then she laid her hand on his shoulder and gave a gentle squeeze. "You know Peter, you're just like I was," she said with a sigh.

He looked up.

She was gone.

***

He found that his mood soured the rest of the day.

Even though it bothered him not to monitor Jim and Emily, he gave in to the compulsion to sneak out the back of the store and walk a wide perimeter about the area. It was a crisp, clear day, and he didn't want to waste it regurgitating old frustrations to new strangers on the dark side of apocalypse… Or so his thoughts ran as he scowled and shook his head while he walked the woods.

Before returning to the store, he stopped at a spot he had not shown Jim. It wasn't far from where they had burned the stranger; it was a spot he knew well. Secluded behind a cluster of evergreens a small bowl of ground hid the bones of the other bodies he had burned. He wondered what Jim would think if the pit were dug up; it was a notion that filled him with unease. There were more than just bones in that pit—memories hid among those black ashes, dark, nightmarish and chaotic from those early days when things had fallen apart.

He leaned on a tree and crossed his arms on his chest. How could he ever explain something like this, this pit and what it contained? He wondered what Emily would think if he showed it to her, but then he rebuked himself, ashamed that he had even considered putting her in the seat of judgment in his head, the seat where he had bound his wife's ghost.

Then his eyes widened, because in that moment he saw the twisted irony of his existence. He'd always been a private person, remote in everything but his devotion to his family, and had always made a point to keep his home life guarded. Outside, in the society and world he viewed and tolerated with such disdain and contempt for its waste and decrepitude, he had kept his presence before others sanitized—through conscious effort, he tried to make his life so that those outside his home knew nothing of it, and therefore held no purchase or intrusion upon that which he valued most, that which he saw as the only reason for tolerating the world without. For if the life he lived had been different, if he had not met his wife, he knew he would have succumbed to those other things whispering in him, and would have resigned from society.

Yet now that society was gone, now that he was so alone, now that he had the very existence about which the darker parts of his heart had always fantasized, now that he could be perfectly isolated within himself, he found that *who* he was and more important *what* he was he had, without intention, mapped on the landscape around him. It was here in the pit, it was there in the charred area of the parking lot, it was over the hills where he had built his secret little cinderblock fortress, it was back on the store's supply room computer where he studied the last news reports of the world-that-was on an Internet that lived careless of human absence, it was scrawled in paint back in the recesses of the store's automotive aisle, and it was there in the manager's desk where he kept the caffeine pills to avoid long sleep and the nightmares that went with any lapse of consciousness.

And it was in other places, within him, but tapped now on his surface, his wariness to outsiders lost in the length of his isolation.

He sat on the ground, took out his notebook, and began to write.

So the question remains, and it is about me, from within me. All those years in that hospital lab, me and all those complicated machines, my little pets. Like people, those machines were complicated, but unlike people—unlike me—those machines, no matter how temperamental their delicate workings of electronics, pneumatics and mechanics, no matter how obtuse their errors, they all in the end followed some logical path to whatever state they were in. Not so with people, not so with me. Things go wrong, and there is no sense to it. A plague ends the world, cuts down the living without care or attention to who is taken and who is left behind, but still I go on. I do not live, I exist, yet all around me I see things in this space I occupy that display me, that show me as another wanting, illogical living thing rather than the metered, mindless, mechanical existence I pursue.

So yes, the question remains, and it is about my loneliness, and Jim, and Emily, and what I am going to do with them.

Have I become more human, being alone, or, in surviving, have I somehow become less human?

Have I become honest with myself, have I decided for myself?

Am I man, or monster?

***

He wandered back to the store in the late afternoon to find Emily and Jim in the store's electronics pen. They had pulled over two cashier stools and sat there, leaning next to each other over the counter. The slender telescoping pole of an antenna reached up over Emily's shoulder and as he neared he could make out the scratchy static of a radio.

"Almost, almost," she said under her breath as Jim studied her profile. "I know this is the frequency."

Jim blinked, but then turned when he noticed Peter coming up behind them. "Hey Pete. Emy-lou says the government's been broadcasting to bring people in."

"I know," Peter said, drawing a surprised look from Jim. He waited until Emily turned away from the radio. "You'll never get the signal sitting in the store. You have to go up on the roof."

"Wait a minute! You knew about the government broadcast?" Jim stood from his stool, trying to catch Peter's evasive glance. "Whenever I mention anything about a community or going south you blow me off. And you knew all along the government was out there?"

Peter slung his rifle. "When I heard the broadcast it was a loop. I figured it was just some broadcast left running like all the others that I picked up. Nobody home, all dead. So I gave up and turned the radio off. There didn't seem any point."

Jim shook his head. "You know, I just can't figure you. The more sense you make, the less sense you make."

Peter gave him a sidelong gaze. "Are you sure about that?"

Emily turned to Peter. "So you get a signal on the roof?" she asked, intent on the radio.

Peter nodded.

She grabbed the radio. "Show me," she said and waited until he moved. Jim followed close behind. Peter led them back into the store's warehouse and up a metal staircase to the roof door. Using his keys, he opened the door and they walked out onto the wide gray roof of the building. A short distance from the door sat one of the building's large air conditioner units. Upon closer inspection they could see that Peter had loosened one of the aluminum side panels. Walking over to the unit, Peter flipped the panel up to reveal a small shelter. "Home center," he gave as a blunt explanation to the work he had done. Within the unit's housing he had stored a sleeping bag, a telescope, a pair of binoculars, a beach blanket printed with cartoon characters, a terrestrial radio, and a satellite radio as well. A plastic tote box of batteries and bottled water sat beside the radios.

Emily and Jim looked at him, Jim shaking his head once again. "I repeat myself," he said under his breath, "the more I know of you, the less sense you make. You're so clever and so crazy at the same time. Nice beach blanket, by the way."

"We can stay for a little bit," Peter said, ignoring Jim, "but then we have to go back to the woods."

Emily shook her head. "No way. I need to be here tonight, at about one thirty in the morning."

Peter looked up to the sky. "And just who will be passing over us at that point?"

Emily stepped by him and crouched before his little shelter to inspect the satellite radio. "There's a satellite the government's been using. NSA used it to tap into the satellite radio networks to get another communication conduit, but it's only up when the NSA satellite goes by. Too many of their specialists died, so this is the best they can do for now." She looked over her shoulder to Peter. "I'm staying up here tonight."

"It's going to be cold tonight," Jim warned. "You can smell it in the air."

Peter shifted on his feet, his eyes darting between the radio and Emily. "Fine. Not alone, though. I'll stay up here with you." He looked to Jim. "You can sleep in the manager's office. It'll be warmer in there."

Jim stared at Peter. He hesitated, glancing once at Emily before looking back to Peter.

She didn't notice; her attention was focused on the satellite radio in her hands. "Actually, I would prefer Peter stay up here with me," she said, breaking Jim's lock on Peter. "It's his equipment, and he has the firepower if we need it." She looked over her shoulder to Peter. "Unless you want to give the guns to Jim so you can sleep in the office?"

Peter's eyes narrowed on her. He frowned before he bowed his head, his gaze rolling to Jim. "Jim, you have to understand—"

"I don't want the guns," Jim interrupted. "I told you. I could be here with a friggin' tank if I wanted to. You think I never came across guns on my way down from Boston? Hell, I could have had an arsenal in my pack if I wanted, but I don't want anything to do with guns. You know how it is with guns, Pete. They make people crazy," he added on the sly, but slapped Peter on the shoulder to break the tension. "Look. You two play recon; I'll cook up some dinner for us and bring it up."

Peter waited until Jim left the roof before turning on Emily. "You ask dangerous questions! Give the guns up? You know that's a power play to create tension. People who have guns don't give them up. You made me look like some survivalist psycho with that question."

Emily stood, but looked down and opened her hand to the shelter he had made. "Well, you are kind of a survivalist, aren't you?"

"You know what I mean," Peter said, his aggravation breaking through. "Don't do it again."

"Sorry. I didn't mean to upset you."

"I'm not upset, I'm annoyed," he corrected. "When I lose my temper, you'll know it. Just don't create little power struggles where there are none. I told you—this is *my* little world, and you and Jim are just guests. You're here on my good grace, nothing else," he said, but hearing the tone in his voice, he took a breath and relented. He shook his head. "Look, I didn't mean that so harshly. Being alone, I'm sure you understand, it does an odd thing, crippling the way of the world-that-was to develop a slow dialog with someone. Dialog is a forgotten art in this world, you know, taking time to say things in the proper way. You have nothing, or it just spills out. That's not proper."

She waved off his discomfort. "It's the way of the world now," she said with grace. "Part of the human social need to connect. The world is a very, very lonely place to be these days, and that puts us off balance, because most of us have grown to be wary of strangers, something you could do when there were so many people in life who were not strangers." She paused, her eyes rolling up to the sky as evening came in a hurry. "That's why we need to pull together, Peter. Everyone has a little psycho inside waiting to get out, selfish and wanting and impatient, and loneliness brings that little psycho to the surface because there's no external check. That's why we *all* need the company of others, why we need to be together in some kind of society or community. We'll all go crazy, disjointed and disconnected like this, you know what I mean?"

***

Her statement lingered with him.

They sat and ate together on the roof, which, to his surprise, and despite himself, turned into an enjoyable evening. They talked until the stars came out, sitting the whole time around a bucket-sized citronella candle, draping themselves with blankets to keep out the chill of night. For the most part they reminisced about the world-that-was and their lives as they were, Jim and Emily providing most of the conversation as Peter's old reservations for discussing his family resurfaced and kept his talk to stories that did not penetrate too deep. He noticed, though, that Emily dodged any question pertaining to what she did for a living before the plague. They talked as well about what they did in the last days as things fell apart, and how they found their respective ways in the following months. By the time Jim was yawning and they all felt heavy with sleep, they parted as if they were long friends, and not strangers who had just met. It was the immediacy of their company, Peter decided, the immediacy of companionship combined with the vast emptiness of the world.

It brought him back to her statement, still lingering among his thoughts for those hours, waiting to return to his consciousness until he sat alone with her under the clear night sky.

"What are you?" he blurted, his voice shattering the cold.

Sitting next to him within the roof shelter to conserve their warmth, she nevertheless jerked awake with some surprise at his question. She turned to him. "How do you mean?"

He kept his gaze on the stars in the black void above them. "I know you said you're doing a survey for the government, but I want to know your real specialty, what you did in the world-that-was. You made a point before not to talk about it."

She took a deep breath before answering. "I did behavioral studies for the FBI, as a consultant."

He hesitated before answering. "I see," he said, uncomfortable at once.

"I'm sure you do. You're not a stupid man, Peter. In fact you're one of the most resourceful people I've found so far. And you have the fiber of resilience in you. I saw it, when you helped me."

Despite himself, he smiled at what he took as a misplaced compliment, but he nevertheless concluded she was playing a game of mental chess with him, and this was just another round in that game. "You bounce back quickly yourself," he conceded. "What you went through the last two days, that man chasing you, I thought you'd be a little down, at least for a day or two."

"Nope."

He looked to her. "That's it?"

She turned to him. "Let's make a deal," she said, but when he seemed confused, she poked his shoulder with a finger. "If I explain myself to you…"

He took a breath and set his jaw.

She tipped her head, her widening gaze boring into him. "If I explain *my*self…"

He looked away. "I'm not playing games."

"Neither am I." She waited before opening her hands. "God, Peter! Come on! In all this loneliness, isn't the curiosity to know about someone else killing you?"

He held his silence.

She shook her head. "Well you're better than I am, because the curiosity is *killing* me."

He looked to her, annoyed with himself when he found her waiting stare.

She grinned. "I'll go first." She rolled her shoulders. "Now, I'll bet that you think you're the only one who has come to relish this mess we live in, right? No. My life as it was… I wrote reports and studies about all these wild things people did—not necessarily illegal things, because my work wasn't limited to that—and it made me think that I wasn't living, that I was just witnessing life, that everything was just this big vicarious thrill ride to me. I wrote about it—*life*—sitting in my little office, wearing my little business suit, wearing my glasses, my hair in a bun—confined, confined, confined. I felt it in my work, in the news at home, in movies I saw, in books that I read. The world was this *thing* that seemed to spin away under my feet, and there I was, just watching it all go by.

"And then it all ended," she said with a snap of her fingers. "Just like that. And for some reason I was left behind, maybe, I thought, because I was never really part of that world anyway. But now, because of this genetic fluke buried in me that gave me immunity, I'm left, I'm a *remnant*. That's what the government calls survivors: remnants. I hate that, it implies that we're still part of something that *was*, not the start of something that *is*. Some of the remnants fear the world as it is now for its uncertainty. Not me. I'm empowered by it. I finally feel like I'm living. Running from that psycho, you bet I was terrified. Absolutely. But now? I'm *invigorated*. That should be wrong. I know that. But that conclusion is another part of the old world, that standard is part of the old world. Now," she began, but shook her head, "now life is one big bungee jump—the lows just give me these springing highs."

She looked to him. "Okay. Your turn."

He licked his lips, but he found himself still digesting what she had said. Either she had an analytical skill that bordered on mind reading so that she could play him, or she was telling the truth, and the reservation he felt, the anxiety he felt sitting beside her, was the unsettling notion of kinship. Debating that, he became aware of his silence, and turned to her. "I'm sorry, it's just that this isn't easy."

She nodded. "I know. It was a strange feeling when I admitted to myself those things I just told you. But hey, I'm a stranger, right? It's easier to tell things to a stranger."

"You're not a stranger," he said, but bit his lip.

She knew enough to look away, her eyes rolling up to the stars. "You said you had a family. I never had that, a marriage, kids. What's it like?"

He looked to her, studying her profile before he looked out across the empty expanse of the roof. It seemed unreal, surreal, sitting there with this woman he had rescued by shooting a man he would have respected as an embodiment of order. He felt as if he were drifting away from himself, and when his voice came, he found it hard to believe what he was saying. "My wife was a better person than me," he said, somewhat embarrassed with himself. He had never thought of himself as a good speaker, particularly with women, when his nerves and innate

reservations had so often served to undermine him. But in that moment
he found himself somehow powerless to stop, despite his instinct that he
was making a serious error in judgment. Nevertheless he took a breath,
and then he heard his voice, low and even.

"She was a far better person," he repeated. "I always looked to her as
my moral compass; I always judged my thoughts and actions on the basis
of how she would react to whatever I said and did. I never thought of
that as my being subject to her," he said, raising a finger, "but only as the
honesty of my vows to her. She was a good person, and I would never
want to do anything to shame the bond between us, to make her realize
there were other things inside me." He closed his eyes, forcing a dry
swallow before he opened his eyes and continued. "But those things are
all around me now."

He felt his muscles tighten as he heard his words echo in his head. He
felt naked, he felt shamed, and yet he felt impervious to the old
reservations that would have shut him down with ease in the world-that-
was. He turned to her, his heart pounding in his chest. "You want the
truth? Then listen. This stunt you pulled before, mentioning the guns,
and who would hold them, do you have any idea what kind of a nerve
you were tempting? I possess all the icons of power here! I have the food,
I have the shelter and water, and I have the guns. I have all the things
that grant me power over the three of us, and in this microcosm we have
of what the world *used* to be there can only be one outcome, that the
world-that-was will return with its ghosts of greed and power and lust!

"You think the promise of a future is the remnant of a world that's
been destroyed?" he said, ridiculing her optimistic idealism, and no
longer able to contain thoughts that had boiled so long within his heart.
"No! The memory of innocence is the remnant we carry within us no
matter what world we create, because all that ever remains is the clinging
filth of humanity. The good never get the pardon they deserve! Reality is
a careless creature, and its ultimate cynicism is shown every time
calamities destroy the good with as little regard as they destroy the bad.
What I did before, killing that animal chasing you, it's justified by the
obscene accident of this mess that we have been condemned to live in,
and yet I still feel it has bound us to something that is completely wrong.
I don't regret killing that man. I regret only that it would disappoint my

wife, and I regret that hypocrisy within myself, that despite her judgment, killing that man… It meant nothing to me, it was nothing to me."

He fell silent, and she gave him several moments before she looked to him. "You think you're crazy," she said.

He met her gaze, but he had nothing to say to the stark simplicity of her observation.

She lowered her head, but kept her eyes on his. "You know what? You probably are, but so am I. We all are. Jim, with his misplaced hippie pacifism and its latent aggression, he's crazy too. It's just like you said, Peter, what the real remnant is."

He stared at her. He was not sure what to think.

"Come back with me," she said, her eyes intent upon him.

He swallowed and looked to his feet. It would be so easy, and he knew as surreal as it would be with her, he nevertheless wanted it, craved it. No one would know, except him. He found it to be the oddest of temptations; misplaced, displaced, disconnected, immediate and yet distant, all serving to remind him how fractured he was and how he clung to his past. In all practicality, he wondered, what was the use of his wife's ghost in his mind's seat of judgment? Had he not, in some way, been judged, and that was the reason he still existed when his family had died? How long could he last in this moral slipknot before he had the major mental breakdown, the calamitous moral collision with himself, that he feared in the dreamless comfort of his caffeine pills?

She leaned into him, pressing her shoulder to his as she craned her head to get a look into his eyes. He could smell her, could smell the clean soapy smell of her shower. It was intoxicating.

"Peter?"

He squeezed his eyes shut and bowed his head. "No," he said, making his decision. "My memories are the only good things I have left. I can't turn my back on them."

"You'll never be able to move on that way." She tucked her hair behind her ears. "I've brought in more loners than any other government scout, and almost all of them presented in the same way. But none of them, *not one*, is anything like you, is anything like the paralyzed walking contradiction that you are. Would you really choose to stay out here, to linger in some emotional retro-limbo, to keep oaths you made to ghosts, when you can start over again?" She sighed the moment she finished the question. She looked away as her head sank. "It figures," she said in defeat. "For all the reasons I think you're worth it are all the reasons you're untouchable."

He thought of the pit. He thought how good she smelled. Then he thought how she might smell *in* the pit. The easy, almost comical, brutality of the thought shocked him enough to blink.

"I'm sorry," she whispered.

He swallowed. "Me too," he echoed, but not for what she thought.

She rubbed her hands on her arms as she trembled. "I'm cold."

He glanced at his watch. "It's almost time." He looked to her. "For the satellite."

"Really?" She laughed. "You know what? I just wanted to get you alone." She waited a moment, tipping her chin up as a warm smile drew across her lips. She patted his leg. "Peter, you'll have to forgive me. There's no satellite," she confessed and walked away.

***

He woke to find Jim unfolding a lawn chair beside the roof shelter. He leaned to his side, his hands stiff from holding his rifle in the cold, his legs numb from sleeping cross-legged. Jim sat down in the chair, handed him a thermos of coffee, and nodded a good morning, his eyes lingering on the spent blister pack of caffeine pills Peter had left in the open.

"Why take them if you fall asleep anyway?" Jim asked.

Peter winced as he stretched his legs out. He needed a shower. He needed something warm, his breath condensing in the morning air. He took the thermos of coffee and held it under his face to breath in the hot vapors. "No dreams," he croaked at last.

Jim frowned, but did not look at him. "I'm no shrink, but that can't be a good thing."

"I know."

"How'd it go with the radio?"

"It didn't," Peter said, but then looked about the roof. "Where's Emily?"

Jim hooked a thumb over his shoulder. "In the shower." He sipped his coffee. "You know they have mattresses in this place? Couldn't believe that one. Slept like a baby last night. Emy-lou set down on the display bed next to mine. She says I snore like a chainsaw!" He laughed, but then quieted down and shook his head. "Funny thing is, no rat swarms. No rat swarms and no radio. So, really, no reason to sleep in the woods," he added.

Peter tipped his head back. "It's too bad you didn't get to be a lawyer. You really seem to enjoy cross-examining me."

Jim held up a finger. "Pete old boy, I've been nothing but honest with you. I'd just like the same in return. I know I got on your case about shooting that guy, but even with that, I was up front with you."

"I don't trust Emily," Peter said.

Jim looked at him. "How many fires have you set?"

Peter scowled and looked at his feet. "What difference does it make?"

Jim laughed to himself. "Now, you see, if you hadn't set any other fires, you would have gotten all defensive. So obviously you have set other fires."

"What difference—"

"I don't know if I can trust either of you two," Jim interrupted.

Peter nodded. He debated with himself, his eyes falling to the satellite radio. Taking it in hand, he stared at it, something rising from the sleepy wash of his memories.

Jim stood and grabbed his chair. "I'm gonna start heading south again. If you—"

"Four," Peter admitted, looking up to Jim.

Jim studied him.

Peter held his silence.

Jim sat down again and took a deep breath. "You are a crazy bugger, you know that?"

"Doesn't stop you from hounding me," Peter said.

Jim grinned. "How about that? I guess I know you wouldn't hurt me."

"What makes you so certain of that?"

"Because I'm a good guy," Jim replied and opened his hands. "Besides, you're not a real psycho killer, because you talk around it too much. The real psychos, they just do it."

Peter sipped his coffee. "You've grown brave since yesterday."

Jim shrugged. "Part of being in this world of ours these days is seeing all sorts of dead people. You know, mangled in cars, choked up in buildings, chewed up by rats, bloated under a toasty summer sun," he rambled, studying Peter for any reaction through the course of his graphic description. "Seeing the actual death, though, now that's something different altogether." He nodded. "You're a little crazy, Pete, but you make things seem alright. You've got, I don't know, presence, I guess. So what's this about Emy-lou?"

"Did you say you were leaving?" Peter asked, at last understanding what was happening.

"That's the plan. When I woke up I went to the automotive aisle, got a battery off the shelf, and checked it. After my coffee I'm gonna pop it into one of those cars in the parking lot, gas it up and fill up some extra jerry cans, gather up some canned foods, and off we go."

Peter stared at him.

Jim nodded. "Yes sir, Emy-lou's coming with me." He turned to Peter. "Got room for one more, Pete. Like I said, you seem to be a handy guy to have around, and you could have a future. Emy-lou said the same thing."

"Did she?"

Jim tipped his head. "Yes she did."

"She put you up to all of this, didn't she?"

Jim shrugged. "Well, it wasn't *all* her. We were talking about you when we woke up. We want to help you. So with all that 'we' going on, I guess you could say the idea was mutual." He stood and sipped his coffee. He studied Peter, struggling to figure out how to say something.

Peter opened his hands. "Out with it."

Jim fidgeted, swirling his coffee before taking another sip. "When I went for the battery, you know, I wandered around the store a bit, and I found some things…"

Peter went still as stone.

Jim cleared his throat. "There was an aisle with picture frames, and all the dummy pictures, you know those goofy fake family pictures, they were all missing. There were some mirrors at the end of the aisle, and they were all broken. And back in automotive, there was some stuff painted on the walls, poetry stuff, like low-rent Shakespeare or something, babblings about guilt and death and shame," Jim tried to explain, opening a hand.

Peter remained still.

Jim cleared his throat again. "Yeah, uh, okay then. Ah, I should get moving, you know, got a lot to do."

Peter looked off to the distant woods.

Jim folded the chair and began to walk away, but turned and came back. "Look, Pete, you're hurting. I see that. But despite the death threats and the killings, I really think there's still a decent, honest guy inside you. That guy, the Peter Lowry I think you were, still has a chance. You stay here, alone, and I promise you, that's gonna fade away. Don't forget, you may be a handy guy, resourceful, all that, but winter's coming on. This is the Northeast man, and you know the winters are a bitch. You've been scavenging, not really surviving, and let's face it, none of us know shit about *really* surviving, you know, hard-core survival skills. One thing goes wrong this winter, and that animal you like to think you are, you really will become that animal, and the Peter Lowry you were will be gone."

Peter rubbed his chin and looked back to Jim. "I don't know why I let you say these things to me."

Jim held up his hands. "Because I'm a good guy, remember? That's why you let me say these things. Because I think inside you, I remind you of who you once were."

Peter looked back to the woods. "The things I've done... I belong here." He turned to Jim. "There's a white crew-cab pickup truck behind the store. Four wheel drive. I used it to move supplies from the home center. It runs well. Keys are under the driver's floor mat."

"See that?" Jim said. "You are a good guy."

Peter closed his eyes. "Go away."

Jim raised his coffee in thanks and walked off. Peter frowned and looked to the distance, watching as the trees swayed in the breeze. They were almost bare, the only reminder of their once rich foliage the last brown leaves of autumn.

***

Guilt.

He stared at the one word he had written in his notebook. The afternoon sun deepened the contrast between the empty white page and the black ink of his pen. From the chill of the morning the day had grown unseasonably warm, but remained cloudless. He snorted at the combination of those observations.

Frowning, he put the notebook away and looked down from the roof's edge where he sat. Jim had moved the pickup in front of the store and spent the rest of the morning putting a diamond-plate tool chest at the head of the pickup's bed, which he loaded with two shopping carts worth of canned foods and bottled water. After that he came out with six five-gallon jerry cans, put them in the bed, ran the rig over to the mega-mart's gas station, and topped off the truck and the cans with gas. He used a credit card from a dead person's wallet; it was a trick Peter had shown him earlier. Other than that, though, Peter did nothing to help. He waited until Jim settled in the pickup bed with a can of soda for a break before deciding to leave the roof to take a shower.

He stood for some time in the stall, letting the water run down his back as he stood with his forehead resting on the cold tiles. Eyes closed, his thoughts churned away, but they were fractured, broken bits of irrational, corrupted still frames from his past. Similar moments always came in the shower; it was the sound of the water, the feeling of being wet—it brought him back, back to that miserable, magical last night huddled under the picnic table in the rain with his family before he was sundered from the life he had treasured to the nightmare that had so often served as his apocalyptic fantasy. After that night, there was only the surreal silence of the morning, and with it, the utter, irrevocable loneliness.

Without looking he groped behind him for the choke valve on the hose between the shower's head and the bathroom's sink. The water gurgled in the hose and stopped. He stood for a moment longer before turning and opening his eyes. He cursed in surprise.

Emily smiled at him as she brushed her hair. She looked back to the mirror she had hung over the sink. "Peter," she greeted.

He blinked as he snatched the towel on the sink's ledge to cover himself. His eyes darted from her to his clothes, and beside them, his handguns and the rifle he had leaned against the wall. But despite his paranoid twitch his eyes were drawn back to her as she stood before the sink, clothed in a yellow sundress and sandals. "How—what—how'd you get in here?"

She put the brush down before looking at him and crossing her arms on her chest. "I made a copy of the key after I showered this morning. There's a key machine down in the hardware aisle," she said, a finger poking out to point to the floor.

His eyes shifted about. He wanted to stare at her, but he was ashamed to be so blatant, and he felt vulnerable, so exposed before her. His hands clutched the towel around his waist. "So you found the women's wear, I guess."

"I'm sorry I lied about the satellite."

His eyes darted from the floor to her before sinking back to the tiles. He shrugged.

"But it was nice to talk, wasn't it?" she continued.

"Yes, it was nice to talk." He looked back to her, but this time he did not look away again. "It's been a long time."

She smiled with grace and tipped her head. "That's okay."

"Since I've really talked to someone," he added, but reddened with embarrassment.

She stared at him for a moment before she found her voice. "I want you to come with us," she whispered, leaning towards him.

He forced himself to swallow and squeezed his eyes shut. "I'd like to get dressed now."

She smiled. "You're avoiding the question."

He felt the redness of his face in the burn of his skin. He trembled. "I'd like to get dressed now," he repeated.

"Okay."

The door opened and closed. He laid his hands on his face and sank to the floor.

***

"Check it out!" Jim chirped when he saw Peter coming toward him. They were in the electronics pen; Jim had hooked up a television and a DVD player. Emily came up behind him with a large bowl of microwave popcorn and a six-pack of imported beer. "Movie time!" she said with glee.

Peter stood there with his rifle slung on his shoulder, feeling very foolish as he watched Jim and Emily settle down in two large, wheeled office chairs they had brought over from the furniture aisle. They put their feet up on the cashiers' stools of the pen. Jim had a pile of movies next to him on the counter by the register and began looking through them. "What's the flavor? Action? Romance? Mystery? Sci-fi?"

Emily tossed some popcorn in her mouth and wiggled her feet to flip off her sandals. "I'll be the traditional female and put up a vote for romance." She opened a bottle of beer and handed it to Jim before opening one for herself. "What do you say, Peter?"

He sighed and looked at the stack of movies Jim had collected.

"Oh, I know," Jim said and looked between Peter and Emily. "We should watch one of those cheesy post-apocalypse movies and see how close it is to the real thing!"

Peter shook his head. "No."

Jim shrugged. "Fine. How about a comedy?"

Emily pointed to Jim. "*Romantic* comedy."

Jim looked to Peter. "Come on buddy, help me out here. I can't believe you didn't have your own movie house going here."

"There is one movie I have," Peter began, but bit his lip, his eyes resuming their nervous dart.

"What?" Jim wondered, studying the DVD remote.

Emily looked to Peter with an expectant gaze.

He closed his eyes. His chest grew tight. Frowning, he walked away.

***

It wasn't so easy to walk away, though.

He went out to inspect the pickup, curious at the return of his old diligence for preparations. It only deepened the schism he felt within, driving a deep scowl on his face as he argued with himself whether or not to finish the inspection. He kept thinking of Jim and Emily laughing before the comedy they had agreed to watch, and it managed to still him somewhat, summoning feelings of the world-that-was, of happiness, of security, of belonging, of a sense of hope in the world. But with that came the darker whispers that had always lurked around him, and he felt the bitterness of Jim and Emily abandoning him, saw humiliation in the way Emily taunted and tempted him, even as he knew these things and more were nothing other than the corrupted workings of his mind. And then a familiar paradox welled up within him, the paradox of consulting with his wife so that she could sort out his confused perceptions, except that having her consultation would have meant she was still with him, and that would have precluded the entire dilemma.

At the back of his thoughts the pit lingered.

He left the pickup with a grunt, skulking through the store to reach his roof shelter. The sun was setting, and with just a thin white undershirt and his cargo pants, the quickening chill of night bit at him. He struggled against it as long as he could before retreating to the manager's office where he pulled on a sweatshirt.

He paced.

He debated with himself.

Night drew on, and with it, the unveiling of things best kept hidden within him, things he wanted to stuff back down, to suppress as he had with such success those years he had lived in the world-that-was. Had he not made it clear to Emily and Jim last evening the kind of creature he was, how his family was such a critical factor in the balance of his old life? Didn't they see the danger they were tempting by inviting the bitter insanity of trying to make this new world anything like the old world, in trying to make it hospitable, in trying to make it cozy and comfortable?

Pacing didn't help anymore. He thought of the pit again.

He left everything in the office and paced through the store, clenching a handgun at his side. As he expected Jim and Emily had turned in. The television was powered off. The store was dark. Only the stark moonlight from outside offered a scant, disembodied glow.

He came to a stop in the bedding department. They were sleeping in their beds. Jim was snoring. Emily had left her sandals next to her bed. Before he realized it he surveyed the scene down the length of his extended arm and the black barrel of the handgun.

His teeth clenched. He pointed at Emily, then at Jim, and then back at Emily, but his finger couldn't pull the trigger. His eyes tracked the gun as he switched between Jim and Emily. In the end, there was only frustration, his throat tightening around his breaths until he closed his eyes and put the barrel to his temple.

It was no use, for a new impulse welled up within him, one long forgotten, and in its welcome return the darker impulses were once again fettered and put in their cages.

He lowered the gun and walked away.

***

Several caffeine pills and two hours later he found himself on one of the cashier stools, transfixed before the television. Nevertheless, in the still darkness he was well aware of Emily as she came up behind him and sat on the stool next to him. He did not, could not, look at her, his eyes locked on the blank glow of the empty television screen.

"Can't sleep?" she whispered, but when he offered no answer she drew her blanket about her shoulders and answered herself. "I have things that haunt me, too. I guess we all do." She nudged him with her elbow. "Finally picked a movie?"

He nodded once.

She sat silent for a moment. "Okay then. Can I watch too?"

He turned to her, his eyes wide and unblinking. He stared at her with a gaze both intent and vacant, his thoughts far away. After a deep breath he turned back to the television and hit the play button on the DVD.

The screen blinked. Then it showed a home video, and it only ran a few seconds for Emily to see that it was a child's birthday party; Peter's daughter, in fact. He felt her gaze on him, and despite the burning sense of self-consciousness that seized him, he ignored it and let the video play in silence for a short time. He hit the pause button when the scene skipped to the lighting of the cake, with Peter and his wife flanking their daughter.

Emily nodded. "It looks like a happy time."

He took another deep breath.

"Peter—"

"I never had any faith in the world," he said, blurting the words. "When I met my wife, I was finally happy, and more than the surprise of her—of anyone—loving me was my own realization that maybe in all the ugliness and mess of the world something good remained. It quieted the darker things in me, but they were still there, and every now and then I withdrew from her in moody fits. But as I told you, she was a far better person than I, because she stayed with me regardless, and always told me to think of our time together. And when our daughter was born, I wept, I wept like a baby, I couldn't understand why I was given this beautiful little life, this fragile little life that looked at me and didn't see all those other things inside me, but only the gratefulness in my heart. Still it didn't hit me fully until her third birthday—this birthday on the video. It was a month before the plague came. That night, after we cleaned up and put her to sleep, I just sat in the dark on the edge of my bed, and I finally believed it, believed there was something good in this world, something of hope and promise for the future, even as the television news behind me mumbled something about rashes of unexplained deaths in Europe and the south."

He looked to the floor and laced his hands on top of his head. "I uploaded this video the next day to one of those picture websites. I figured whatever happened, this way I could always get to it as long as there was a computer and an Internet. I lied to my wife and told her it was for the rest of the family. But I look at it now, I look at that *person* in the video, and I don't even remember being there. I only remember it from this side of reality, as a spectator."

Emily leaned against him. "Thank you for sharing it with me," she said and put an arm around him. "Those of us who are left, you know, we've all had loss, but you need to break away from that." She patted his shoulder. "You need to come in from the cold."

He shook his head. "Not yet."

"Why?"

He squeezed his eyes shut. He wanted to admit what he had done while Jim and Emily were sleeping, but then again, that same temptation carried with it the darker impulse to stifle the shame and humiliation of that confession. The pit loomed in his consciousness once more. He ground his teeth, but the collision within him that he had feared for so long began to beckon. He wanted to strangle himself with his grief.

"Peter?"

He sucked in a breath. "Leave me," he forced out, his voice trembling as he ground the heels of his palms into his eyes.

"Peter—"

"Please! Leave me," he sobbed, almost choking as he tried to contain the devastating grief that pummeled him. "Leave me, go away; go away before something bad happens! God *damn* it all! I'll kill all the rest of the world before it hurts me again!"

She tightened then, separating from him ever so slightly. Her hand lifted from his shoulder. "I think—"

"You can't send me back!" he said, turning on her with a savage gleam in his eyes. "You can't! And this, this *shit* you call the new world, it mocks me every day I have to breathe its rot and stench, every time I have to do anything to remind me that I'm alive, that this isn't some nightmare, that this *is* my life and the world has spat on me one last time by letting me live after they died!"

She kept her eyes on him, but said nothing. Instead, she folded her hands in her lap and just listened.

He trembled, his teeth grinding so hard his face turned red. The pressure in his head was unbearable. And then it was gone, like so much shouting in the vacuum of the world's deaf sympathies. He sagged, his head drooping until he leaned forward and pushed his face into her shoulder. He felt her arms around him. "Please, you have to go before I hurt you."

"You're not going to hurt me."

He bolted upright and glared at her.

"You'll sooner hurt yourself. Don't forget what I used to do. Talk to me; you have to talk it out of you. If we get to Camp David, there are other people there who can really help. I told you, you're not the only one to have loss. Everyone who's left, all of us, we all lost everyone we knew. We help each other. We can help you. *I* can help you, if you'd just let me, if you'd just open up to me."

He blinked. She had hit on the nature of his schism, he knew. Confronting his grief would mean accepting it, accepting its implications in their finality. It was an unacceptable prospect.

He stared at her, speechless as his thoughts knotted within him. And then he was up and moving, staggering, and once more he did not dare look back.

***

He woke in the manager's office, huddled in the foot-well of the desk, clutching his rifle.

Sitting there with his eyes still closed, his imagination drifted to give him a disembodied view of himself. At once depressed and annoyed, he grunted and pulled himself to his feet before running his hands over his head. With a roll of his shoulders he shuffled to the bathroom and leaned on the sink to wash his face with cold water. The shock summoned his senses and he looked up to find his reflection staring back at him from the little mirror Emily had hung. He held there for several moments before jerking away, pulling on his coat, and slinging his rifle.

Cursing under his breath he made his way up to the roof and walked to the edge to look down on the parking lot. It was a morning of featureless gray clouds, a misty drizzle adding a creepy chill to the air. His jaw fell when he saw Jim and Emily by the pickup; Emily was busy loading their backpacks into the back of the crew cab while Jim fastened a tarp over the pickup's bed. In sudden disbelief and dismay Peter fell back a step before charging across the roof, running down the stairs, and hurrying toward the store's front. Despite himself he slowed to his usual walk before appearing from the frozen aisle where they could see him. Emily smiled and waved; Jim turned and nodded his head.

"You're leaving?" Peter said before he realized it.

Jim shrugged. "Well, you've watched us pack up. There's room for one more, Pete."

"Plenty of room," Emily added.

He frowned when he noticed Emily was wearing her jumpsuit and boots. "Did you two have breakfast yet?"

Jim nodded. "I went looking for you but I couldn't find you. We figured you were off walking a perimeter."

Peter glanced over his shoulder toward the manager's office. "I was..." he began, but thought how odd it would sound if he told them where he had slept. "I was around," he completed, but frowned again.

Jim pulled a little red rag from his pocket and wiped his hands before stepping to Peter. "Look, Pete, if you want to stay, I don't know, I guess I understand, it's your choice, but I think... Ah hell, just get in the pickup, will you?" He tipped his head in disappointment at the blank gaze on Peter's face. "Well, I took your advice, you know. I found a road atlas and plotted a route that'll take us well away from the cities but keep us on decent sized state routes; hopefully they'll all be open and not choked up with wrecks. I figure maybe two or three days between stops, detours, and downed bridges, and with some luck we should be down safely around Washington." He stuffed the rag back in his pocket and stuck his hand out. "Shake?" He waited, but when Peter hesitated Jim took his hand and shook it. "I can't thank you enough for letting us take all this stuff."

Emily walked around the pickup to come before Peter. "It was a very civil thing to do."

He looked between them, then nodded and reached inside his coat to offer one of his handguns to Jim. Jim hesitated but Peter pressed it into his hand and fished in his coat to give him two clips. "Take it. I've been around New York City. Not many people there, but some very bad people left over. If it comes to it, don't hesitate."

Jim looked down at the gun. "I hate these things, you know."

"Then give it to Emily."

Jim tipped his head.

Emily grinned. "I won't hold it against you."

"Hell, you can have it," Jim said and handed her the gun and clips.

Emily slid the clips into her breast pocket, but pulled on the handgun's slide to give it a quick inspection. Satisfied, she nodded and put the gun into one of her large thigh pockets. Her eyes fell before she glanced at Jim, who shrugged and walked over to the pickup. She looked to Peter. "You know Jim and I had this half-baked plan of knocking you out with sleeping pills and taking you with us, but we reconsidered and thought you might not take too lightly to that."

He stared at her, a dizzying mix of disbelief and rage, gratitude and regret swirling within his head. "That would have been a huge mistake."

She put her hands together before her chest. "I want you to come."

"Still the government scout, bringing home her prize catch?"

She held her calm. "You know that's a cheap shot, and you know it's not that simple."

His eyes fell to the ground.

She stared at him, her eyes narrowing a moment before she eased. "I'll try it one more time: you have no future out here."

He opened his mouth, but had nothing to say. Part of him, he realized, wanted her to stay, but that was one of his darker inclinations, because with it he saw himself driving Jim away at gunpoint and keeping her as his hostage in some skewed hope that he could make her into his wife. He blinked, ashamed of himself. Yet, at the same time, and perhaps more disturbing to him, was the thought of leaving with them and confronting himself. "I can't. Not yet. I'm sorry."

"Me too," she said. She took his hand and squeezed it. "Me too, but I'll be keeping an eye out for you."

He watched her walk around the pickup and hop inside. He glanced down at his hand before looking up again. Jim settled into the driver's seat and fished in his pocket for the keys.

His heart pounded in his chest. "I know you came here looking for me," he called out, Jim and Emily turning to him. "When you ran here you didn't come here by dumb luck, you were hoping you could get help. It was the satellite radio, you picked up the subscription activation when I did it on the Internet and tracked the website's cookie to the store's computer."

Jim looked to Emily, but then looked back to Peter.

"What else did you see?" Peter asked. "Did you see when I downloaded my daughter's birthday video? Did you see all the pictures of my family I downloaded? Did you people think that you knew me because of that?"

Emily sat with her head down. Jim turned back to her, but when she looked up she glared past him at Peter. "It gave me hope. You didn't secure the computer. I'm sure you know how to do that. I think you *wanted* to be found, Peter Lowry of Long Island."

He had no response.

Jim looked to him. "You take care of yourself, Pete."

He nodded. Jim pulled around and drove away. Emily shifted in her seat, staring back at Peter from the cab's rear window. He frowned, but turned his hand up to give her a single wave.

"I'll keep the fire burning," he said.

And then they were gone.

***

As Jim had warned, the winter cold came on double-quick, and things turned sour.

Peter just made it through the middle of December before the power to the store failed one dark, cold night. The noon temperature stayed just below freezing, so he left the frozen foods in place and kept a careful check on the temperature readings in the freezers. As a failsafe he wheeled a small freezer to his secret cinderblock fortress in the woods, hooked it up to a generator, and stuffed it with as many meals as he could. Nature made a mockery of that plan, though, when a warm front passed through, lifting temperatures into the fifties for a solid week, destroying his sacred stash of food in the store and with it much of his confident plans for making it through the winter in relative comfort. He kept the generator running, but quick calculations told him without the return of the cold he was going to run out of his gas supply. When the front passed temperatures once again plunged below freezing, and he hauled the freezer out of his fortress to let nature do the freezing for him.

He found it difficult to stay warm, despite the progressive layers of clothes he added, and the frigid winter winds howled through the store's broken window fronts to suck the heat out of every room, no matter how secluded. Seeing the futility of staying in the store, he retreated to his fortress, grateful then more than ever that he had taken the effort to construct it in the weeks before he had met Jim and Emily. But that proved little comfort, for regardless of his handiness, he was not an expert at construction, and even with the fortress half buried in the lee side of a hill, it still proved a most uncomfortable way to live.

The pipes froze in the store, robbing him of any ability to wash.

He resorted to log fires to keep warm and saved the generator to power an electric heater when weather forbade any foraging for wood. By supplementing the remaining frozen foods with canned foods and thawing them over the fire, he found he was able to eat quite well, and settled into thinking that he could make it through the cold in good shape after all. Confidence in that plan was destroyed when he was struck with a case of food poisoning from one of the frozen meals. After several devastating hours of diarrhea it took days for him to recover some semblance of strength and proper hydration. Seeing little choice, he emptied the freezer and buried the food. Forced to rely on canned foods, he repeated his calculations and came to the grim conclusion that even with strict rationing he would run well short. He raided the store, rounding up whatever dried food he could find, and came away with a box of beef jerky, a case of trail mix, and a case of peanuts. He regretted consuming the cereals during the warmer months.

So it was in late January that he found himself with little fuel for the generator and a strict ration of repetitive foods so high in salt that he had to watch his water consumption, as the once endless supply of bottled water in the store grew lean. Half starving and freezing as a relentless winter pounded him with snowstorm after snowstorm, any thoughts of attempting to drive south were destroyed. All his plans, his meticulous considerations, were revealed as a series of horrendous and inexperienced judgments. He lost track of time, lost track of himself, lost track of his place in the world.

For one week at the end of February it grew cold enough that he had trouble starting a fire and the gas he had stored for the generator turned into a thick mess in the jerry cans. His trips to the store ended when one trip left him fearful of frostbite in his numbed hands and feet. Once again, finding his options spent and his choices choked, he holed up in his fortress, set a fire, and bundled up in blankets and sleeping bags. He was cornered, trapped between the pitiless, unrelenting cold outside and inescapable hunger inside.

That was when it happened, when at last the break came within him, shivering before that little fire, starved and delirious, as bitter winds moaned in the sleepless night. There, in his hour of decrepit need, devoid of all comforts of the world-that-was, he stared wide eyed into his fire and finally let it go, let the world-that-was go, let it be in the past and with it let his resentment seep away. The grief of his family, of his wife and daughter and that horrible last night he had with them, that was an indelible mark, but it became manageable, for he could see the borders and delineations within his feverish thoughts that his nature so desperately craved. There was a sense of his life, the life he had known with his family, but that, like all the other things in that life, were memories now, his to pick and choose. Yes, he could remember his moments of joy once again, and no, they did not drive him back into fits of anger and depression. He was that person of his choice memories, free of those darker voices that always threatened to subvert him, that always feared and craved the obliteration of the world in his contempt for its despotic nature, because now that he was living in the bleak, unforgiving midst of that obliteration, those voices lost their seductive purchase upon his imagination. And he found it fitting, it made sense in its own logic that he had to stay the winter, that he had to let himself suffer deprivation to dispel and quell those voices within him so that he could evolve and define himself in the empty world about him. It could have been the better wisdom of his subconscious, deducing how he could reclaim his life, but he came to a different conclusion, one he accepted with greater ease: it was the memory of his family that had saved him, and for that, he learned to cherish them in a new way.

He thought of Jim and Emily, for the first time in a long time. They were good people, he admitted to himself. He wondered, hoped, that they had made it past the cities to Camp David. He found himself filled with a deep and sudden ache to see them again, to apologize to them for his odd behavior, to thank them for waking his old self and honor his family by sharing memories of his old life with them.

The pit and the evidence of his crimes it held, they were no longer part of him.

He closed his eyes and drew the cartoon character beach blanket around his gaunt, bearded face.

***

It was a struggle, but he managed to survive the winter. By the time the first thaw arrived in late March it felt like a tropical heat wave, and just as Nature about him seemed to stir in anticipation of the coming warmth, so too he emerged from his little fortress and for the first time in several weeks made the walk to the store. There were leaks in the plumbing, but enough water still flowed for him to take a cold and meager shower. He shaved off his ragged beard and clipped his hair right down to his scalp. The filth seemed to come off in layers, a disgusting process that left him scrubbed pink and pristine. Having grown accustomed to the cold, it didn't bother him to walk through the store with nothing but a towel around his waist to pick new clothes off the store's racks and dress himself.

As the weather eased he set about a new plan, that of relocating from his decrepit fortress back to the manager's office of the store. With that done he set about his next task, one he knew was of dubious value, and that was to find a car that would start after sitting all winter. For all his planning, it was the one thing he wished he had remembered, but considering his mindset going into the winter, it didn't surprise him, just as it did not surprise him that not a single car would start. He dismissed the idea of driving out, as he was not a mechanic, and even if he charged a battery using the generator, if anything else failed on the car he could be stranded in an unknown area. No, he decided, he would have to resort to his alternate plan.

Over several days, and at great effort, he moved a load of cinder blocks, one block at a time, out of the home center and into an empty corner at the front of the store's parking lot. Once there he laid the blocks out, painted them red, and returned to the store.

With the little gas that remained for his generator he got it running and ran a precarious chain of extension cords to the computer he had used before the winter, the one that held his pictures and movies. To his relief he was able to get a slow but stable dial-up Internet connection. It was a gamble, but he began downloading his family pictures again, and at that point he was thankful for the slow connection, as it would increase the time the computer was visible on the Internet. After three hours the generator quit on him, his fuel supply at last spent.

The next day he cut down several small trees and started a large fire in the parking lot.

The day after that he woke early, made his way to the roof, and sat down in the folding chair Jim had used months ago. He looked across the parking lot. The fire he had set continued to issue a tall pillar of smoke in the sky. The cinder blocks, laid out in giant letters representing his initials, gleamed with their paint under the May sun. He thought of the lengthy download, and hoped the government was still searching the Internet for traces of computer activity.

He looked back to the fire he had set, and was struck by how the meaning of it had changed. In times gone by the means by which he hid his crimes, it now served as the beacon of his optimism. It reinforced the necessity of the timing he had chosen. It would have been his daughter's birthday, and in another week, his wedding anniversary.

He took out the worn little notebook from his pocket. Since his awakening that desperate winter night he had not written a word, deciding it had served its purpose. Now it was the only possession of value to him, the one thing that, even in his absence, someone could read and understand that his family had lived, and that their lives had not been inconsequential. The one thing it lacked, he felt, had been a title, and now it came to him.

He opened the cover, clicked his pen, and in neat little capital letters wrote one word:

REMNANT.

***

Hours later he returned to the chair from a meal of what little food remained to him: trail mix and canned string beans. His stomach growled. His tongue felt sticky from the salt of the canned string beans, but he was down to only one case of water, and it was too precious to waste. After the sickness he suffered during the winter, he was loath to resort to catching rainwater and attempting to boil it for drinking. He had a few more days, by his estimates, and then he would have no choice but to start walking south. Given the condition he was in, he doubted he would get too far; by now, any bounties of the old world were gone to rot or ransacked. It reminded him how his clothes hung from his body.

His eyes scanned the horizon.

"Come on," he said under his breath. "Come on, Emily!"

He sat and waited.

The sun began to set.

And then he heard it, the rhythmic thump of a helicopter.

So life begins anew...

He stood and waved his hands in the air.

About the Author

Roland Allnach, after working twenty years on the night shift in a hospital, has witnessed life from a slightly different angle. He has been working to develop his writing career, drawing creatively from literary classics, history, and mythology. His short stories, one of which was nominated for the Pushcart Prize, have appeared in several publications. He can be found at his website, rolandallnach.com, along with his published stories. Writing aside, his joy in life is the time he spends with his family.

7909707R0

Made in the USA
Lexington, KY
21 December 2010